The Smuggler

CYNTHIA KEYES

VINCI
BOOKS

Vinci Books

vinci-books.com

Published by Vinci Books Ltd in 2025

1

A CIP catalogue record for this book is available from the British Library.

Paperback ISBN: 9781036702632

By Cynthia Keyes

Regency Romance

The Meadows

The Smuggler

The Spy

The Heiress

Bride of Montrose

This book is dedicated to my mother, Martha, and my mother-in-law, Edna. Two women whose fierce determination was exceeded only by their ability to love.

Chapter One

Lady Osbourne glanced down at the fraudulent documents one more time and smiled. They were perfect. It would be difficult, even for an expert, to realize the forgery.

Setting down her teacup, she pushed a stray bit of her steel gray hair behind her ear and gave a satisfied sigh. "We have done it Adrienne, and nothing could be more suitable to me. My grandson Theodore will acquire a young lady for a bride who is worthy of him."

"But will he suspect?" Countess Myrell shifted forward and examined the documents one more time. Like Lady Osbourne, she was in her golden years, but there the similarities ended. Where Lady Osbourne was a buxom woman, with a personality as blunt as her solid body, the countess was tall and slender with an indolent air. "After all, he will never have heard of betrothal papers supposably written up all those years ago. Will he not wonder why an agreement like this one has never been mentioned? And even if he accepts these documents as real, he could find ways to avoid the arrangement."

"He could. Sadly, the world has changed. People are prone to take these contracts less seriously than in the past. A grave mistake in my mind." Lady Osbourne shook her head, causing her heavy jowls to tremble. She grasped an ornate cane at her side and gave it a little thump as if to emphasize her words. "But not to worry, Theo will never suspect me of fraud. If I say it is true, he will accept it. Besides, he is ready to wed. He has the responsibility of producing an heir. If he must find a wife, then why not Arabella?"

Lady Osbourne grinned conspiratorially and continued. "And of course, there is the trivial matter of money. He will gain a considerable fortune from my estate if he agrees. Theo is an astute businessman. He loves nothing more than managing money." She snorted. "And your Arabella, will she be a problem?"

The countess waved a languid hand dismissively and smiled. "My Arabella needs a husband. And she needs a marriage settlement to help her salvage Harwood Place. Since our Aran left on his tour, she has been quite dependent on me." She took a sip of her tea and considered the problem. "And like your Theo, if she must marry, then why not an earl? It is perfect for her."

Lady Osbourne thumped her cane sharply once more and ignoring the countess's wince, added, "Well then I see no need to delay. We will speak to our respective grandchildren." She shot the countess an assessing look. "You must be firm, Adrienne. Insist. With Aran gone, she is your ward. Therefore, you have the final say."

The countess lay back against the sofa cushions. "Do not worry, Amelia. I know how to handle my Arabella."

"Excellent. I will attempt to bring Theo to Harwood Place as soon as I can manage it. We have done an excellent piece of work this morning." She nodded, her heavy jowls quivering. "I doubt either of them will suspect the authenticity of the documents. Certainly, neither of them would consider their loving grandmothers capable of a forgery. Our families will be joined at last."

The countess gave a lazy smile as she helped herself to a dainty from the tea tray. "What is a little forgery if it brings about such a happy result? Besides, there is no one more suitable for the young earl than my Arabella. She is a paragon of womanly gentility."

"Move your arses!" Arabella yelled from the bulwark. "She is coming up fast! Rig up the foresail to the bowsprit. We will need all the speed we can muster to outrun her!"

"Aye aye, Cap'n Ara. We got her coming." Arnold and another sailor hustled to do her bidding.

Arabella hurried to the stern pulling her telescope from its loop at her belt to get a reading on the revenue cutter. Her first mate, Jem, joined her at the rail. She smiled when the lugger lurched forward as the foresail caught the breeze. The Bella was designed for speed, and she did not disappoint. She was gaff-rigged. The smooth lines of her carvel hull cut cleanly through the water. Even loaded with tubs of brandy as she was today, she was able to skim through the water.

Arabella kept the scope trained on the revenue cutter, feeling her stomach twist with dread as she took in the might of their pursuer. "This will be a damned hard run, Jem. Even the Bella will have a race against that monstrous cutter. That ship is fast enough to catch us."

As a smuggling captain who worked England's eastern

shores, Arabella was confident she was one of the best. Jem had trained her well. She and her twin Aran had been sailors since birth. Arabella had always been more skilled than her brother. Today she knew her skills would face the ultimate test.

"My god, Jem. She is seventy tons at least." Lowering the scope, she turned to her crew who were scrambling with the rigging, and hollered, "Hustle up, boys! Full sails! We're going to need all we can muster on this run!"

The sailors responded instantly. Canvas sails popped as they found the wind. The lugger cut through the waves.

Arabella watched her crew move with precision as they rigged out for full sails. As captain, she had always maintained her male persona aboard the ship. The moment she donned her captain's gear, she was Ara. Her persona at sea was no longer a role to be played but had become an identity. When Ara had first taken over from her twin Aran, it had not been her gender that concerned her crew but her youth. With each trip to the mainland, she had slowly won their trust. Today, with a cutter on their heels, there was no one better at the helm and they knew it.

She was tall for a woman, and slender. She prowled her ship with an agile physicality. If she could swing from the rigging to move about, she did. It was as though she relished the freedom from her inhibiting skirts. She wore a peaked felt hat pulled tightly over her head. The hat sported tattered frills at its back to disguise the bulge of her braid. A tattered red sash covered her lower face, its ends flapping in the winds. Her red faded long coat was fastened with one button at her chest; its lapels flapped open wide to reveal the cutlas and telescope attached to a sturdy belt. Fitted trousers were tucked into tall boots.

Arabella handed Jem her telescope. Jem stretched to his

full height of an awesome six foot seven and squinted into the lens.

His weathered and scarred face twisted as he focused on the ship in the distance. "She's a big one, Ara. And she's moving."

He handed Ara back her spy glass, and she raised it to her eye once more, focusing it on their pursuer. She estimated the distance quickly. Turning towards the English coast, she saw her deliverance rolling in from the north. Fog; a thick band of it hugged the rocky coast. And the sun was setting soon. But knowing the winds would still as they neared the foggy coast, Ara decided to make a separation from the revenue cutter now.

She turned to her first mate, Jem. "We'll make a hard run. Then I need to take her in close to the shore, to hide in the fog." Ara swore under her breath. "But the Bella can't be steered in until we clear Bergen's point with its rocky reef. We have a battle, and she's going to be a close one, Jem. Call up our spotsman."

Arabella grabbed the rigging and swung lithely across the deck. Let the cutter come. Her place was in the bow, at the helm.

She muttered, "Please god, let us get safely past the reef and into the fog before the damned cutter can catch up to us."

Her spotsman, Jamie, climbed to the stern of the boat and braced himself against the railing. His talent was essential now. She trusted him above her telescope. Jamie knew this coast better than his cottage on shore. He would holler when she could veer in towards the shore. Still, she trained her scope on the shrouded coast once more, trying to identify the exact moment they passed the reef.

Arabella spun around, raising her spy glass to check the cutter. She was gaining.

"Damn and blast!" she swore into the salty spray. Grasping the wheel, she swung the ship hard to starboard. A rush of icy water struck her full in the face, the salt stinging her watery eyes. Without taking her hands from the wheel, she rubbed her face against her sodden sleeve.

"Tighten her up, boys. We're going to take her to the limit! Full speed ahead." Arabella felt the hull beat hard into the waves, as they zigzagged into the wind. The port side hull was tilted dangerously close to the waterline as the Bella crashed into a wave. Water cascaded over the deck. She turned the Bella sharply starboard. With a head wind, they needed to zig-zag forward, executing tight turns to accelerate.

Timing was everything. It would determine the fate of all aboard. One wrong maneuver could mean death to the crew; first from the sea, and then, if they survived, from the law. Being boarded by the revenue cutters could mean that all aboard would be sentenced to death for treasonous smuggling. If they were lucky, they could be pressed into the British navy as a galley slave, a fate which too often was also a death sentence. There would be no defense. Now was not the time to be faint hearted; it was the time for extreme risk.

Though her heart pounded in her chest, and her stomach knotted, she showed no outward signs of fear. At each turn, Arabella pushed the ship to the edge of its capability. And with each turn, the water was inches from the top of the hull. The Bella raced forward at breakneck speed. Arabella kept a steely grip on the wheel.

She needed to clear the reefs to safety and soon. Her hands became slick with sweat. Arabella had to pull her right hand from the wheel to wipe it dry on her coat.

She urged her ship forward. "Come on, baby!"

Jem shouted into the fray, "Hang on, boys!"

A massive wave pounded the hull as the lugger took a sharp turn to starboard. Water rushed across the deck, forcing the crew to brace themselves against its fury. She was at top speed.

Arabella gripped the foremast with one hand and held to the wheel with the other, first peering coastward, then swinging to check the revenue cutter once more. She could see nothing of the shoreline through the thick fog to her left, but they had gained some ground on the King's men.

Another huge wave approached from the portside. She was just able to turn the bow into its crest before it smashed into the ship. The ship was precariously over-powered. So far luck and precision had been with her, but one slight error and they would capsize.

Thankfully, the load was tight. She carried a cargo of gin and brandy tubs, with some extras of silk and lace. Had the stock in the hold been able to shift, it would have been enough to tip them into the sea. Arabella was thankful now that she had carefully supervised the packing.

At last, Jamie screamed from the stern, "We are past the point, Cap'n."

"We'll pull her in," Arabella shouted to the crew. Though she could see nothing, even with her telescope, Arabella trusted Jamie's expertise. Jamie would not call it unless he was sure. Arabella swung the ship sharply to the portside.

The ship swerved into the safety of the thick fog. From here on, Arabella would rely on her memory to guide them along the coast. This was her home stretch, and she knew it well. Beneath her mask, she smiled in triumph. They had outrun the revenue boys. The setting sun would be further cover for them.

Arabella expelled a long breath. It had been a close one.

Jem approached her and laid his massive hand on her shoulder with silent approval. The spotsman stood on her right. His job now was to watch for the signal from the shore.

Jem leaned down and spoke quietly into her ear, "That was a near miss, Ara. That cutter was seventy tons at least. We have not seen her like in some time. I heard rumors about a cutter of that size in our midst but hoped the tales were exaggerated." He shook his shaggy head. "Worse, this is the third time we have been spotted on as many trips. Something's not right. There's a leak somewhere. We'll need to keep our ears to the ground. We don't want to meet her in the open sea. She's too fast for us."

"She was that. And you're right. The bastards were waiting for us." Arabella looked at the darkening mists swirling around her. "But he won't catch us today, Jem."

She would address the worry of the new cutter in time. Tonight, she had to concentrate on bringing the ship safely into port.

Her timing was right. They would see the signal light soon for the unloading. The night's smuggling job would not be complete until the goods were safely on shore and stored in the caves until Jem could arrange their transport.

As she suspected, the breezes had died closer to shore. The sea had calmed to an eerie stillness. The ship glided silently through the comforting blanket of fog.

Tremble Inlet was their destination. At high tide, the inlet allowed them to dock and haul off the cargo without the aid of beach crews. Tremble Inlet was a secret known only to the crew. It was tucked along the coastal cliffs of her

Yorkshire home, Harwood Place, safe from the prying eyes of the community and difficult to spot, even from the sea. The fewer people who knew of it, the safer it would be.

The Bella was built for speed not cargo. She was a mere fifty feet from bow to stern with a capacity for carrying only ten tons. It would be quick work to get her unloaded and sail her around to dock at the village.

Arabella knew the revenue cutter still prowled the coast, searching for her prey. She twisted her salt-ravaged face into an arrogant smirk. The fog and the dark would hide them.

Still, she sighed with relief when the spotsman hailed the signal flare and they maneuvered into the inlet. Grabbing a lead rope, she leapt to the ship's rail and hollered, "Drop the sails. She's calm. We'll dock her cliff side. Make fast work of it, boys. We can't have the damned cutters spot us now!"

Theo sat up and slowly swung his legs to the floor. By the look of the sun through the gauzy curtained window, it was already late morning. His head hurt. He ran his hand through his tussled blond hair, pushing it back from his forehead. He had consumed far too much brandy, again. His mouth was dry. The sweet smell of Dierdra's perfume mixed with stale sweat clung to his body. It nauseated him.

He squinted down at Dierdra. She was the latest in a string of mistresses. The morning sun was not kind to her. Her blonde hair lay snarled across her pillow, heavily pomaded locks now stiff and misshapen. Her rouged cheeks and lips stood out sharply in the harsh light. Her makeup betrayed her. Instead of enhancing her beauty, as it had in the soft light of the evening, it now emphasized her aging skin.

But it was not her age that concerned him. It was her cloying possessiveness which had convinced him the arrangement they had was over. Last night, she had irritated both he and the predatory mamas of the marriage mart by clinging to his arm all evening. Finding a suitable wife with Dierdra at his side would be impossible.

She stirred, looking at him through eyes opened in narrow slits, and groaned, pulling the sheet up over her head as if aware of her disheveled state.

He was bored with her. Knowing what would be next, he sighed. There would be the scene with its tears and recriminations and finally the gift. He wished he could simply walk out and never return. But she was a widow in good standing in the ton and could make life a misery for him. That she had begun to make claims on him publicly could only mean she had aspirations; she hoped for a proposal. Theo had made it clear to her at the start of their affair he had no intention of involving himself in a committed relationship with her. She had agreed. He resented her obvious manipulations.

Rising from the bed, he grabbed his shirt off the rumpled heap of clothing on the floor. The scene with Dierdra would have to be saved for another time. He had promised to luncheon with his grandmother. Getting home and making himself presentable before she arrived was his priority. Things would not go well for him if she saw him in this state.

As he buttoned his trousers, Theo smiled at the thought of his formidable grandmother. She had messaged him to inform him of her arrival to discuss a matter of great importance. He was not concerned. Every discussion was a matter of importance to his grandmother. He was fond of the old girl. She had taken the reins after his parents had died. He and his little sister Lizzy had been in firm, but loving hands.

Two hours later, Theo sat rigidly at the table in the breakfast room staring at the faded contract in front of him. It was outrageous.

"You cannot be serious, grandmother. This is positively medieval."

His grandmother had said little while they lunched, strategically waiting until the meal was concluded before presenting her case. Her silence during the meal had been suspicious but never had he suspected this bombshell to be dropped into his lap.

"It is a contract. It was signed in good faith by your parents and those of Arabella Forsythe. I have had it checked. It is legal and binding." She gave her cane a solid thump.

He winced. She used her cane like a judge's gavel. It had never boded well for him. Once the cane had hit the floor, her mind was made up. She would entertain no further arguments.

Theo's first instinct was always to resort to charm. It usually worked for him. He tried a winning smile. "Surely you don't think to hold me to this, Nana. And think of the poor girl. I have not laid eyes on the lass since she was a child. All I can remember of her is scraped knees and pigtails."

He laughed at the memory. The last time he had seen Arabella Forsythe, he had been fifteen and she was about eight. She had swung at him from a tree branch and plopped down at his side to ply him with questions. She was curious about everything—could he ride? Why had he been sent to school? Did he miss his home? Could he sail a ship? Indeed, his most enduring memory of her was thinking that she was the most annoying brat.

"She cannot be eager for this arrangement," he said.

"She is willing." Lady Osbourne rested her cane on the arm of her chair and laid her hands on the table. "Think of it, Theodore. You are thirty. It is time you took your responsibilities seriously. The Earldom must have an heir. You have scoured the town checking out the young ladies each season. None have appealed to you. Had you found a young lady to your liking, I would never have brought the contract to your attention. But you have not. It is time. Unless you have someone that appeals to you..."

She left the question hanging and looked curiously at him.

Theo thought of Dierdra. He gave a bark of laughter. "No. God, no."

He continued to smile as he thought of Dierdra's reaction to the news. It would certainly solve his mistress problem.

He had no idea who would best suit him as a bride. The responsibility weighed heavily on him. It had been on his mind since the marriage of his best friend Ambrose. Lately, he felt he was the last of his companions to find a suitable spouse.

Marrying was his responsibility. He needed an heir. He loved women, almost all of them, at least for a while. Each time he thought he found the one, he became bored. To choose someone to spend the rest of his life with was next to impossible for him. He had considered the new crop of ladies this year with interest, but soon found the games played by them and their mamas a burden. He could not stomach machinations and manipulations.

He was an earl and therefore a fine catch for every girl. And he had money. This season, Theo's attendance at the soirees and balls had signaled his interest in finding a bride. The mamas had gotten wind of his intention to seek a bride. There was no end to the line of eligible ladies who had thrown themselves at his feet. Literally. Last weekend, a young woman had actually fainted in front of him. He had been obliged to catch her and haul her to a chair while her mother smiled approvingly. It was too much. He had given the business of finding a wife a serious try but found the games impossible to tolerate.

"Theodore. If you must marry and you have no one in mind, then why not honor this agreement? Your problem will be solved."

Theo looked down at the contract once more. It was real. It laid out the marriage settlements precisely. "What do you know of her?"

His grandmother smiled. "She is twenty-three, neither too young nor too old. She is an intelligent, spirited young lady. Like you, she lost her parents as a child. And she is lovely. I have heard she takes after her maternal grand-mother who was an acclaimed beauty."

Theo was skeptical. "Then why has she not been snatched up?"

His grandmother shrugged. "She had many offers in her first seasons and declined them. Her grandmother has much indulged her. This past year, she has apparently been helping to manage her brother's estate and not moving in social circles. And then, of course, there is the trivial matter of money. She has none."

Theo glanced down at the contracts. Money was defi-nitely something the woman would gain if they honored this agreement. Theo considered the exorbitant price he would pay for this bride. He winced. But it would be worth it if this damnable search for a wife was over.

His grandmother appeared to read his thoughts. "And speaking of money, there is also the little matter of my inheritance for you. I would be willing to grant you half of my sizable estate. I must of course hold a portion back to settle on your sister when she weds, but it is a generous amount." She paused to let him consider the deal before adding, "Harwood Place is floundering. I think it may need a capable manager to bring it about."

Theo raised his eyebrows. It was not like his grandmother to offer up funds. She had always been tight-fisted and conservative with her money. Indeed, he had had a battle with her when the time had come to manage his inheritance from his parents.

He thought about the challenge of bringing an estate back from the abyss. It intrigued him. Over the years he had made a considerable fortune buying enterprises that were struggling for rock bottom prices, turning them into viable businesses, then selling them for a profit. It was both a talent and a passion. It accounted for a sizable portion of his considerable wealth. Certainly, when added to his inheritance, he would be considered one of the wealthiest gentlemen in England.

"You very much want this arrangement, Grandmother. Why?"

She gave him a rare wide smile. "Believe it or not, I want you to be happy. I know the young lady's family well. Her mother was a woman of strength and integrity. Her grandmother and I have been lifelong friends. I have an instinct for these things and am seldom wrong."

"When was the last time you saw the girl?"

"I knew her as a child. Her personality was set. Trust

me. She will be a lovely young woman and make a fine wife. Her grandmother assures me she is very much the gentile lady."

"I will meet her." Theo shrugged. "I will even offer for her if that is what you want. I need a wife. I need heirs. I seem to have had no luck managing the task so far."

His pronouncement surprised him. He had been flippant and hasty.

His grandmother leapt at his agreement before he could change his mind. With a thump of her cane, she announced, "It is settled then. We will leave for Harwood place next Thursday. I will send a letter to the countess today."

Theo glanced at his grandmother. If nothing else, he had pleased her. She now leaned back in her chair and sipped her tea with an air of satisfaction. Theo too, found himself relieved with the betrothal. If Lady Arabella were the demure, gently raised woman his grandmother described then his search for a bride would be over.

He pictured a shy young lady, raised in the country. She would be blushing with pleasure at the thought of marrying an earl, forever thankful for his proposal. He imagined a soft, gentle creature. A woman who would happily manage his household, enjoying her role as wife and mother. It might all work out for the best.

Chapter Two

Arabella stood with Jem admiring the new colt. "It's been a damned good year for the stable."

Jem frowned. "Watch your language, missy. There is no need to play Captain Ara here."

"Sorry, but she is a beauty, Jem. Strong and healthy." As if to underline her words, the little filly wobbled to its mother to suckle. "We have four new foals this season. It is a fine start for us."

Arabella rested her arms on the rails of the pen and smiled. The stables with their carefully selected breed mares were the one part of the estate which was flourishing.

"Aye, it is that," Jem replied, his scarred face twisting into the hint of a smile. "But we have a long way to go to make this place stand on its own."

Arnold approached. "Lady Adrienne wishes to see you in the sitting room. She has asked me to fetch you."

Arabella frowned. It was not like her grandmother to rise early, especially having just returned from a trip to

London. "I best be hurrying then. I mustn't let her majesty wait."

She laid her hand on Jem's shoulder in farewell and turned to do her grandmother's bidding.

Her grandmother's request could only be trouble, she thought to herself, as she walked into the sitting room. The countess was reclining on the sofa. On the end table before her a tea tray had been set. She was sampling an array of chocolates. Choosing one, she used it to motion in Arabella's direction.

"Sit down, my dear. Pour a cup of tea. We must have a little talk this morning."

Arabella perched on the chair across from her and poured her tea. To her dismay, her hand shook slightly with the task. In her experience, the more relaxed and indolent her grandmother appeared, the more difficult the conversation would be. In the past, if a reprimand or command was to be administered it was always done with the countess in a reclined position. Arabella was sure it was employed as a tactic to distract her prey. This morning, her grandmother was stretched out on the sofa. Not a good sign at all.

Her grandmother patiently watched Arabella pour her tea and settle it on the end table, then began.

"I have been considering this ruin of an estate your brother and you have been saddled with. My funds are limited. I cannot be expected to subsidize this place forever." She waved her hand, with the chocolate still held in her fingers, in a circular motion. "It is simply not possible to pull it from disaster with the meager income I have."

The countess expelled a long breath, laying her head back on the cushions.

Arabella felt her stomach turn. Her grandmother had dived into the issue without the usual niceties. This could only mean she had a plan in mind. Arabella lived in constant fear of her grandmother discovering her clandestine activities. The countess was the one person who could destroy her thriving smuggling business and put her beloved Harwood estate in jeopardy.

She turned to Arabella. "With your brother away on his tour, it is my responsibility as your guardian to manage your future."

Arabella looked down. Her twin Aran, unbeknownst to the countess, was not on a tour, subsidized by her deceased father's old friend, Admiral Hews. He had been caught at sea smuggling contraband. Like many in that circumstance, he had been conscripted into the British navy. Only Aran was not serving as a sailor; he was serving as a spy. Admiral Hews was not his benefactor, but his captor.

"In my estimation we have only two alternatives. We can sell this place—"

"Never," Arabella gasped.

"Let me finish." Her grandmother gave her a stern look. "Or you can do your duty and find a profitable marriage. One which provides a sizable settlement which can then be invested into Harwood Place."

Arabella found herself looking at her slippers again. She knew she must do this duty. She was committed to Harwood. More than anything else, she wanted to honor her family. All her exploits at sea had been directed to this very goal. To lose Harwood Place was not an option. Her twin would never forgive her, and she would never forgive herself.

She could hardly tell her grandmother she planned to restore the place with funds from smuggling. She was caught. Her grandmother had the power as guardian to sell the place if it was in the best interest of the heirs to do so.

With the estate in the condition it was, there would be no argument to forestall her.

"Now then." The countess took a small bite of her chocolate. "The season is in full swing in London. I think we shall pack up and journey to town. You will have this one chance to find a husband to help you save this place."

Arabella felt a wave of panic. "Oh, Nana, you know the trouble I have had in the past finding a suitor. When it is discovered I have no dowry, any young men melt away. I am left with old men. Those men willing to dump a large enough settlement on me are invariably of the merchant class looking for a brood mare with good bloodlines."

Her grandmother looked unmoved, taking a bite from her chocolate, and then discarding it, to examine the tray for a more pleasing dainty.

"Please do not insist on this. I do not display well in town." Arabella leaned forward. "There is no one more awkward than me in society's endless soirees. I will fail."

Arabella thought of the evenings in London, attempting unsuccessfully to flirt with men she had no interest in, and shuddered.

"No, my dear. My mind is quite made up. I have thought long and hard about the responsibility I bear to the two of you, my grandchildren." She sighed, closing her eyes, and rested her head on the cushions propped behind her once more, before making the effort to continue. "You are twenty-three years old, darling. The choice is no longer yours. I have neglected my duty in not insisting you do yours."

She reached for another dainty. "Do not look so glum. London will be a welcome change for you."

"Grandmother, surely, we can hang on a little longer. When Aran comes home—"

"No." The countess softened her reply with a smile. "Things are not so hopeless, Arabella. I am sure you will not be forced to sell the estate. London will have plenty of available men for you." She bit into another chocolate and considered. "There was that man, Mr. Cleves. He had plenty of money and certainly was interested."

"Grandmother, he was a widower with five small children. Five."

The countess smiled again, selecting another chocolate with exaggerated care. "And there was the other fellow, the merchant, now what was his name? Mr. Bumbleman, or Bramblebum—"

Arabella groaned. "It was Bramblemen. He was fifty and needed two chairs to sit down."

There was a long silence while the countess ate her chocolate with relish. Arabella could not help but glare at her. Her world was crashing around her, and her grandmother was nonchalant.

"I am sure there will be plenty of suitors like those we have discussed. For now, my dear, you need not worry. Simply pack your bags and prepare for the trip."

Arabella's cheeks burned with indignation. Her eyes flashed with a surge of anger. Only her grandmother could put her in this helpless position. It infuriated her. She rose slowly from her chair feeling utterly defeated.

"There is one other option darling."

Arabella paused and looked at her.

"Sit down, my dear, and I will enlighten you. I think you will be pleased." The countess swung her legs onto the floor, adjusting her skirts. For the first time in this discussion, she appeared to be engaged. Her eyes sparkled.

Reaching over to the side table and collecting a piece of

parchment, the countess laid it next to the tea tray, smoothing its frayed edges carefully.

"This is a marriage agreement. It was signed by your father and the former Earl of Pembroke twenty years ago. It is a contract complete with a generous settlement to be paid to us when the marriage is completed. There is more than enough here to revive this beleaguered estate." She placed her finger on the line indicating the cash settlement.

Arabella looked at the figure and took a breath. "But this is a sizable settlement grandmother. Why did you never tell me?" She looked again at the contract. There on the paper was the funds she needed for the estate. No reasonable excuse could be made to deny this opportunity. She realized she should be thrilled with this development. Instead, her heart sank. There would be a price to pay for this settlement and she was unsure if she could pay it.

The countess smiled at her reaction. "I thought to give you the opportunity to select a mate of your choice before I brought it to your attention. But since you have not..." She shrugged, leaving the rest of her statement dangling.

She cleared her throat and beamed at Arabella. "Honoring this agreement would be honoring the wishes of your deceased father, my dear. It was he who arranged it for you." She paused, allowing her a moment to digest this information.

"And the earl has agreed to the contract, provided you meet his requirements. He has been searching for a suitable wife. The earl is thirty, I believe. By all accounts, he is a handsome and charming young man. I have heard he is much pursued by many female admirers. His grandmother described him as a fine gentleman, a popular man about town. I think you will be pleased."

"If he is such a prize, why has he not taken one of those admirers?"

The countess only smiled and rose to her feet. "Read it. Think about it. If you have not decided by tonight, then begin your packing." She strolled to the door and rested her hand on the frame, adding, "He just might be the answer to all your problems," before leaving the room.

Arabella read the contract several times. Her stomach ached. How was she to continue her work on the Bella with a husband underfoot? Indeed, with the money for Harwood provided by this agreement, would captain Ara even be necessary? She quickly squashed the thought. As her grandmother had pointed out, this agreement was indeed the answer to her problems. The countess had made it abundantly clear to dismiss it meant selfishly denying both her father's wishes and her beautiful Harwood Place. And worse, if she did not accept the contract, she would be carted off to London immediately. Arabella scowled.

There was only one person who could understand her dilemma. She snatched up the documents and hurried back to the stables to consult Jem. He had been a surrogate father to her and Aran all these years. He knew about her career on the sea. And he would have her best interests at heart.

She found Jem in the stables where she had left him. After telling him of her predicament she waited patiently for his response. Jem slowly set aside the tack he had been assembling and looked down at her. His ravaged face was without expression.

"This is a good arrangement for you, Arabella. It is what your father wanted." Arabella eyes burned with unshed tears. Jem too was in favor of this agreement. She had longed for him to say that all could remain as it was.

That together they would make the money for Harwood on the sea.

He put his heavy arm around her. Her head reached only to his chest. She lay against him, comforted by his massive strength.

"My girl, it is time you married. If as you say he can give us a good settlement, you should consider him. And he is an earl. A fine catch for any girl."

She stepped back a pace. "But Jem, what about the runs to the mainland? How will I manage it with a husband?"

"The runs must stop for you, Arabella. It is too dangerous. We have lost Aran because of the trade, and we cannot lose you. Think of that massive cutter, my girl. He can take you down. If as you say this earl will give you funds, then there is no reason to take the risk."

"I am hoping he might marry me and leave me here to do as I please. Or perhaps he will find me unsuitable."

Jem gave a snort of laughter. "You are a beauty, Arabella. There is no man alive, sane or otherwise, who would leave you here to live out your days on the sea. And as to him finding you unsuitable, I canna see it." He sighed. "No, Arabella, it is time you had a husband. And if you can find one like this fellow who can save this place from ruin, then I say aye."

Arabella scowled. That Jem had agreed to this match surprised her. She had been sure she would find an ally in him and hoped to hear the opposite. He knew the difficulty she would have balancing a husband and her life at sea. She was not willing to give up her role of captain. Not yet. She would have to find a way to make it work.

Jem looked down at her from his massive height. As though reading her mind, he added, "Your days as a captain are numbered, Arabella. It is past time you lived your life as a woman. You will be a wife and very likely a mother. You must learn to be satisfied with that."

She sighed. "I will look at him. If he suits me, I will consider him. But I don't know Jem, if I am able to be the submissive wife this man will surely want."

He gave her arm a reassuring squeeze. "It is only right for woman to find a husband. This will be a good thing. A thing your father would have wanted for you, lassie."

——————

Before the end of the day, Arabella had been able to give her agreement to the contract.

Her grandmother smiled at her. "It is a wise choice, Arabella. You will have a fine man, and Aran when he returns will have an estate which will support him." She hugged Arabella. Leaning back from her, she said, "You know I want the best for the two of you. This agreement provides that."

She took her arm. "Come, let us go to supper."

At supper, the countess made another announcement. "It is time I moved back to London. I have suffered this place for ten years with only an occasional visit to town. It is enough. I have done my duty to the children of my son and feel entitled to a life of my own." She raised her glass and swirled the dark red wine about, watching it intently. "You will be nicely settled and there will be no need for me to remain. My friend Lady Osbourne has offered me a room while I look for a proper residence in London. This arrangement will have worked out perfectly for all concerned."

Arabella looked at the countess suspiciously. She was a

sly creature. As much as she loved the old woman, she would be relieved to have this bit of distance between them.

"If you are pleased, then I am happy for you," Arabella replied politely.

Her mind turned to her prospective husband. Fighting her apprehension, she resolved to make the best of this situation. She would try to be the perfect young lady for him. At least until the wedding. Then she would strike a bargain with him. If he were a man accustomed to the niceties of town life, he would readily agree to leave her behind at Harwood while he enjoyed the entertainments of London.

Captain Ara would be back in business. She hoped.

Chapter Three

Arabella stood at the full-length mirror in her room as Celeste adjusted her undergarments. She was excited to try on the gowns her grandmother had brought from town. She loved the new dress styles. The heavy brocades of the past had not suited her. They were confining. If she had her way, she would not have worn even the corset.

But Celeste insisted. "You have very little for a decollate," she said, waving her hand to indicate her breast area. "We must make the best of it. Yes?"

Celeste gave the corset strings a sharp tug, cinching Arabella tightly, forcing a little cleavage to appear between her meagre breasts. Celeste was small in stature, yet in all matters of dress and men she was not to be argued with.

Arabella resigned herself to tolerating the corset. It was a light burden compared to the full chested one she wore to disguise her breasts as captain of the Bella. It was wiser and safer to always remain in her persona as a male when working the Bella. And if that meant a restraining corset, then so be it. Celeste had been more horrified by that restrictive garment than she had been when she had stumbled upon the evidence of Arabella's persona as Captain Ara.

Celeste had been Arabella's personal maid for a decade. Since her father's death when Arabella was thirteen, Celeste had ruled as her upstairs maid. She was not surprised by Arabella's antics. She had learned to waste no time attempting to curb Arabella's adventurous nature, but she would not tolerate a faux pas in style or on her favorite subject, men.

"We must look our best to meet your young man. Yes?" Celeste's eyes glowed with excitement. "It is past time you had a man, eh?"

She gave Arabella's shoulder a nudge and cackled happily.

Still grinning, Celeste reached for Arabella's new gown, which she deftly pulled over her head. The gown was a soft turquoise silk, covered with an airy film of a pelisse which could be removed. It had short, puffed sleeves, off the shoulder as was the new fashion. It sported a low wide neckline, remained tight across the bosom, then fell to the floor. Arabella loved it. She could not resist a twirl to admire the freedom of the loose flowing skirts.

"It is lovely. *N'est ce pas?*" Celeste stepped back to admire her charge. "Yes, it is quite all right. You look like the portrait of your grandmama, a Spanish belle."

Arabella looked at her reflection critically. She was not an English beauty. Her father had always said there was nothing of the Saxon in her. Family legend told how her grandmother on her mother's side had been a Spanish princess. Like this grandmother, her skin was olive, partly inherited, but also tanned from her days in the sun and wind at sea. Her eyes were dark and slightly tilted at the corners. She had full lips. She smiled. Her brother had nick-named her *imp* for that mischievous grin. She hoped the earl was not expecting a classic English beauty because he would not find it in her. Perhaps a little rouge. She reached for the pot.

Celeste slapped her hand. "No. Not for you. You have no need of it. We will leave your skin fresh. Now for the hair. Come, Arabella."

She pulled back the chair from the dressing table. Arabella obediently sat.

"Now what shall we do?" Celeste picked up the long black hair and examined it as though she had not styled it daily for the past ten years. "I think we shall go with simple elegance. He is to be a husband; it is what he would like best."

She did not wait for a response but began brushing. "A French braid at the sides, and we will do a braided bun just here."

She poked Arabella at the back of her head.

As Celeste worked her hair, Arabella thought about the night to come. It was to be a private formal dinner where the engaged couple could be reacquainted. Just the couple and their respective grandmothers. The earl would be appraising her to see if she suited. Arabella thought it could only be an awkward evening.

"*Voila*! Elegance." Celeste admired her handiwork. "You are perfection, my lady."

Arabella sighed. It was time to face the inevitable. For a man to accept this offer he will probably be distasteful in any number of ways, she thought to herself. Her grand-mother's description was not to be credited. If the man were such a catch, he would not be here tonight willing to take an unknown woman for his bride. For her, the choice was made. Knowing she could not do better in London meant he would have to be completely unacceptable for her to reject him.

Her best hope was that he was one of society's fops. A man dedicated to town life, with its many entertainments. She had seen many of those creatures in London, particularly amongst the titled gentlemen of wealth. Most were only interested in the cut of their suit or a new arrangement of their tie. She grimaced. That brand of man had never appealed to her. But if the earl was of that variety, then he might be eager to complete this wedding and return to his role in town. It would solve her problems. Arabella stood and walked to the full-length mirror. Her black hair shone and was indeed elegant. Her deep brown eyes looked black and too large on her face. She realized with distress, she was nervous, perhaps even a little afraid. She would need to handle the situation with some delicacy. It was essential she portray the modest young lady perfectly. He had to accept her as a bride.

If she could play the part of Captain Ara, then surely, she could play the part of the demure young woman, take this man's wealth, and have him leave her here where she belonged.

Chapter Four

Theo stood at the fireplace with one arm casually resting against the mantle, watching his grandmother and her old friend chat as if the evening were solely designed as an opportunity for them to enjoy their chance to reunite. He had assumed this would be an awkward meeting but had underestimated the social skills and resolve of those two harridans. He smiled. His grandmother would hate the word.

He looked around the room. It was decorated in a style which could only be described as genteel shabbiness. The furnishings were expensive, but sadly out of date. The Persian carpets were of a fine quality, but they had begun to fade. All around him was evidence of a formally wealthy family in need of funds.

Theo had wondered why the young woman would agree to this marriage and now he was sure he had his answer. It did not bother him that her intention was to make use of his money. It was part of the contract. Without her need for his funds, he doubted she would have considered the arrangement.

The last few days, his impending marriage had become increasingly acceptable to him. He had even begun to anticipate the match. He would no longer have to suffer the parade of eligible females at every function he attended.

Dierdra had been angry. She had pouted and stormed. Fortunately, he had been able to confide to her that this marriage had always been his destiny; he had no choice in the decision. He'd cheerfully handed her his parting gift, knowing there was little she could say or do in the matter. He had been vastly relieved. The problem was solved.

He only hoped his fiancée was not a complete frog. He admitted to himself he wanted her to be acceptable in appearance. And he prayed she was not an empty-headed miss. His grandmother had assured him she was an intelligent, gentile creature. She was usually right. He reminded himself if he found her unappealing, he could back out, and he would.

Across the room the subject of his thoughts arrived at last. She stood still at the threshold, unnoticed by the grandmothers, and fixed her gaze on him.

Theo's breath caught. The woman was stunning. He was not sure what he had expected but it was not this. She was tall and slender with black hair which shone in the lamp light. With her olive skin and black eyes, she had the look of a foreigner. She was beautiful—he could not take his eyes off her.

"Ah, Arabella, at last. Come and join us. Arnold, a glass of white wine for my girl." The countess held out her arms to her granddaughter.

Arabella strolled across the room and took the woman's hands.

His grandmother greeted her. "My dear, it has been too long. Time has been gracious to you. You have become a lovely young woman as I knew you would."

Lady Osbourne pulled Arabella close to kiss her cheek. His grandmother could not resist flashing an 'I told you so' look at him over the girl's shoulder. He realized his jaw had dropped and snapped his mouth together quickly.

Lady Osbourne released her and indicated him. "And of course, you must remember my grandson, Theodore. Quite grown up now as you can see."

Arabella turned to him with an impish grin. His stomach flipped.

"So, I see. It is a pleasure to meet you once again, my lord." She gave him a formal curtsy, perfectly executed.

Theo bowed and took her hand to raise it to his lips. Usually adept at these situations, he suddenly found himself tongue-tied. For a few seconds, he just held her hand. He cleared his throat, finally able to mutter the required response. "The pleasure is all mine."

When he met her eyes, a shock of recognition reverberated through him. He had seen these eyes before. He had no idea where, but he knew he had looked at them and seen arrogance and disdain reflected there. He shook off the feeling. Perhaps it was a memory from their childhood encounters.

"Shall we go in for dinner? I believe all is ready," the countess interjected.

He realized he still held Arabella's hand. He let it go quickly and cursed himself for behaving like a dolt. She was a beauty. This was the woman who would soon be his wife.

Theo stole another glance at her. She was not the typical society belle, so familiar to him. There was an air of confidence about her, almost a regal countenance in her stance. He could not imagine her engaging in the shallow flirtations he had become so accustomed to.

He looked down at her hands. She did not even carry the stylish little fan most debutantes maneuvered in accomplished coquetry.

His signature half smile returned to his face. He offered her his arm to escort her to supper. "Shall we?"

She laid her hand on his arm. A surge of possessiveness washed over him as they walked together to the dining room in silence. The moment Arabella laid her arm on his, the decision was made. He would accept this contract. For better or worse this was the bride he would choose. He felt a strange sense of finality.

His apprehension dissipated. In its place was a determination and resolve to make this engagement a reality.

At the dinner table, the conversation inevitably turned to the matter of the impending nuptials. Both elderly ladies assumed the matter was settled. They began to discuss the specifics of an impending wedding. His grandmother was insistent on a quiet and quick affair, while Lady Myrell preferred a society wedding.

"As I said, we come prepared. Theodore has a special license should it be required," Lady Osbourne said.

"But a society wedding, in London, would be marvelous. It could be the event of the season as I have so hoped," Lady Myrell objected. "And why so rushed? Really, Amelia, must everything thing be so abrupt with you?"

"Well, I believe we should leave this decision to the young couple." His grandmother looked at him. "What is your preference, Theo? You must have an opinion."

Theo could hear the growing irritation in her voice. It was clear she hoped to have this arrangement finalized and fully expected an ally in him. His grandmother would want to leave no room for last-minute reversals. In her mind, the sooner the marriage was completed the better.

Theo looked at Arabella who had kept her head lowered. She was the picture of the shy young bride he'd imagined. For the first time, he wondered how she must feel about acquiring a new husband. Was she disappointed? Angry? Resigned? Would she even accept him? He found he needed to know. The grandmothers were premature in their assumptions that the contracts would be honored so readily.

"I would like to speak to Arabella alone before we make these arrangements," he said.

Arabella raised her head, giving him a relieved smile.

His grandmother shifted nervously. "Yes, I suppose that is only reasonable." She glanced at Arabella with some trepidation.

Lady Myrell objected with a long-suffering sigh. "Arabella is committed to this arrangement. I see no reason we cannot progress to the planning. Now then—"

Arabella interrupted, "I too would like to speak with Lord Pembroke before we commit to these plans."

She turned to him. They shared a smile.

It is a start, Theo thought. If nothing else, they both had grandmothers who were adamant in their determination to force their choices and decisions upon them.

Arabella stood. "Could you join me in the library, Lord Pembroke?"

"I could." He rose and took her arm.

He glanced back at the grandmothers. Both wore an identical look of concern on their faces. He smiled at them. He could not help but be pleased with the disruption he and Arabella had made to their schemes.

It will do the old girls good to wait and worry while we make our decision.

34

Chapter Five

Arabella held her breath as she walked with Theo to the library. Somehow, she must get what she wanted from this arrangement. First, she needed his agreement to the betrothal. His money would bring Harwood back to the viable estate it had once been. If he backed out now, she would be in London, searching for a rich husband—a disastrous scenario.

But if she could convince him to marry her, then leave her here in her beloved Harwood, she would have the best possible deal. She could be here to travel to Gravelines to receive word from Aran and her life on the sea would be uninterrupted.

She indicated a chair by the settee. "Can I get you a brandy? I think the evening calls for one."

"Yes. Thank you. I couldn't agree more."

Arabella gave him a healthy dram and poured some for herself. He raised his eyebrows at her unwomanly choice of drink. Women drank madeira, or sherry, never brandy. She was tempted to swig the entire glass but thought it might be a little too shocking for him. She chuckled. Now was not the time to show him she was not quite the perfect lady he may want.

Theo tilted his head quizzically as if suggesting she might share the joke. She felt a ridiculous urge to giggle. She coughed to hide her mirth and waved her hand in front of her face.

"Nerves," she choked out. She pulled herself together and looked at him.

He wore a curious expression which almost set her off again.

"I am so sorry. I don't know what has come over me." She took a quick drink, then a long breath to settle herself.

I am nervous, she thought to herself. If I must bargain, I will need to control myself.

She shifted in her chair and straightened her shoulders.

"Are you all right?"

"Yes. Yes, I think so." Arabella sat and stared at him. "I am afraid I do not know where to start."

"It is difficult. But is it really so different than most marriages of the ton? Everyday marriages are arranged by families between two individuals who hardly know one another. I think it might be wise to remind ourselves our situation is the norm and not the exception." He flashed her a smile and tilted his head. "Don't you agree?"

Theo took a sip of his brandy, addressing the issue immediately, he said, "Now then, I am willing to accept the betrothal, if you find me suitable. And you Lady Arabella? What is your choice?"

"I too will sign the contracts. But there are a few things we need to discuss." A wave of panic flooded her. Had she just agreed to a marriage? The situation felt unreal. "It just seems so rushed," Arabella watched him carefully. The earl had handled his proposal like a business deal. It was not what she had imagined, or what every woman hoped for in a proposal, but she supposed under these circumstances it was the best choice for them both. Much less awkward.

He seemed pleasant enough. She was surprised and relieved by his appearance. He was attractive; tall, with a young healthy body. His blond curly hair was brushed back from his forehead and tied at the nape of his neck. She decided the best way to describe his face was engaging. He sported a smile as though he was interested, but also slightly amused. He was definitely charming.

She continued, "You must admit most couples do get a period of time for courting."

"Ah." He sipped his brandy, then swirled it about in his glass. "Is that what you want?"

He was so much more than what she had been resigned to accept in this agreement. She had spent the week squashing any girlish dreams she had about a future husband who could be appealing to her. But this man was attractive, she decided. It was both a relief and a worry.

"What I want is to know why you agreed to this marriage. You are an earl. You have money and by all accounts you do not lack for female admirers. You are not even a disaster in appearance. Why would you choose me?"

He laughed loudly and looked at her with his blue eyes shining appreciatively. She found she could not resist a smile in response.

"Well, it's good to know I am not a complete disappointment for you." He chuckled. "It is a worthy question."

He took another sip of brandy as though debating his answer.

"I need a wife. It is time I had an heir. The contract is a handy solution." He sighed and leaned back in his chair.

"All of these reasons but most of all, I'm weary of the entire process of searching for the right match."

He looked at her and grinned, "So you see it is all very convenient for me this way. And you, Arabella, why did you agree?"

He seemed to have been completely honest with her. For a second, she wished she could do the same. She could give him at least part of the truth.

"I need your money." She flashed him her mischievous smile.

He threw back his head and burst into loud laughter. Arabella decided she liked the sound. He laughed with such heartfelt ease. Again, it was impossible not to smile in return and she did. She waited until he had finished before she continued.

"I do. My twin Aran owns Harwood Place, but he has left me in charge. There is so much to be done and no funds. With your generous marriage settlement, we could begin the task of making this place self-sufficient. So yes, there is that."

Arabella took a good swallow of her brandy. Now came the hard part of her bargain. "Which leads me to my second reason for signing the contracts. My grandmother is moving to town. I need to be here. I cannot move from Harwood for at least six months or until my twin returns home." She looked at him to gage his response. "I cannot, as a young single woman, be left here alone without a proper chaperone. My grandmother would not hear of it. As a married woman I could stay and manage the estate as I must."

She waited while he digested the information. She decided to underline her point. "I would need to stay here at Harwood for the time being. Not forever of course, just the next six months."

She was at a loss. She could not confide to him she was needed here to make runs across the channel. Even if she did not smuggle goods, she had to make her trips to seek news of her twin Aran. When Aran had been caught running a load of contraband and captured by the British navy, being pressed into service as a spy meant their contact with him was limited. Only through messages left at the smuggling port of Gravelines on the French coast were they able to receive precious news from him.

Whatever their agreement, she was simply not ready to leave her life here at Harwood. To lose Captain Ara, to forgo all contact with Aran, her twin, and to not be here to see the improvements to the estate would be too much to give up. At least not immediately, she thought, feeling her stomach churn.

He furrowed his brow. He had obviously not considered leaving her here after the marriage.

"I see." He looked at her curiously. "Have you considered an overseer? Many estates are run by an agent; indeed, most estates are operated in that way. There are many talented managers to be hired."

Without thinking, Arabella said, "We have a good overseer, or I mean, Aran has hired an overseer. Jem McAlister is one of the best." Realizing her mistake, she stared at her hands, desperate to produce a reasonable explanation for her request. It would have been much easier if she had said there was no proper administration here at Harwood.

Arabella decided to ignore their conversation about an overseer. He was right of course; a good manager could handle the estate, but it was not an option she cared to consider.

She tried again. "It is not so unusual. Many men marry and leave their wives at their country estate. It is exactly the same except in this instance it is her family estate." When he said nothing, she pressed on, "It is the one part of our bargain I must have."

"That you must have?" Theo raised an eyebrow.

"Yes. I am afraid so." Her cheeks were burning. It was so hard to explain to him what could not be explained. Until this moment she had not realized duplicity was an issue for her. Outright lying was different than her persona as a male captain aboard the Bella. When she was Captain Ara, she submerged herself in the role. It was a truth, in a strange sense.

Now she found she could not make up a reasonable explanation for her need to remain at Harwood. She realized, with a wry smile, she was fortunate it was Aran who was acting as a spy and not her.

Theo watched her carefully, then rose and walked to the brandy decanter on the cabinet. He raised the dispenser. "May I?"

When she nodded, he poured himself a glass and took a drink.

"This is exceptionally good brandy." He raised his glass to the light and swirled it. "French. And some of the finest."

Arabella stared at him blankly. Good French brandy could only be purchased from smugglers. The war with Napoleon had ended the trade. Though illegal, most of the homes of the wealthy somehow continued to get their hands on it.

"My... my grandmother finds it medicinal," she stammered.

"I think we can manage six months." He leaned against the cabinet, taking a sip of his brandy.

Arabella was stunned by Theo's abrupt agreement. She released a long breath she hadn't been aware of holding. He had not asked her the uncomfortable questions she would not have been able to answer. She was thankful for that. She had no idea why he had accepted her condition, but he had.

"I have a codicil to add. If we are to reside here, I want to help you restore this estate. I don't relish the idea of lounging about for six months in the wilds of Yorkshire with little to do."

Arabella quickly interjected, "But you wouldn't have to. You can return to London and enjoy your life there. Then in six months—"

"No," he interrupted.

"No? But it would be ideal for you. You wouldn't have the burden of looking for a wife. And I, of course, would be no trouble to you far from town." Arabella was taken aback by his assumption the two of them would reside here together. She had assumed he would be a creature of society, eager to be in London amongst his peers.

He took a sip of brandy, looking at her over the rim, then slowly set it down on the cabinet beside him. She watched him, hoping he would see the benefit to him in this arrangement. He seemed to be considering it.

His next words belied the notion. "Having made this decision, I'm eager to begin the endeavor. Leaving you here alone is not an option. It is off the bargaining table. I will not consider it." He smiled at her. "Besides, I'm curious to see what can be done to save your Harwood Place. Restoring enterprises to prosperity is a passion of mine."

Despite the smile, there was a firm resolve to his words. He was serious.

She sighed. It was going to be a difficult six months with a husband underfoot. She debated declining the entire contract. But the money, with the opportunity to restore Harwood it provided, loomed in her mind. She scowled. If she backed out now, she would be in London within the week, sitting in a ball gown, looking for an elusive husband. One who could provide her with everything this man in front of her could offer. It was the endless soirees in town, and the image of Mr. Bramblemen, which finally swayed her.

"Fine. You will be here with me working on the estate. But I want to be clear. I will need six months." She paused. "Unless my brother Aran returns sooner than expected."

His eyes sparkled. Clearly, he was pleased with her capitulation. She shot him a nasty glare.

He laughed. "I will want access to everything, Arabella. In management, the answers usually lie in the accounts. If I am to be of some assistance while I'm here, I will be interested in doing a thorough job."

"Fine. I agree," she grudgingly replied.

"Now then." He returned to his chair. "Have we hammered out an agreement?"

Arabella laughed, partly in relief and in part because of his exaggerated businesslike attitude. Striking a bargain was not new to this man.

She sobered as she considered him interfering with Harwood. She had not expected it. A shiver of apprehension went through her. The earl might not be as manageable as she hoped. Assessing him once more, she examined his impeccable dark tuxedo and polished hessians. He was the image of the man about town. This man would soon lose interest in country life and return to town life.

"I think we have an agreement." She bit her lip as she considered. "There is one more concern, but it is only a concern, not a condition."

"Surely not."

Arabella looked at him sharply. He was smiling. It was a joke. She smiled a slow smile. He had a sense of humor which could only be a good thing.

"I was hoping we could have a little time to get to know each other." She hesitated, unsure of how to go on. "We mentioned courting. Or I mean that there had been no courting, between us, you see. I know the grandmothers will insist on a wedding as soon as possible. I have no objection to that. But I had hoped we could have a little time before we...That is..." She felt herself redden and gave up.

Theo laughed. "We will manage, my dear. I am sure I can muddle through an attempt at courtship, even after the marriage, if it is what you want."

Whatever the outcome, the bargain was struck. She had done what she must. She had not been able to get all she had wanted, but she had managed to negotiate for the most significant elements. She hoped it was a deal she would not regret.

He offered her his arm. "Shall we return to the grand-mothers?" He grinned. "Though it pleases me to make them a little uneasy, I don't want to torture them too much."

Arabella laughed. "Yes, I suppose we cannot hold them in suspense too much longer."

They found the ladies in the dining room where they had left them. They were enjoying a glass of madeira. Both looked up with similar expressions of apprehension. Arabella allowed Theo to lead her to her chair and take his seat across from her. She decided to let him make the announcement.

Theo cleared his throat. "We have both decided to honor the agreement."

There was a palpable release of tension in the room. Her grandmother leaned back in her chair and smiled.

Lady Osbourne was not yet satisfied. She would have the marriage completed before she was content. "Now then, as I said, Theo has a special license. I propose we complete the process by having the ceremony as soon as possible." She looked at each of them in turn as though assessing the degree of opposition she would face. "I see no point in further delay. A quiet wedding here at Harwood could be achieved in a few days."

Arabella met Theo's eyes, waiting for his response.

He shrugged. "I too prefer a quiet wedding. I have no interest in a large gathering. But of course, it is up to Arabella. If she wishes to travel to London and put on a grand affair, then that is what we shall do."

Arabella gave him a faint smile. She turned to her grandmother. "I know it is your fondest wish to have this grand affair. I don't like to disappoint you. But I think I would prefer to be married here, quietly at my home." She reached over and grasped her hand. "Particularly under these circumstances."

Lady Osbourne's cane came down on the hardwood floors with a resounding *thump*. Arabella flinched. Theo could not suppress his grin.

Lady Osbourne said, "It is settled then. The local chapel. And there is no call for delay. We can get this business over and done in two days."

The countess gave a long-suffering sigh and looked at Arabella. "I had hoped for something a little more elaborate for you, my dear."

"It is perfect," Arabella said, patting her grandmother's hand.

And that, thought Arabella, is that.

As the ladies discussed the niceties—the invitations, the flowers, the food, and whatever else—Arabella contributed little. The details held no interest for her. Instead, she marveled at the abrupt change her life was about to take.

Theo too seemed to be lost in thought. She wondered if this were a decision they would be able to tolerate, or if both would forever regret their hastiness.

She had managed to beguile him as planned, but there was no thrill in the victory. In her heart she knew she faced a lifetime of deception or a difficult farewell to Captain Ara and all the persona provided to her.

Chapter Six

Celeste loosened the stays on Arabella's corset and pulled it over her head. "I confess I took a little peek at your man. Ooh la la. He is a prize for you. Yes? I like him. He has a good smile."

"He does. I hope to like him too, Celeste," Arabella said as Celeste helped her wrestle out of the chemise and put on her nightie.

She thought of her future husband, feeling a tingle of butterflies in her tummy. He was much more than she'd thought he would be. She found him attractive and appealing. Maybe this marriage could give her some enjoyment.

Recalling her smuggling career dashed her dreams in that direction. She shook her head and pressed her lips into a determined line. Instead, she would hope he became bored with managing the estate and return to his life in town. Aspirations for a happy married life were not for her. She could never be the lady he wanted. If he ever found out about her life as Captain Ara, he would be sure to look upon her with disdain. Discovering her true identity would certainly be a cause for divorce.

She sighed and squashed her daydreams; a true marriage was not for her.

"Have a good sleep, my *cherie*. You will have much to do tomorrow. Me, I must find the perfect dress for you." Celeste set the lantern on her bedside table and left the room.

Arabella got on her knees, reached beneath the mattress, and pulled out a crumpled letter. It was the last letter she had received from Aran one month ago. She smoothed it carefully and read.

Dearest Arabella,

I hope this letter finds you well. In receiving this you will know at least part of my mission has been successful. You have in your possession an object of extreme importance to England. I ask that you deliver it to the smugglers port at The Meadows in Kent. At the unloading when the password, "The Ides of March" is given you may give it over in good faith.

I had hoped to return after this mission and indeed it was the promise given to me. I have been too efficient in my work. My language skills, especially my fluency in Spanish and French, have been both a boon and a curse. Admiral Hews has requested that I complete another task before I return. It will take me some time. I cannot be certain of when I shall return, but I have been promised I will be pulled from this assignment before the Christmas season.

I am well and in good spirits. There is danger, but I know I am safe and expect to return home in good health. My worries lie with you and our beloved Harwood. It is my hope all is well. I ask that you limit your time at sea. I could not bear to hear news of you being taken as a smuggler. I know you will be travelling to Gravelines to receive word from me but again I ask that you do so infrequently so I may be assured of your continued safety. Appeal to our grandmother for funds if they are needed. I rest easy knowing you and Jem will do all possible to manage our estates, but you, dear sister, are more important to me than even Harwood.

You have my love, Arabella. Please do not send a letter in return. I fear it would only cause me danger. And know too that if an opportunity exists for me to send you word of my continued good health and safety, I will. If you hear no further word from me by the new year, or if you must contact me, go directly to Admiral Hews at the Home Office.

With much love,
Your twin Aran

Arabella carefully refolded the letter and returned it to its place under the mattress. The night at the wharf on The Meadows flashed across her mind. There was something nagging at her memory about the transfer at that docking.

She brushed it aside. After a long day, it would be a relief to say her prayers and get some rest. As always, her first prayer was for the safety of her twin. Tonight, she also prayed for herself. She had chosen a husband. She hoped it would be a marriage which allowed her the freedom to continue her life here at Harwood.

"I am to be married," she murmured to herself. "How strange."

Arabella had never been a girl who dreamed of love. Perhaps it was her upbringing. She had spent her childhood with Aran and occasionally some of his companions. She tolerated her girlfriends but found them and their interests boring. Though she had been forced to endure endless lessons on decorum, an element of her education her grandmother had refused to ignore, she preferred the company of males.

Arabella had competed with Aran her whole life. Sometimes she won. Like him, she could speak fluent Spanish, French, and Latin. But he had a talent for accents which she could not master. Both had received a strong education in history, geography, and mathematics, but again he had been the better student. She was the better swordsman, and she was also the better sailor. She knew with a certainty that had she been at the helm the day he was taken by the revenue cutters, she could have outrun them.

Before falling asleep she thought of Theo. He laughed easily and loudly. There was an ease about him, a charm she found appealing. But there was something bothering her —something familiar about him, almost as though she had met him before.

Impossible. She closed her eyes with the image of his lazy smile in her mind.

———

Morning found the staff of Harwood in a flurry of activity. Besides the upcoming wedding breakfast, the countess had decided to take up Lady Osbourne on her offer of a lift to town. They would be leaving immediately after the wedding breakfast. The countess had insisted Arabella be moved into what had formally been her suite.

"It is only right, my love. The adjoining rooms are made for a couple," she had said.

Poor Celeste was in a temper, supervising the move and preparing a trousseau for Arabella. The upstairs rooms were a hub of activity. Arabella had a quick breakfast in her room followed by a dress fitting. The gown was to be a light gold silk in the modern style. A sheer veil and pelisse completed the ensemble. Her hair would be worn long, with small braids at the sides pulled back to hold it in place. Celeste declared it, "Simple and elegant, your hair down as a bride's should be. Perfect for my *cherie*."

Arabella joined the grandmothers in the library to discuss a guest list.

"We do not have time for an extended guest list. A few neighbors will have to suffice. The invites will go out within the hour," Lady Osbourne said with a thump of her cane. Thankfully, her chair rested on a thick Persian carpet, muffling the sound.

Her grandmother emitted a long-suffering sigh. "Amelia, must everything about this affair be so hasty? It is tiresome."

The countess leaned back and folded her legs beneath her on the sofa. She was the picture of indolence. Arabella found it hard to believe that the two of them were friends. They seemed the complete opposite in nature.

Lady Osbourne ignored her and turned to Arabella. "Get a pen and paper, my dear. We will make a list." She waited until Arabella sat behind the desk and prepared her quill and paper. "Now then, I have sent word to the Vicar, Mr. Berg. Theo will be visiting him now to apprize him of the details. Apparently, he is new to the community. Does he have a wife, my dear?"

"He does."

"And who for neighbors will you wish to have?"

Her grandmother roused herself to attend to this chore. "Let me see. We will not be able to ask people from afar, therefore we will limit it to a few neighbors. We shall ask the Bradfords, of course, the baron, his wife and their two daughters who have been friends with Arabella. And the mayor of the village, Mr. Dewberry, and his wife Margaret. With the Vicar and his wife, that is a sizable crowd on short notice." She rubbed her forehead. "Oh, and our new neighbor, whatever is his name? Oh, yes. We shall extend an invitation to Mr. Sheffeld. He is residing on the property past the gulley, near Bergen's point. He is a single man, I believe."

"Is there anyone you would like to add, Arabella?" Lady Osbourne asked.

"Yes. I would invite Jem Mcalister, our overseer, and a friend."

"Good. That was simple. Unfortunately, Theo will have to make do with me for a guest. It is simply too far for his crowd to attend. Now then, I expect you to have the invitations written up and sent within the hour, Arabella."

Arabella waited for the signature thump of her cane and was not disappointed. She could not suppress a smile.

Lady Osbourne continued, "A handwritten notice from the bride will be a nice touch. Be sure to use quality paper, my dear. A good parchment speaks volumes. Now then, let us leave her to work. Come, Adrienne, we need to finalize the menu."

Arabella smiled as the two ladies left the room. There was nothing the two of them could not accomplish. She made short work of the invites, sent them off, and went to find Jem to hand deliver his.

She found him by the stables in a close conference with Arnold and Jamie. At her approach, the conversation ceased. All three of them looked as though they had been caught stealing fruit.

Something was wrong. It did not escape her that Jamie

and Arnold were crew members of the Bella. Arnold also worked for her as a footman; Jamie was a stable hand.

Arabella did not waste time on niceties. "What has happened?"

Jem responded, "The Mrytle was caught last night. She was on the way out, carrying wool and coins to France."

Arabella stared at him. The Myrtle docked in the village. She was manned by sailors from the area.

"What is the fate of the crew?" she asked.

"It is not to be known. Jamie only picked it up from his cousin, a crew member of the Mrytle."

"What! What does this mean? Not to be known?"

"Hush. Keep your voice down, Ara. Your boyo is in the stable, just now home from the Vicar's. Come, let's walk a ways." He led the little party down the fence line a few feet where he pretended to examine a gate. "Tell us, Jamie."

Jamie cleared his throat. "The Mrytle ran into the cutters on her way out to sea. They had a load of wool and gin for trade. She had only just cleared the point. It was a short race. They took her down and boarded her quick-like. They were lying in wait for her. My cousin Bart is sure of it. They had no chance. She took 'em fast, she did." Jamie paused. "He says they were sure they were done for. He and the boys had their hands on their cutlases, but it was the oddest thing you see."

He waited to be sure he had their attention.

"Get on with it," Ara ordered.

"They weren't taken up. The captain, the revenue man, he ordered the goods transferred onto his cutter. A full cargo of wool meant to be traded at Gravelines. Lucky for them the bastards hadn't found the gold. Then the boys were told if word leaked out, they'd find their deaths."

"And?" Arabella asked.

"And that's it. That's the whole of it. The scoundrel cutter left. Took their wool for themselves, the dirty thieves. Bart and his boys came back to the village. The Myrtle is docked. It's all to be kept quiet. No one's to know. Bart says his captain is raving. And there's more. We are all sure there is a traitor in the village. It was too handy by half. Everyone is suspicious."

Arabella was outraged.

"The bloody thieves!" She muttered another string of curses.

Jem scowled at her foul language before saying, "Something is up. The Bella has been chased three for three and now the Myrtle. There is a rat, Arabella. We cannot do a run until we find him."

"There are new people in the area. The Vicar and his mousy wife for one. I don't trust 'em." Jamie scowled. "And my cousin agrees. Says the new Vicar is the quiet sort. He only spews the scriptures. What kind of Vicar is the quiet sort?"

He snorted.

Jem rubbed his chin thoughtfully. "Again, the cutters hide just beyond Bergen's point. It's where we have seen them too. If there is signaling going on, it must be from the high cliffs beyond the village. The vicarage sits above the village but still a signal could not be made past Bergen's heights. The Vicar could see the departures and make a fast trip to the cliffs, tis true. But it would be a hurried and hard trip for him. He'd be seen." He ran his big hand across his grizzled jaw. "No. There must be a spotter on the cliffs relaying the signals to the cutter beyond."

"Am I interrupting?" Theo walked toward them. He was looking at them curiously.

Arabella realized they made an unlikely group.

She felt her cheeks flush. "No. I was just delivering Jem my personal invitation to the wedding tomorrow," she replied, reaching into her pocket, and handing Jem her inscribed card. She turned to Arnold. "And it is back to work for you two."

The lads hustled off.

Arabella took Theo's arm. "My lord, I would like you to meet our overseer and my friend Jem Mcalister. Jem, this is my fiancé, Lord Pembroke."

Jem nodded, "Good day, sir."

Arabella noticed Theo wince as they shook hands. Jem towered over her future husband; his face impassive as he slowly eyed Theo from head to toe.

Theo looked up at Jem with an expression of amazement. Jem was an unlikely overseer. He had the look of a prize fighter or a bodyguard with his bulky form and weathered, scarred face.

Arabella smiled. Jem was the most intimidating man she had ever known. His hard look alone could scare off any threat. Just now he was assessing Theo with that look. Jem had been her father's batsman in combat. When her dad had returned from the peninsula a broken man, Jem had taken it upon himself to see to his children. He took that responsibility seriously.

Theo recovered slowly. He cleared his throat. "Ah. The overseer. Arabella has told me you do a fine job. I should like to see the estate. I took a trip into the village this morning. The land here is rougher and rockier than I expected. I'm curious to see what it looks like away from the coast."

"Aye," Jem said. "I'll be checking a fence line this afternoon. Come if you want."

"I will."

"Then we'll meet up here in two hours." Jem gave him a

final hard look and walked back into the stables without another word.

Theo watched him leave with an expression of horror.

"Huh." He turned to Arabella. "Will I survive that encounter? It would be nice to live until the wedding at least."

Arabella laughed. She took his arm. "Jem is a little protective. You must remember he's like a father to me. He is family, and I love him dearly."

"It would have felt better had your father figure been a little less...less of a giant. I feel as though he could crush me with his little finger and worse, he would take pleasure in the task."

Arabella laughed again. "He could and he would. But enough of Jem. Would you care to take a walk with me? I could show you the gardens. They are in a sad state, but there is much potential."

"I would." Theo gave a final glance at the stables as though assuring himself Jem was not in sight and took her arm. "I want to practice some of the courting skills I promised you last night. You look lovely today, my dear."

He lifted her hand to his lips and kissed it as they walked.

Arabella blushed. She was unused to flattery. "Thank you, my lord."

"You must call me Theo. My lord is a bit stuffy for a future husband, don't you think?"

"Thank you, Theo." Arabella was unsure what to say to him.

Theo seemed aware of her discomfort. "Let's get to know each other a little. Tell me what interests you. What is your favorite thing to do?"

"Oh, that is an easy question. I love to sail. Aran has a

lugger. She is docked in the village. I take her out as often as I can." Her eyes shone with enthusiasm. "Being on the sea is everything to me."

She looked at him and raised her chin with a smug expression. "And I am the best. I captain her. My Bella is slick in the water." She looked at him with excitement. "You will have to come out with me while you are here."

"I will. I have sailed but I am afraid, unlike you, I am not the best." He smiled at her. "I have been wondering what we could do after our wedding breakfast. Since we're not going away, perhaps you could get a crew together and show me your skills."

Arabella clapped her hands. "Wonderful idea! We shall. Oh, you'll love my Bella! I will talk to Jem and arrange it."

"It is settled then. We shall have a honeymoon cruise." Theo reached over and took her arm. His grip was warm as he pulled her tight against him.

They walked in silence. His closeness was disconcerting. She glanced at him from beneath her lowered eyelashes. His jacket fit snuggly over strong shoulders. His face had chiseled features. He was not rugged, like the Yorkshire men she knew, but there was strength in his firm jawline and high cheek bones.

She searched her mind for something to say. For the first time, she regretted she had not practiced flirtation like all the other girls. It was what she wanted to do now. She decided to give him a history of the gardens instead. "When we reach the gardens, I am afraid you will find they are quite overgrown. It is my last priority you see. But they once were beautiful and will be again."

"May I ask what happened to the estate?"

Arabella considered. "It has been a long decline, I am afraid. There is no one thing which brought us down, but several. I suppose it started when my mother died. My father lost interest in everything." Arabella grimaced. Even his children, she added silently. "He spent a few years just letting the place slide before he bought a commission and entered the fight against Napoleon."

Theo said nothing. He tightened his hold on her arm and let her speak.

"He left us with an overseer who robbed us blind. All the livestock was gone. He had taken high rents from the sharecroppers and most of them left as a result. The land lay bare. Nothing had been repaired or replaced. The mill had stopped operating and the miller disappeared. To this day we are forced to haul what little grain grown to the village. Aran and I were too young to do much of anything about it."

She sighed. "It was challenging times. We had no idea the extent of the overseer's pillaging until well after he left. Then when father returned, he was a broken man. He didn't care about the estate. For months he stayed in his rooms. His mind had been damaged. Jem took care of him, but it was not enough. He fell from the second story window."

Arabella stole a glance at Theo. Her father's death had looked suspiciously like a suicide. It was a family secret. Theo did not meet her eyes but held her arm reassuringly.

"Since then, Jem has tried to help us restore the place, but it's been difficult. There has been no income and only expenditure for more than a decade. With no money it has been next to impossible to recover."

She decided to try to lighten the mood. She had not intended to give him this long sordid story.

"But enough of that. I plan to spend a good part of your marriage settlement on Harwood. It will be a new era.

And you, my dear, will have helped us rebuild," she said, squeezing his arm lightly.

They walked through a gap in a ten-foot hedge near the back of the yard and entered the gardens. A wide tiled patio extended from the house at least thirty feet and ran the length of the mansion. Its side edges sported a wrought iron railing that doubled as a trellis for climbing roses which were currently in full bloom. Someone had given the patio some much needed attention. Its floors were wet and freshly scrubbed. The area nearest them held several large potted plants. The patio was prepared for the wedding, adorned with tables laid with cloths and empty vases. Near the building preparations had begun for the buffet.

"If the weather permits, this is where we shall have our wedding breakfast." She looked at Theo. "The grand-mothers decided it would add a little charm. Do you approve?"

Theo grinned. "I would be a fool to even attempt to disagree. I am sure the gavel has been struck on this issue."

Arabella found herself laughing again. She shot him an appreciative look. She understood at once why her grand-mother said he had a throng of admirers. He was enter-taining.

Arabella looked around the garden. "I think our grand-mothers have been busy. And it looks as though they have brought help in from the village."

A freshly cut lawn stretched out from the patio an addi-tional thirty or more feet. It had only this morning been reclaimed from the wild and was therefore brittle and sparse. A servant was trimming and cleaning the rose beds. Another was raking the pathways. Beyond that the grass grew tall. Trees and shrubs long overgrown littered the area. In the distance, half shrouded in foliage, a fountain peeked out. To the far left, a gazebo could be glimpsed through a haze of gnarled shrubbery.

"My maternal grandmother loved the gardens. It feels so good to see at least part of them again." She gave him a wide grin. "I have just decided I will hire a gardener or two. It is time to take this back."

Her black eyes danced with excitement.

Theo looked at her with approval. "An excellent idea."

"You must see the gazebo!" She hesitated. "If we can get there."

She took Theo's hand and led him across the yard. His hand felt large and strong in hers. They both walked carefully through the tall grass skirting the larger obstacles. Eventually they came to the gazebo, half-hidden near the garden's perimeter. It was a white marble structure, long since turned dull gray from layers of dust and grime. It was Etruscan in style. Its half walls sported benches which were interrupted by carved pillars reaching a domed ceiling. She led him inside.

Letting go of his hand she did a little spin in its center, her shoes tapping on the marble floors. "My Spanish grandmother had it constructed in Italy, then shipped it here in pieces to be reassembled." She grinned. "I always thought it was beautiful."

"There is much beauty here and not all of it is Italian marble." Theo took a step closer to her, gently putting his hands on her shoulders, and pulled her close.

Arabella breathed the tantalizing mix of his fragrance, a spicy blend of cologne and a scent which was unique to him. She looked into his eyes, seeing gold flecks in a blue base. She could not look away.

Very slowly, with his gaze not leaving hers for an instant, he leaned in to taste her lips. She gasped. He rained soft kisses along her lips, then gently sucked her bottom lip into his mouth and pressed it between his teeth.

Arabella's heart was pounding. This man would be her husband tomorrow. Feeling a curious excitement, she lifted her arms to his shoulders.

Theo smiled and deepened the kiss. His hands moved to her waist, grasping her more tightly. Reaching her arms around his back, she held him close to her body.

He left her lips and began to kiss her neck. His hot breath and wet kisses were intoxicating. She needed to touch him. With a heady recklessness, she pushed up his jacket and shirt to slide her hands inside. His back was smooth and hot. Touching his bare skin felt decadent and exciting. She ran her hands down the length of him, feeling his muscles harden beneath her fingers. His warm breath tickled her neck.

His hands found her breasts and he kneaded them as his mouth moved ever so slowly across her chest. She threw her head back and closed her eyes, her chest arched towards him, her hands gripping his shoulders. She thought only of the way he was making her feel.

He leaned back, grasped her dress by the shoulders, and eased it carefully past her breasts to her waist. For a minute, she was shocked and stunned. She felt exposed and vulnerable with her arms trapped at her sides. He raised his eyes to hers once more before he placed a hand on each of her small breasts and held them.

"You are beautiful," he murmured.

She could only stare at him wide-eyed. A tremor that was almost fear rippled through her body. Leaning forward, with his hands still cupping her breasts, he kissed her long and hard.

Then he pulled away from her, carefully returning her

dress to its former position and meticulously arranging her sleeves, before reaching up to cup her chin.

Looking at her intently, he said, "I apologize, Arabella. I lost my head. I hope I haven't offended you."

Arabella was speechless. The only kiss she had ever received had been from Aran's friend Andrew, who had grabbed her and forced it on her. He had received a solid kick to the shins for it. This was not the same at all. Theo's kisses left her body trembling. She wanted to touch him. And it was strangely exhilarating to feel his hands on her. She shivered.

Arabella did not know what to say or do now. Her cheeks flushed with embarrassment. She looked up to find him watching her. It made her discomfort worse. She quickly turned her eyes to the floor.

"I..." she stammered. "It... your kisses were...exciting."

He laughed loudly and joyfully, reaching out his arm. "Come on. I will take you back to the house. God knows I better not be late for my tour with your Jem. I can hardly tell that massive behemoth that I was romancing his girl, can I?"

Arabella laughed too. It was a relief from the tension of the last few moments. Besides, the idea of confiding the events of their interlude in the gazebo to Jem was ludicrous. She took Theo's hand. It felt warm, comfortable, and right.

But in her heart, she knew she played a dangerous game. Theo was far too appealing. It would be a battle to keep her distance from this man.

Chapter Seven

Theo looked across the patio at his new bride, who shimmered in a gold dress. Arabella looked for all the world like a Greek goddess: tall, slender, and beautiful in her olive skin and mysterious dark eyes. Her blue-black hair fell straight and long to the center of her back, its only adornments a few sprigs of baby lace tucked into two tiny braids like a miniscule laurel wreath.

He chuckled to himself. He was behaving like a besotted schoolboy. In the gazebo yesterday afternoon he had allowed his curiosity about his bride to overwhelm him. He had had to taste her. Yet having done so, he found the image dominating his thoughts. And Arabella had responded to him. This above all else consumed him. Whether it was because of her beauty, or his knowledge she was his, he could not stop thinking of her. He had been with many women, but never had he felt this draw, this strong urge to be with her and to make her his.

Arabella was everything the society girls he had met were not. She was fresh and exuberant. She did not play coy or flirt with him in the traditional way. He thought of the brandy she had poured for herself at their first meeting. No sweet feminine sherry for her—and she made no apologies. She was an innocent and a mature woman simultaneously.

He wanted to move slowly. Arabella wanted a courtship before they became intimate, and he was determined to give her one. It was little enough to ask. There could be no more kisses like the one in the gazebo. He again felt his body respond as he remembered those small firm breasts and the feel of her hands on his back. She was an innocent, but she had clearly wanted him. And that was the most powerful aphrodisiac of all.

He was relieved to see the party was breaking up. Arabella came to stand beside him to say farewell to the departing guests.

The Vicar and his wife, Mr. and Mrs. Berg, were the first to leave. He had been surprised by the effort his new wife had made to get to know the couple. He supposed as the gentry in the community, Arabella felt it her duty to make the connection. The Vicar seemed to be a man of few words and his nondescript frail wife had been equally close-mouthed.

Next, Mr. Sheffeld made his departure. He seemed an unpleasant man. Tall and hefty, with a pale face half hidden by a thick red beard, he wore the old-fashioned short pants and hose of a country gentleman and a permanent scowl. He kept himself distant from the other guests, meeting any attempts at polite conversations with monosyllables. There would not be much in the way of neighborly entertaining for Arabella and him there.

The Baron and his family were entirely the opposite. The Baron, Lord Bradford, was as noisy as his daughters. His voice boomed above all others. And the girls, Rebecca,

Clarice, and their mother, were in constant conversation. The family, together with the mayor and his wife, left as one, leaving the patio in sudden blissful silence.

Theo's grandmother pulled Arabella to her and kissed her on both cheeks. "I could not be happier, my dear. You make a fine new granddaughter. My Theo will take excellent care of you. And if he does not, you need only to come to me." She smiled broadly at the two of them. "Now then, we have had a little luncheon and we are ready to go. The coach is loaded and waits only for us."

When the countess strolled over to say her goodbyes to Arabella, his grandmother pulled him aside for a little chat. "You will have to come to town in a few days. The funds must be transferred. It will be all in readiness for you, but it must be done."

"I will. Have a good trip, grandmother." He leaned in and kissed her cheek.

"You may write me a long letter to thank me for this day."

Theo laughed. "I might surprise you and do just that." He watched the two old girls depart. Draping an arm around Arabella he said, "Jem has left to prepare your lugger. He says he can put together a small crew. Are you still wanting our honeymoon cruise?"

"I am more than ready. Though I suppose we should change out of this finery first." Arabella spun around and made for the house. Turning back, she called, "Five minutes. It is all the time you have."

Laughing, she hurried on.

He stood and watched her run to the patio doors, her gown trailing forgotten behind her, and considered the strange mix of child and woman she was. She was beguiling and hugely sexy. When her lips curled into a knowing smile his stomach flipped with anticipation. But just now she was the young hoyden who had run wild on this isolated country estate.

The seas were calm. It was a gentle breeze that saw the ship round Bergen's point. Arabella was at the helm. Theo watched her with open admiration. It was apparent she was both talented and experienced, with a crew that was efficient and more. Arabella's sailors were entuned to her every word or motion. And they called her captain with such ease he knew they had sailed with her many times.

He was watching the wind play with his new bride's hair and thinking about how alive and powerful she was at the helm when Jamie hollered from the stern. "We've gotta cutter, Cap'n Ara. She is coming in hard."

The phrase Captain Ara jolted him. He had heard it before. This was the second time he had experienced this sense of déjà vu concerning Arabella. His thoughts were soon lost amid the hustle of the crew at the sighting of the incoming ship.

Arabella let him take the helm. He turned in time to see her climb to the rails at the stern to get a clearer view. It was a dangerous and precarious stance. Theo was about to yell a protest when to his surprise she reached up to the rigging and swung through the air to the deck. He could only stare open-mouthed. This was an Arabella he did not know.

The crew stood in readiness, waiting for her orders.

"What is your plan, Ara?" Jem asked. His face was calm but like the rest of the men, he had about him a palpable intensity.

"Let her come, boys. Drop the sail. Lay anchors. They

can board us today. The earl," she said, nodding in Theo's direction, "our captain, can explain our business to the cutters."

The message was clear. The boys dropped the Bella's sails and she slowed.

Arabella stood closely beside Theo. "To save ourselves a lot of unnecessary trouble, today you will be the captain, taking Lord Forsythe's boat out for a honeymoon cruise." She looked at him to be sure he understood. "Trust me in this. The cutters can be a bother and a female at the helm will be much more suspicious than an earl."

She gave him a smile and tilted her head while she waited for his response.

"Just call me Captain Theo." He grinned back at her.

The revenue ship pulled up beside them. The crew stood motionless on the deck as lines were thrown from her hull to theirs. They were being boarded. Two men from the larger ship, in the signature green uniforms of the revenue men, jumped lithely to their deck and secured the lines.

"Here now, what is all this?" Theo called out in his most haughty voice. "I demand to see your captain."

"Oh, and you shall," a burly sailor replied.

He and his fellows laughed as they pulled a gangplank across the hulls. Four more sailors in green uniforms came across to the Bella. They were followed by their captain. He stood arrogantly on their deck and looked about.

"Search her," he said. "Leave nothing to chance. I want her checked from top to bottom."

"Wait a minute," Theo said in a commanding voice. "Stop."

The captain glared at him. "What is your business here today? And do not tell me it is fishing or lobster. I see no nets or cages."

Theo took a step forward and replied, "I am the Earl of Pembroke." Arabella had been right. For a moment, the captain looked startled. Theo continued, "I am taking my new wife on a honeymoon cruise. I demand to know why I am being harassed in this way."

The captain looked at Arabella. To Theo's surprise she stood shyly behind him, half hidden by his body as though afraid. She seemed to have shrunk. Her head hung low in a show of submissiveness.

He suppressed a smile. He patted her on the shoulder. "It is all right, my dear. Do not be afraid."

She peeked up at him meekly, but her eyes held a vicious glint. He had to bite his cheeks to keep from laughing.

"We are doing the King's business," the cutter captain said in more moderate tones. "We had word that a crew of smugglers were headed out to sea. We'll be searching your boat and then you'll be on your way." He smiled slyly. "That is, you will be on your way if we find nothing."

"What is your name captain? I will be reporting this to the Home Office."

The captain huffed. "My name is captain and that's all ye need to know."

Theo became suspicious. A request for his name or qualifications was reasonable and accepted procedure.

"Your name, captain?" he repeated.

The captain sneered at him and said nothing. He shifted his feet, clearly disconcerted by Theo's presence and rank.

A resounding crash came from the cabin. Theo spun around and went to its doors to check it out. A revenue man brushed past on him on his way up. Theo paused.

"All clear below," the revenue man hollered to the captain.

"Check the bow."

"Aye, Captain Berg," the revenue man muttered as he passed the captain, heading for the bow.

The captain shot his man a glare and spun around to see if Theo had heard. Theo quickly turned his gaze to the men searching the bow. The revenue captain scanned the deck for anyone else within hearing distance. The only other one near enough to hear was Arabella. The captain looked at her suspiciously. She stood huddled behind the helm, gripping the wheel as though she was about to faint. Her head was bowed. Like Theo, she gave no indication she had registered anything.

"She is all clear, captain." The searchers had returned from below.

"Clear here too," yelled the man from the bow.

The revenue boys hustled back to their cutter.

The captain smirked and said, "I will leave you to your cruise," before following his crew back to his ship.

The entire encounter had taken only a few minutes.

The ropes were pulled, the gangplank slid back, and the King's ship began to drift past. The crew of the Bella watched silently as she raised her sails and moved off into the distance.

Theo looked at Arabella, raised his hands from the wheel, and gestured with both arms that she should take over.

She smiled at him. "I do not think so, my love. You have definitely earned the right to take the helm."

"I will if you remain the shy little miss I met when we were boarded." Theo raised his eyes in a mock question.

Arabella let out a peal of laughter. "You wouldn't like her. I know you wouldn't." She punched him lightly on the shoulder. "Take the wheel. You deserve it."

"Raise the sail, boys," Theo hollered.

It was a calm day with a gentle breeze. Still, he concentrated hard on maneuvering the ship. After watching Arabella's expertise, he wanted to at least be adequate.

After some time, he realized Arabella had left his side. He scanned the deck. She stood at the stern behind him with Jem and several deck hands. They were engrossed in an intense discussion. He could not hear the words at this distance, but several times Arabella gestured with angry swipes of her arms. Theo had the uncomfortable feeling they had moved as far as possible from him to avoid him overhearing.

He turned back to the bow and grimaced. When he looked behind him once more, Arabella caught his gaze, left her crew, and strode towards him with a smile. He pushed his suspicions aside. It was his wedding day. Today he wanted to enjoy his new wife. But he could not shake the feeling Arabella was more than the innocent country miss he had anticipated.

Chapter Eight

Theo sat upon his bed and looked around his room. It was a standard men's suite in a country house. He had the usual furniture, a fireplace, a cabinet with several decanters of spirits and glasses should he desire a drink, and a full-length mirror next to a dressing room on his left. A huge four posted bed with matching side tables dominated the room. His eyes rested on the door to his right. It opened to Arabella's room.

Theo stared at it. It would be so easy to do the one thing he most wanted to do; open that door and seduce his beautiful wife. The memory of her dark skin and small breasts, with their nipples swollen and ready, haunted him. His body ached with need for her. He pictured her nude in her bed with her silky black hair spread across her pillow. His heart began pounding in his chest and his body tightened and throbbed.

Theo closed his eyes and sighed. He needed a drink. He decided a brandy might help him sleep.

He had promised himself he would give Arabella a

courtship and some time to get to know him and he was determined to accomplish it. Their day together, barring the incident with the revenue cutters, had been one of the best.

Once docking the Bella, they had gone for a twilight picnic in the hills for supper. After eating, they tried to relax, but they were still too new to each other. Their conversation was stilted and self-conscious.

He'd decided to fix the problem.

"Come here," he'd said holding out his arms.

She had stood up awkwardly and taken a careful step towards him, uncertain of his intentions. He put his hands on her hips and turned her away from him before pulling her down to sit between his legs.

"There. Now rest yourself here." He shifted her body so that her back was against his chest. "I think we may be better able to communicate this way."

It had worked. She'd relaxed against him. Feeling each other's bodies pressed close against each other, while not making eye contact, allowed them the intimacy they needed to converse more freely.

He told her funny stories about the society men and women he knew. He found she laughed easily, and he loved the sound of it. She talked of her brother Aran and their playful fighting and romping in the hills of their home.

When she bragged of her ability to beat her brother with either swords or cutlas, he laughed and said, "Well, you hardly needed me to sign that contract. You could have gone to town and dragged a man of your choice home at knife point."

She squeezed his thighs hard, giving him a charley horse.

"Ouch!" He looked at her, shocked. He hadn't had one of those since grammar school. "You fiend!"

He grabbed her, while she laughed, rolling her with him off the picnic blanket and into the grass. He ended up on top of her. With their bodies pressed together, he looked down at her and almost gave in to temptation. But instead, he had been true to his word and rose to his feet, offering him her hand.

"Come on, it will be pitch-dark before we get you home."

She'd held his hand. Together, they'd walked to the manor house as the sky darkened. By the time they reached her doors the stars were out.

He took both of Arabella's hands in his. He wanted to be romantic with her. His other lady friends had always raved about his 'romantic charm.' And so, he searched his mind for a poem to give her. He brought her hand to his lips and quoting the famous bard said, "She's beautiful, and therefore to be wooed."

To his surprise, she'd laughed and said, "She's woman and therefore to be won."

It pleased him that she was quick-witted and educated enough to complete his quote. There was much to learn about this young woman.

And now, alone in his room, he propped up his pillows, lay back against them, and sipped his brandy. He was satisfied with this match. Arabella was everything he had not known he wanted. He enjoyed her. With every new encounter with her, he discovered more of her independent nature.

He smiled wryly, congratulating himself on his tolerance and even his appreciation for her unorthodox ways.

But she was also his sweet innocent bride. Again, he remembered her as she had been in the gazebo. She had arched her back towards him, wanting his touch. He saw her black eyes glowing with passion. He groaned. It would be a long night. It was not the wedding night he had always pictured, but she wanted time, and he was willing to give it to her.

He drifted off to sleep, feeling pleased with the bargain he had struck.

The next morning, he awakened, determined to begin to assess this declining estate. If he were going into London to sign the papers required to transfer funds, it might be wise to see what else could be purchased or accomplished while in town.

At breakfast, he said, "Arabella, where are the accounts? I would like to look at them today."

"So soon? I would have thought you might want to relax for a few days." She chewed her lip. It was apparent his perusal of the accounts made her nervous.

Interesting.

"I think if I am to help with this recovery, I best get on with it. Don't you?" He watched her struggle with the problem, lowering her gaze to think.

"You will find there are many deposits from outside the estate. You must remember my grandmother has been providing the funds to keep us afloat." She looked up at him, her face and shoulders stiff with concern. He wondered what was bothering her.

There was only one way to find out. After breakfast,

Arabella showed him to the library with its large mahogany desk. In the light of day, it looked much different than it had when they had negotiated their deal. Outside of the desk, which was neat and wiped clean, it looked as though the room had not been used for some time. There were tall shelves lining the walls, but the books were covered with dust. The fireplace had long been cold.

Arabella flung back the curtains. A haze of dust swirled in the ensuing light. She smiled apologetically. "I am afraid this was always Aran's domain. I avoid it if I can. I spend enough time here to do the necessary entries and that is all."

He looked at Arabella. "Do you have a housekeeper?"

"No. I have Grimes, our butler. He handles the house-keeping staff. Occasionally we bring in girls from the village to do a thorough cleaning. I do have a cook, and a kitchen helper," she added. "Celeste and Arnold help with the other chores. Since we closed the west wing, it has been unnecessary. There are the stable hands and Jem."

"Then you should go to the village and hire some extra help. The place could use a good cleaning. You can afford a housekeeper now."

"I suppose I can. I may just do that this morning. There is a woman I have in mind," she said, pleased.

She pulled out the right-hand drawer of the desk and lifted the heavy account book. "Everything is written here. If you need me, after I return from the village, I shall be with Jem at the stables." She stood awkwardly at the door. "Accounts are not my forte."

He smiled at her. "I will find you if I need you."

Theo spent all morning poring over the accounts. He decided to go back several years. Until two years ago, there had been next to nothing listed in the account books. This was not a surprise. If the overseer was robbing the place, he was unlikely to document it. But since then, the estate had made meager money. Indeed, it had been working at a loss. There was no livestock. Most of the land lay vacant. There were notes jotted in the margins—a cottage needed repair, or a farmstead updated before renters could be brought in. From what he could tell, the Forsythes had only a half a dozen renters currently. And those premises had only been improved and rented in the last two years. It was a start. Arabella had not exaggerated when she had told him the land lay bare. He sighed.

Quarterly deposits had been made, with the initials of the countess scrawled in the margin. Each time this occurred, the wages were paid. What was left had been barely enough to keep the place open.

Then several huge investments had been poured into the stable and horses. That was promising. But income from the sale of any offspring would not occur for a year or two. Other deposits went into preparing the half a dozen homesteads which were now rented.

A decent effort had been made to restore Harwood to its former glory.

Two years ago, she had been as close to bankruptcy as she could be. Nothing, it seemed, had been operational. Then a series of deposits amounting to over ten thousand pounds. He whistled. And later, even more lump sums. They had brought Harwood out of the abyss, but there was still much to do. What the estate needed now was a dependable yearly income from the land.

That her grandmother had continued to invest in the place, and in hefty amounts, was a surprise to him. It would have been more prudent to sell the estate. It was odd too that before two years ago, she had covered the quarterly wages, but little else. He was not sure of the old woman's financial status, but the deposits suggested the estate would have been a crushing burden for her. Just the quarterly wages would have been costly. The other improvements more so.

A sizable amount of money had flowed into the place. Though there was no note to identify the source, it had to have been the grandmother. He could find nothing on the estate which could have generated that much cash.

Yet even now, they would need his investment to get the place sustainable. He leaned back in his chair and began to take notes. The first priority would be to get more farm-steads to a condition where they could be rented. The rents would begin to make the place sustainable. Then there would be livestock to consider. Cattle or sheep, pastured on less arable land would add another layer of income.

He decided if Arabella agreed he would hire a crew to begin the necessary repairs to the cottages. He would also look into farm workers to rent the homesteads. They would need to prepare the land for spring seeding. It would be a start.

He had seen enough for now. He put the heavy journal back in the drawer and went to find his wife.

When he walked into the stables, he was surprised to see a gathering of Arabella, Arnold, Jamie, and Jem. They seemed to be in a dispute.

"But it can be done! It can be done if we keep to the coast and come to port from the north," Arabella was insisting in a raised voice.

Jamie nudged her and she spun around to look at Theo. He began to feel uncomfortable with all eyes turning towards him. He tilted his head quizzically in their direction. It seemed as though he was forever finding the four of them in deep discussion.

Jem put a hand on his wife's shoulder. "We'll do all this talk of fishing later, lass. I see your husband wants a word with you." He turned to the young men. "And it is back to work with the two of you."

The big man turned away and went about his chores.

Arabella walked towards Theo. She seemed flushed.

"Do you take the Bella out to fish then?" he asked curiously.

"We do."

"Do you make a decent income from it?" he asked. When Arabella looked at him with surprise, he explained, "I just wondered if it might account for some of the deposits into Harwood."

Arabella blushed. "It does. Fishing brings in a good amount of cash."

He was curious as to why the topic of fishing was such an embarrassment to her. He had the impression something was not right—she was keeping something from him. He sighed. Hopefully, she will begin to trust me, he thought. He shrugged it off. He wanted to spend time with his new wife, especially if he had to travel to London this week.

"I came to see if you would come riding with me. Jem took me for a tour, but there is still much I would like to see."

She smiled. "I can do that."

Theo forgot his concerns when he looked at her. He was still amazed by her beauty. She wore a vest cinched tight across her chest and belly with a light blouse beneath it. Her skirt was dark gray and flowed around her. It all seemed normal enough for a day's work on her estate.

Yet there was something about her, even dressed as she was, that was stunningly attractive to him.

Maybe it is because she is mine. She is my innocent young bride. It will be such a pleasure to learn all about her. And it seems the more I learn about my lovely wife, the more pleased I am with her.

Chapter Nine

Jamie helped Arabella and Theo saddle the horses. Arabella decided to take them to the height of their land, a place where they could see the length of the gully with its green rocky pastures and behind them the gray stone walls of Hardwood, facing the sea beyond. They rode for the first few minutes in silence.

Arabella stole a glance at Theo.

My husband, she thought. How strange.

She was glad he had not come to her bedroom last night, but oddly she was also disappointed. They had said their vows, yet it didn't feel as though they were really married. She sighed. You cannot have it both ways, she chided herself.

"I thought we might take a route along the top of the draw. Does that suit you?" she asked.

"It does."

Some of his wavy blond hair had escaped the tie at the back of his head and blew across his face. He brushed it back behind his ears. He wore a loose long-sleeved shirt, white and open at the neck, with tight trousers tucked into tall boots. Dressed casually, he looked outrageously handsome.

He caught her examining him and flashed her a wide smile. Her heart did an involuntary flip. She gave him a shy smile in return.

She searched for something to say. "It is a beautiful path. You will love the views."

"I find I quite like the view already," he said with a smile. Then he winked at her.

He was a charmer. *I wonder how many women have been enthralled by this man.* He was too handsome. This was never good in a husband.

As they rode, she began to point out the little farms, both the arable and derelict ones. "And this one we have just rented. It was in no condition to be let when we started but I think the cottage is livable now. The farmer has even seeded his crop already." She gestured to the plowed fields, conspicuous amongst the grassy, buck bush covered land surrounding it, "I was extremely excited to see him prepare the land so efficiently and fast. It gives one hope for the future."

He cleared his throat and turned to her. "I wondered if I could use part of your money to hire a solid crew of workers to repair the cottages? I was thinking of hiring from the village. I would pay initially, then when the funds are transferred you can reimburse me."

"Could you?" Her eyes gleamed with enthusiasm.

"Then while in London, we will use an agency to find some farm workers to rent some of those cottages. If we have a crew working on the repairs, they will be available sooner. You need the income, and they need to prepare the land for spring seeding. They might even be able to take off a hay crop or two this season."

"Oh, Theo that would be grand. This is so exciting! It's the best part of being married."

Theo laughed. "I hope not, love. I hope you can find something you might consider at least a little more appealing."

She looked at him and flushed. "I'm sorry. I am sure there will be something."

"It seems I have some courting to do. I want to be more thrilling to you than home repairs," he said with a grimace.

She laughed. "You are. Very thrilling indeed." With a jolt, Arabella realized she meant it.

They came to the top of a rise. Down below was a wide valley. It stretched from the sea inland and curved away in the distance. At its bottom, a narrow river flowed. There was a tall white mill next to a bridge and a trail that climbed up the other side of the gully.

Arabella slid off her horse and looped her reins on the branch of an oak beside her. He did the same. She walked to the precipice where he joined her. It was an awesome sight, one that never failed to inspire her. She took a deep breath of the clean crisp air.

"It is beautiful, is it not?"

"It is." He scanned in the valley. Then he looked at her and smiled. "Not as beautiful as you, my wife."

Arabella turned to him. The wind had loosened more of the hair from its ties at his nape, and it curled along his jawline. His shirt too had blown partly open, exposing a smooth expanse of his muscular chest. Her heart skipped a beat.

She felt a powerful urge to kiss him. She wondered if he would take offence. She was interested to know if Theo could still make her tingle as he had in the gazebo. And she was curious about the whole physical part of marriage. She knew the basics. She had been raised in the country. Somehow, she could not imagine such a circumstance between her and Theo.

She leaned in and kissed him tentatively on the lips. He stood very still as though not wanting to frighten her. She put her hands on his shoulders, then slid them around his broad back. He felt wonderfully warm and strong. His hands circled her waist. She kissed him again.

This time, Theo kissed her back. His arms went around her, pulling her close. She felt his tongue against her teeth, and she parted her mouth. His tongue slid inside. He kissed her more fiercely as his hands gripped her bottom. He pushed her tight against him.

She could feel his hardness against her. Slowly his kisses moved farther down her neck. She nuzzled into his shoulder and breathed deeply of his scent; it was intoxicating, a blend of spicy cologne and his own rich maleness.

Theo shifted until his one hand was between her thighs while the other grasped her behind. He pushed his hand between her thighs, and she widened her step to accommodate him. The cloth of her dress grated against her skin as he slowly moved it back and forth against her nether regions. She shivered with the strange sensations he created. And all the while he kissed her, rough and demanding. It was overwhelming. She moaned softly against his mouth and held tight to his shoulders.

Then he pulled away, letting her skirts drop down once more. With his arms around her back, he held her. His kisses became slow and tender. He gently took her head and held it to his chest.

She found that she was panting, trying to catch her

breath. Theo was motionless, yet she could still feel him pressed against her belly, swollen and hard. He arched back and looked at her.

"You must tell me to stop now. If you don't, I'll make love to you right here. It's not how I would have you experience it for the first time." He rotated his hips against her.

"You must stop now," she gasped.

He held her close, pressing her against his body for a few more seconds before he finally let his arms fall from her and backed away. His withdrawal was almost painful for her. She wanted to throw her arms around him again.

She walked unsteadily to her horse and took the reins. Without a further word, he helped her mount, then lifted himself into the saddle of his horse.

They began the trek back to the manor. Neither said anything until they were almost back at the stables. Arabella was considering the way he could make her feel. It was as though her body wanted him desperately. She lost all sense when she was in his arms.

"Would it feel the way it does if I kissed just anyone? I mean, would every man make me feel as you do?"

He looked at her and laughed. She felt her face redden. She did not want to appear ignorant before him.

He became serious. "I am sorry I laughed, my love. It was such a fine compliment that you gave me. I could not help but be delighted by your words."

He paused, considering. "There is something special between us. I lose my mind a little when I touch you, my beautiful wife."

Arabella nodded. "That is how it is with me. Nothing else can make me so vulnerable." She sighed. "When you asked me to end it, I could hardly do it. I am glad it is only you. I don't know if I could handle feeling this way with everyone."

He laughed again. "Oh god, me as well." He looked at her seriously. "I will keep trying to give you the courtship you want, Arabella. But if it is what you genuinely want then we have to be more careful."

She grinned at him. "No more kisses then?"

"Definitely not."

This time it was her turn to laugh. There will be something to enjoy in this marriage, she thought happily.

But that night at supper, she found it hard to concentrate on him. The dining room was gloomy and dim. They were seated at opposite ends of the long table.

"You look lovely tonight," Theo said, raising his voice to be heard from across the long dining table. "Yellow is the perfect color for you."

When she had only mumbled a response, he had added, "Indeed, you are the only spot of color in this cave of a room."

"Excuse me?"

"I said you are the only spot of color in the room."

He sounds irritated, she thought. She looked around the room. It was dark with the chandelier unlit, and only the wall sconce and a set of candles on each end of the table for light. "It does resemble a cave. Usually, I eat in the breakfast room. Often Jem joins me there. I have never really used this room."

"I understand why."

She looked at him with a confused expression.

He raised his voice. "I said, I understand why."

After that, he gave up all attempts at conversation and quietly ate his meal.

It is just as well. I have much to think about.

They were going on a run tonight. The captain of the Mrytle had sent word they needed assistance. When they had been caught by the revenue boys, a shipment had been left awaiting them in Gravelines. They offered gold for Ara to purchase the load and bring it back to be unloaded into the Mrytle's stash.

Jem was against it, but she had insisted they would be safe. They would not be carrying a cargo out. If stopped on the point, a search of the ship would produce nothing. The gold would be easy to hide. On return, she would come in from the north, avoiding Bergen's Point altogether. The single run would provide a tidy profit. Once the cargo was unloaded, they would not be responsible for the transportation of the goods inland. It was an excellent deal, a bargain too good to pass up.

She looked down the expanse of the table at Theo. After she finished her meal, she would make her excuses and slip away. Jem would have her captain's gear ready for her as usual. Jem may be annoyed with me, she thought, but he will never abandon me to do a run on my own. He had so strongly disapproved; she had promised this would be her last run to get him to agree.

It would be a quick trip. They would be back by dawn.

She yawned loudly.

"I have a headache," she said, raising her voice. "If you don't mind, I think I will go up to my room and rest. I thought you might check out Aran's library. There may be something to interest you there."

She was thankful for the dim lighting which hid her burning cheeks. She did not relish lying to him, but she could hardly tell him the truth. Besides, this might be her last run in a long while.

Though she had convinced Jem the run would be a safe

one, her stomach knotted when she thought of the new cutter. Meeting him on the open sea would mean disaster—she couldn't outrun him. Added to her concern was the necessity to return to Harwood before dawn. It would be awkward indeed to explain to her new husband where she had been all night if he should see her arrive home.

Chapter Ten

Theo pulled back the dusty curtains in the library and stood looking out at the twilight. It was June. The days were long enough that the world outside was still a soft glow despite the hour. The library was directly below their suite of rooms. It faced the driveway, with the stables to the right.

His eyes caught a movement from the stables. Four figures were leading horses from the barns. The fellow who stood a foot taller than the rest was clearly Jem. Jamie, the stable hand, with his jaunty walk, was next to Jem. The other two he was unsure of. At this distance, in the dim light, he could only determine that one of them wore a strange extravagant hat. He wondered what they were up to. Walking the horses from the stables meant they did not want to be heard.

Maybe they were slipping off to a local pub. It is too bad they hadn't asked me to join them, he thought with a grimace. It would have been more entertaining than going over this journal of accounts.

He opened the books and began to work. It was late

when he finally turned in for the night, but he was satisfied with what he had gleaned from the accounts. He crawled into his bed and turned down the lantern to sleep.

His last thoughts were of Arabella. He hoped she would feel better in the morning. Probably some sort of mysterious women's issue, he thought with a grin and drifted off to sleep.

At dawn, something awakened him. He lay still. He could hear rustling from Arabella's room. He smiled and rolled over, going back to sleep.

———

The next morning, Arabella did not come down for breakfast. And it was Celeste, not Arnold, who brought breakfast to the sideboard.

"Is Arabella still not feeling well?" he asked.

"Oh, she will sleep most of the day today, monsieur. Not to worry. She will be cheerful when she rises, yes?" Celeste quickly turned her back to him and began fussing with the platters of food.

"Please tell her I hope she feels better soon."

"That I will." She hustled from the room.

He decided to go for a ride. He was eager to see more of the estate.

No one was around at the stables. He grinned. The boys must have had a late one last night. First, Arnold had been absent from his usual tasks at breakfast and now it seemed that Jem and Jamie were also still in bed.

He enjoyed a pleasant day roaming the estate. He determined that sheep would best suit the rocky gully. It would be a solid investment for her. But like most of the cottages, the shepherd's homestead in the gully needed a new roof and repairs before it could be rented.

Arabella joined him for supper.

"You look well," he said.

"Excuse me?"

Theo cleared his throat and raised his voice. "I said, you look well."

"Thank you. I feel well."

Again, he cursed the huge dining room table.

This is ridiculous. It is impossible to have a decent conversation when you must shout.

It would be another meal eaten in silence.

After supper, they played a game of cards. He attempted to teach her some of the new gambling games. They used a pile of pennies to bet. She loved it. He noted that she was intensely competitive. He decided that it was a good thing he was not.

"Ha! I got you!" She laughed and threw down her cards. "I had nothing! It was a perfect bluff!"

He watched her happily gather her pennies. Sometimes she seemed like an eager child.

"You are the big winner tonight. Tomorrow, I hope to get my pennies back. But it is late. I think it is time we turned in."

She laughed. "You are just a sad loser."

Together they packed up the board and set it on the mantle with their collection of coins. He offered her his arm and they traversed the stairs together.

At her door, he kissed her lightly on the mouth. "Goodnight, my beautiful wife."

He leaned in and kissed her again. This time, he lingered over her mouth, sucking her bottom lip, and gently nipping it. He felt his body respond to her. It was becoming increasingly difficult to keep this distance between them.

"Soon this courtship must end, Arabella. I want you in my bed."

Her face blushed becomingly. He smiled and traced his finger along her luscious lips. "Very soon," he said.

She seemed dazed. He smiled as he nudged her into her room.

Her black eyes glittered in the soft light.

"Goodnight, Theo," she said quietly before pulling her door closed.

It would be another long night. He was correct when he had told her this courtship must end soon. He did not think he could resist her much longer. He could feel his body throbbing and groaned. He looked at her door as he did every night. He had to stop himself from bursting into her room.

Again, he pictured her there with her black hair spread across the pillow. He squeezed his eyes shut. One more day, he promised himself, then I will become her true husband.

Chapter Eleven

He must have drifted off to sleep. A sound awakened him. He lay silent in his bed, hearing nothing now.

He got up and walked to the window. His room overlooked the cobbled drive and beyond it, the stables. Attached to the stables at the far right was the overseer's residence, Jem's house. A soft orange light could be seen from Jem's curtained windows, indicating he was still up. Theo wondered what he could possibly be doing at this hour. It must be very late.

For a few minutes, he saw nothing. He was about to return to his bed when the glow of a lantern appeared from beneath his window. Someone was crossing the yard. He watched as the figure approached Jem's step. The door of the overseer's cottage opened, and light spilled into the drive.

It was Arabella. A huge man that could only be Jem pulled her inside and the door closed abruptly.

Theo stared at that closed door. Ten minutes passed. What could they possibly be up to at this time of night? A sickening thought wormed its way into his head as he considered the obvious answer. Surely not! He pushed the vision from his mind.

No, it is something else. I am not wrong about Arabella's innocence.

The door to Jem's home opened again and another figure, this one without a lantern, slipped inside. Twice more shadowy figures entered the cottage. This time they were bulky men. Neither of them could be Jamie or Arnold.

Theo felt his guts wrench. He had no idea what meeting was going on inside. The one thing he was becoming certain of was his innocent wife was not so innocent. She had secrets. He waited by the window unsure of what he should do. He could confront her. He considered it.

He thought about the four people sneaking off last night and his stomach turned. And today, she, like her staff, had been indisposed. Repeatedly, he had seemed to interrupt her, Jem, Jamie, and Arnold in some sort of discussion. The same group had acted as crew members for Arabella aboard her ship. All of it began to look suspect. And now, tonight, at least four men, besides Arabella, had surreptitiously entered Jem's house.

But to confront her now would surely mean she would be forced to lie to him. He did not think he could tolerate that.

He thought about her aboard the Bella. Whatever was going on, she was not a helpless victim in it. She was in charge. She had been the undisputed leader on that ship.

The ship. That was the key. He felt sick. It could only be two things if the ship were involved, neither of which were easy to think about. One was smuggling and the other was spying. They were at war. Napoleon raged on the continent. England was engaging him on the sea and in Spain.

Theo shook his head to dispel the ugly thought. Spying? Surely not. Her father had fought in some of those battles. She lived remotely here. Arabella would have little information to pass on even if she were a spy.

He thought about her negotiations with him in the library a few days ago. Arabella blushed when she was rattled. She would make a terrible spy.

He balled his hands into fists. He had been duped. He had been walking around in a haze of infatuation and desire. He swore under his breath.

It was time he took control. First, he would need to find out all her secrets. If smuggling was what she was up to then it would be he and not the revenue boys who would end it.

Theo took a deep breath and tried to calm his raging mind. He was being premature. He must be sure of his suspicions. It might be an innocent meeting of some sort. First, he had to be certain.

It was time for action. He decided to search her room. He picked up his lantern and went to her door expecting to find it locked but it swung open easily. Setting his light on her cabinet, he looked around the room. It was the perfect twin of his except that rather than the dark shades of green and brown which adorned his room, Arabella's was decorated in soft lavender and cream.

He could smell her, both her distinctive fresh scent and her perfume. To his exasperation, his body responded. He grimaced. There would be no more thoughts of that.

He went through her closets, cabinet, and bedside tables. There was nothing out of the ordinary. He scanned the room again. Finally, he walked around the bed and slid his hands under her pillows. Nothing. He knelt and peered under it. Again, there was nothing. He reached between the mattresses. His hand touched parchment. He pulled out a crumpled letter.

Taking the letter to the light, he read it carefully. He read it again several more times, until its contents were seared on his memory. Numbed by the insinuations in the letter, he returned it to its place and went back into his room, closing the door softly behind him.

Stunned, Theo poured himself a brandy and pulled a chair up to the window to watch and wait. Taking a deep breath, he went over the letter in his mind. The exchange of papers at the Meadows, which her twin referred to in the damning letter, was familiar to him. He had been at The Meadows with his friend Ambrose to pick up the code book. At the Old Bailey hotel, he had stood with his friend Ambrose again while they confronted the smuggling crew. The captain had sneered at him with an arrogance which had enraged him.

Theo suspected he had seen the lovely black eyes of his wife before, and he had been right. Damn those eyes! There was no mistaking them. Arabella had been dressed as a man, a captain. He grimaced. She had looked like a bloody pirate—his wife. There was no question it had been her.

My god, she was the captain of a smuggling crew!

Standing beside Captain Ara that night had been the giant of a man who could only be Jem.

Had he not seen Arabella on the water the day they were wed, he would not have believed it. An image of his lovely wife using the rigging to swing to the deck crossed his mind.

He threw back his head and barked a bitter laugh. His grandmother had assured him his new bride would be a woman of strength and intelligence. But this? This was too much.

Before long, the cottage door opened, and four figures melted away into the darkness. A few minutes later, the door swung open again. It was his Arabella. The lantern bobbed across the yard the way it had come.

Theo gulped the last of his brandy and poured himself another full glass. Rage flooded his body.

He heard the soft click of a door closing in the adjoining room. Like last night, he could hear the rustling of her moving about, undressing. What a gullible idiot he had been.

He took another long swallow of brandy. Picking up his lantern, he walked to her door and flung it open. It hit the wall with a crash.

Her eyes widened with alarm as she sat up in bed. Her long black hair floated around her. He set the lantern carefully on her cabinet.

"Theo. It is...What is it you want?" She pulled her bedding tightly around her.

Theo looked at her. She was the picture of innocence with her big brown eyes, her hands holding the sheets discretely around her neck. This time he would not be made to look the fool. All promises were off. She had had what consideration she was going to get.

For an eternity, he stared at her while he contemplated his next move. He thought of the nights he had spent looking longingly at her bedroom door, while she was in all probability at the helm of her ship, pleased to have a gullible fool for a husband.

First, he would have his wedding night. Negotiations and promises be damned.

"What is it I want?" He smiled grimly. "I am here to have what is my right. I came to take my bride."

She could only look at him in shock. "But I thought... I hoped... That is, Theo, I thought we had agreed—"

"Would you like a brandy, my dear?" He swirled the amber liquid around in his glass watching with exaggerated interest as it caught the light. "A favorite drink of yours, isn't it? And it is excellent French stock. The absolute best. Only available as a smuggled commodity."

She shook her head, pulling the covers more tightly around her neck. Her eyes were dark pools which followed his every move.

He shrugged. Walking over to her, Theo set his glass on her bedside table with exaggerated care. He stared down at her. Then in one swift motion, he grabbed her bedding and threw it back.

She let out a little squeak and hugged her arms around her body. She wore a soft lacey nightgown which was in sharp contrast to her dark skin. Whatever his young wife might be, a renegade or smuggler, she was beautiful.

He shrugged off his dressing gown and pulled his bed shirt over his head. He stood before her completely naked. He was aroused. Her eyes traveled the length of his body and widened, before returning to his face. She was afraid.

Good, he thought bitterly.

Theo knelt on her bed, grabbed her nightgown on each side of her hips, and yanked it up and over her head in one quick motion. She gasped and wrapped her arms across her chest, covering her breasts. He slid in beside her and pulled her stiff body up against him. She said nothing, but he could feel her trembling.

He felt a pang of remorse. Taking her this way was not what he wanted. Some of his anger melted away, but he was still determined to end this farce of a relationship. He would be her bloody husband. Tonight, was the beginning of her learning what it was to be a proper submissive wife.

But he knew, despite his bravado, he could not take her unless she wanted him. Pulling Arabella close to his naked body, he pressed the full length of her against him. He ran his hands slowly up and down her back until her body relaxed and her breathing slowed. Burying his face in her hair with his lips against her neck, he breathed her soft scent. Minutes crawled by as he waited for her to accept him, all the while rubbing her slender back from her hips to her shoulders.

The feel of her skin pressed against him was intoxicating. Now it was his body which began to tremble. His sex pressed against her, throbbing with need. Just when he was certain he could not survive another second, she put her arms around him. He felt a dizzying relief. She had accepted him.

He kissed her neck first, tasting her sweet saltiness. As he found her mouth, kissing her long and hard, Arabella's arms tightened around him. Rolling on top of her, he slid down to suck her breasts, reaching down with one hand to find her center. She was wet and warm. He stroked her while his tongue played with the hard nubbins of her breasts.

He brought his hands to her waist and rested his head on her belly. Her body was slender, strong, and lovely. He wanted all of her. A wave of fierce possessiveness shook him. Pirate or not, she was his, and he would have her know it. He groaned and sank his head between her thighs, kissing and sucking until he heard her gasp and whimper.

He reared up and replaced his mouth with his hand, sliding his fingers carefully into her, stretching her. She trembled.

"Say my name," he demanded.

She moaned and her arms found his shoulders, her body curling towards him.

"Say my name, Arabella," he repeated.

"Theo...my husband," she gasped.

He could wait no longer. He braced himself over her. Using his hand, he guided himself into her body. In one quick thrust, he drove deeply into her.

Arabella squealed in shock and tried to squirm away from him. He held her still with the length of his body, waiting until he heard her breathing calm before he rose and pushed further. She was impossibly tight as her muscles closed around him.

All intentions of gentling Arabella this first night were lost to him. Unable to control a wave of passion, he bucked and drove into her. When he lifted her legs up high, she wrapped them around him. He slammed into her with a rage and an urgency he did not know he possessed.

Arabella's eyes were closed, and she panted, her lips slightly parted. He kissed her hard, his teeth bruising her lips. Her hands dug into his shoulders. His body was slick and wet with sweat and still he pounded into her.

At last, he reared up and grabbed her by her slender hips. Pulling her hips towards him, he pressed deeply. With a loud groan, he pumped his seed into her.

He collapsed on top of her.

Theo could not believe what he had just done. He had lost complete control. It had never happened to him before. Rolling to her side, he simply held her, keeping his face buried in her neck. He realized he was afraid to look at her and see a wounded expression.

Finally, he braced himself up on his elbow and gazed

down at her. Her eyes were huge and darkly luminous in the lamp light. He reached out and touched her swollen bottom lip.

Leaning down, he softly kissed her. To his relief, she put her arms around his shoulders and kissed him back.

Once more he kissed her, then drew back to look at her face. She gave him a tentative smile.

Theo's stomach churned with regret. He had hurt her; he was sure of it. A woman's first experience should be magical, and he had ruined it. Taking her when he was hurt and angry was a mistake. The soft and gentle lovemaking he had imagined and planned when thinking of his innocent bride was not what he had given her. He swore he would make it up to her.

For now, he had to hope he had not destroyed their budding relationship.

"You survived," he whispered.

A blush stained her cheeks. Her eyes had a drowsy softness. Her hair clung damply to her face, and he brushed it back from her forehead. This was his woman, his wife. Theo felt as if she had entered his very being. Somehow, he would tame this renegade of a woman. Looking at her now, it was impossible to impose the image of the smuggling captain he had met at The Meadows on this soft and vulnerable creature.

He sighed. He could not deal with this problem tonight. Whatever she was, tonight she had been his innocent virgin wife. She deserved better from him.

Rising from the bed, he pulled on his dressing gown. He found a cloth and a basin of water on her dressing table.

When he turned to the bed, he saw she had discretely drawn the sheets up over herself. He pulled them back and began to wipe her. The cloth came away from her body red with blood. She gasped and tried to close her legs.

"It is fine." He placed a hand on her leg and gently held her open. "It's normal. It will only happen this first time," he said, carefully completing his task. He noticed the sheets too were spotted with blood. He pulled the top sheet over it. She grabbed it and pulled it up to her chin again, curling up on her side.

He grimaced at her shyness. This was not one of the many lovers he had had in his past. Whatever happened, this was his wife. Sitting beside her on the bed, he pulled the sheet back below her breasts, cupped one small breast, and rubbed her nipple with his thumb, watching with interest as it hardened.

He looked up at Arabella. Her eyes were wide and intensely black. She watched him intently with her mouth slightly parted as though leery of his next move. Turning his attention to her breasts once more, he leaned down to kiss them. He sucked her gently, then pulled back and blew on her. He slid his hand down her back bringing the sheet with him as he explored the wonder of her firm dark skin. He grasped her narrow hip, then raked his fingers through the soft tufts of hair between her thighs. His body responded. He wanted her again, fiercely. Desperately.

Keeping his hand on her mons, he looked once more into her luminous eyes. He could read nothing in their depths. Her lips were slightly parted, and her breathing had changed into shorter panting breaths.

He knew what he would do to make amends for his earlier brutality. He drew back the sheets and rolled on top of her. He slowly slid down her body until his head was nestled between her legs. His hands explored her rounded belly then worked their way up her body, massaging and caressing, until each hand held a breast. All the while he kissed her on the softness between her legs. He waited until she had spread her legs wide and arched her back before he ran his tongue lightly down the length of her.

He was determined to be gentle. He concentrated on making each movement ever so soft and light. This time he would love her. He would show her with every touch how beautiful she was to him. He kept his arms stretched above him, holding her small breasts, not wanting to touch her nether regions with them. She would be too tender for that.

Theo let his tongue find the little nub at the center of her. He licked, kissed, nibbled, and caressed it. His fingers squeezed her nipples as he felt her excitement grow. She twisted and moaned in his grasp. He had to concentrate hard on not bringing his hands down to stroke her. He kept them on her breasts and used only his face and tongue. He felt his sex throb and fill with need. His hips rose and fell with a rhythm that matched his tongue. More than anything else he wanted her to feel his appreciation for all that was her—to worship her.

She moaned, and he raised his eyes to watch her. Time stood still. There was only his caresses and her smooth beautiful skin.

"Theo. Oh, my god, Theo."

She closed her eyes as her lithe body arched. Theo kept his eyes trained on her, not looking away as he worked his tongue and his lips. She was so wet. Groaning, he rubbed his rough chin along the length of her.

Arabella tensed and shivered. She let out a little scream, throwing her head back as her arched body shuddered. He watched her find her womanly pleasure—her body rearing again and again. It was too much. His own body jerked, and he pressed himself into the mattress. To his surprise, he found his release with her. He laid his head on her soft belly until he recovered.

His beautiful, beautiful wife had a passionate nature. It was a gift he would treasure. He felt an urge to laugh aloud in pure joy. He slid up her damp body and held her in his arms, while their breathing slowed. Neither talked. He held her.

Oh, my god. I am lost completely to this woman. It has only been days and I am entirely enthralled. He felt a moment's panic. *I could never live without her. Even tonight, my shock and rage has turned into this.*

He ran his hand down her smooth back and felt the curve as it rose into her firm rounded butt.

Even now I want her. I want her again. If she were able, I would bury myself in her.

He was stunned.

He stirred and shifted so that he could look into her face. Her eyes were sleepy. She reached up and ran her fingers through his hair, brushing it back from his face.

"Theo," she said in a soft voice, "I like to make love."

She grinned a sleepy smile while her fingers slowly twisted a lock of his hair. "I think I will make it my new hobby. Had I known all this existed I would have married long ago."

He laughed and hugged her to him. "And I will help you with this hobby. It will be a project we can work on together." He was quiet for a moment, then said, "I am thankful for this match, Arabella."

"As am I," she replied, shifting in closer to him.

He reached down and pulled the crumpled bedding around them. The sheets were soiled and sticky. He would need the cloth again before he fell asleep. "Your maid will be horrified when she sees the condition of this bed."

She giggled. It was a joyful sound, making him smile.

"My maid will be thrilled," she said. "She has wanted this for me for a long time. She believes it will settle me down at last."

He ran his finger down her forehead then between her beautiful mahogany eyes. Replacing it with his lips, he kissed the tip of her nose playfully.

"I too hope it will settle you down." He tucked her head into the curve of his shoulder and laid back against the pillows. "Sleep, my love. We will have plenty of time to work on our little hobby tomorrow."

She curled into him. In moments, he heard her deep breathing and knew she was sleeping.

With her body tucked in beside him and her beautiful face relaxed, she looked like a girl. Her activities on the sea seemed completely incongruent with the vulnerable young woman he held in his arms.

He felt confused and at a loss. He let his arm trail along the length of her back. The danger to her at sea was astounding. If caught, she would suffer beyond what she could even begin to comprehend. Once they discovered she was a woman, her torture would take on a new twist. Protecting her was now his duty. He would not let her go out to sea. He brushed the hair back from her face. Losing her was not an option he could contemplate. Arabella had his money now. There should be no need for her to risk her life at sea.

He remembered her twin and silently swore. He understood now why she had insisted on staying at Harwood for six months. There had to be a way. He considered confronting her with his knowledge and decided against it. Now was not the time.

He had to go to London to transfer funds. Taking her

CYNTHIA KEYES

with him was the only option. If he battled with Arabella now, he would never be able to convince her to join him. She could not be left here alone; of that he was certain. He would bring Arabella to town with him, where she would be safe from the risks of her life at sea. No, he wouldn't confront her with all he knew, not yet, but he would—soon.

Chapter Twelve

The sound of the window sliding open awakened Arabella.

"Ooh, la la. Phew. It smells of the chattel house in here." Celeste threw back the drapes.

Arabella squinted as the morning light filled the room. She stretched. The feel of the sheets on her bare skin brought events of last night back in a flood. Her cheeks burned. She pulled the sheets up tight to her chin and glanced across the pillow. Theo was gone.

Celeste stood at the foot of the bed holding her robe. "So? How does my girl? It was a good night, yes?"

She held the robe hostage. Arabella would not be getting it until Celeste had heard how the night had gone.

Arabella propped herself up on the pillows and gave her maid a bright smile. "It was marvelous, Celeste. It was..." She could find no words. She hugged the covers to her. "Oh, Celeste, it was more, so much more than I expected."

Celeste laughed and tossed her the robe. "I knew he was a good man. He has the look. That smile. And those fine strong hips." She pulled back the sheets. "Now up with you. I have brought a bath. Come on, come on, up, up. *Mon Dieu*."

Arabella glanced over her shoulder and felt her cheeks burn again. The sheets were spotted with blood and sticky with the evidence of her night with Theo.

Celeste took her shoulder and nudged her towards her dressing room. "To the bath with you, *tout suite*."

Arabella sunk into her bath. She laid her head back on the rim of the tub, listening to the sounds of Celeste's happy mutterings from her bedroom. She ran a sponge over her body and thought of Theo's rough hands.

Her lower belly clutched. She knew what this feeling was and what she wanted. She smiled. She felt as though she had found a treasure. This part of marriage was an unexpected delight. She would enjoy it. If Theo came to her now, she would find a way to make him give her more of it. She wondered if all married couples felt this way. They kept this secret well. For now, all thoughts of convincing her husband to leave her alone here at Harwood were dismissed. She wanted to enjoy this new aspect of married life.

She reluctantly pushed these feelings from her mind. They were a powerful distraction. She turned her thoughts to the captains' meeting they had had last night at Jem's.

She was not alone in being plagued by the excise men of late. The Myrtle had lost her cargo and she was not the only one. Rumors flowed up and down the Yorkshire coast. A new revenue cutter prowled. Its captain was not interested in turning them in to the law, but instead took their cargos with threats of death and imprisonment should the word get out. Unlike the revenue boys of the past, this crew was vigilant. They were obviously determined to make their fortunes on the backs of the Yorkshire men.

The losses were not sustainable. Smuggling operated like any other retail business. The money from one shipment helped finance the next. Each take by the renegade cutter was a blow to the captains and their crews. There was no legal means of protection or retribution. They had only themselves to police and defend their livelihoods.

"We should capture him and string him up," the burly captain of The Bess had growled. His suggestion was met with a chorus of approval shouted out by the boys gathered around Jem's heavy oak wood table. They banged their pewter mugs against the table and ale splashed across its surface.

They were a rough looking crowd. They wore the woolen shifts common to the native fisherman. Each sported a wide belt from which hung a deadly cutlas. Their leggings were heavy denim over which were the oilskins, leather shields worn to protect them from the elements. They were captains and as such did not wear the short pea jackets of the common sailor but rather long coats in an assortment of colors and varying in wear. All of them, except Captain Ara, sported heavy beards. Two of them wore bandanas, tied at the sides, the others wore the flat caps of sailors.

Captain Ara was the youngest member of the group. If they suspected she was female, it was never mentioned. As always, she kept her face covered with a tattered scarf and her cap pulled low. Her scarf was accepted without question by the smugglers. Initially, Jem had spread the rumor that her lower face had been mangled on a trip to the Mediterranean in search of treasure. Seafarers loved legends.

Somehow the story had changed to a sordid tale, where Ara had gone south for treasure and picked up a case of leprosy instead.

She and Jem had welcomed the tale. It had not only justified her disguise; it had kept others well back. Outside of her crew, no one shook hands or shared a drink with Captain Ara. Her youth, her ability at sea, and the wild tales of her shocking disease had all contributed to the making of a legend. This was both good and bad. Her reputation had leaked far and wide and even the revenue boys had heard of her prowess. A cutter who captured Ara would earn his reputation. She had a target on her back.

Arabella was a respected member of the group, in part because of her exploits, but she also knew much of her respect was given because of the formidable Jem by her side. She too banged her cup in approval before slipping it under her mask to take a long swig.

"Here, here," she shouted. "I'm for hangin' the thieving rogue!"

"Whoa. We can't be hanging him," Captain Barr interjected when the noise had waned. He waited until he had their attention before continuing. "He is a big one. If he ran, the only lugger who'd have a chance to catch 'em is Ara. And when he hung 'em, he'd only bring the revenue boys down hard on us."

He shot her a nasty scowl.

Arabella met his look and scowled back beneath her mask. She took another long drink of ale and brought her mug down hard against the table. The room erupted in noisy debate, with Ara taking no small part.

Jem looked at her askance. Arabella ignored his warning glance. Her shouting and swearing matched and even exceeded those of her cohorts.

What had been an act when she had first taken over the Bella from Aran was now a reality. She was a smuggler. Arabella was the rough and tough captain she had for so long only portrayed. The change had been gradual, but it had happened.

The conversation turned to their suspicions about an informant on shore.

"I got the cutter's name," Ara said in her deep voice, a voice she had practiced and mastered. "It's Berg. And it's a name shared by the new Vicar."

Her pronouncement brought another round of hollering and slamming of mugs.

"We'll tar and feather the scoundrel and run him out of town," Peasley shouted. He was a big man with his bushy gnarled blond hair held back in a gray bandana. His weathered face was covered by an equally thick beard and his eyes were hard.

"Wait," Jem said. "The run-ins we have had with the cutters have all been on the other side of Bergen's point. The Vicar lives high above the village, it's true. He could signal out to sea, but he couldn't signal down the coast. The cliffs are too high and would block it. There must be an accomplice. A transmitter from the cliffs, who in turn signals the revenue boys."

"Aye, you have it there," Captain Barr agreed.

"We'll want to nab that one as well or it will never be safe for us." This was from the hawk-faced Captain Gorge.

The captains, including Ara, eventually all agreed to hold off on the trade until the culprits could be caught. The boats would return exclusively to fishing for the time being. It was the season to fish. Most of the coastal crews had planned to do exactly that anyway. A look out would be placed upon the cliffs each night to attempt to intercede any signals and try to locate their source.

When the captains departed, Arabella used Jem's back room to change back into her clothes. By the time she reentered the room, Jem had cleaned the table. All evidence of the meeting had disappeared.

Jem rested his heavy hands on the back of a stout wooden chair and looked at her seriously,

"Arabella, we'll need to have a wee chat." He pulled the chair back and gestured to it. "Sit."

She smiled her impish grin at him, raised her eyebrows at him, and gingerly took a seat. She could hear a Scottish burr in his voice. This was not a good thing.

Jem grabbed another chair, scraped it across the wooden floor, and sat opposite her. "Arabella, your days as captain are numbered. You're a lady and now a wife. This rough life is not for you. Your father and even Aran would not want this for you. It must stop."

Arabella opened her mouth in surprise. She was speechless.

"You have the money now. There is no need to take these risks. It is over." He took both her hands and held them.

"But Jem," she said, "I must at least get to Gravelines for word of Aran."

Letting go of her hands, he rose and awkwardly patted her on the shoulder with his huge paws. He would hear no arguments. "I don't think it's Aran that keeps you in the trade. I think you have had a taste of captain and don't want to let it go." She shook her head in denial. Jem carefully tucked his chair under the table before turning to her once more. "But you must. As to Aran, we'll find a way. Go now. Go back to your husband and think on it. But know there will be no runs and no Captain Ara."

Arabella thought about leaving her life as a captain. Her stomach did a turn. It was too hard to imagine an existence without the persona of Captain Ara. It had become her identity. She did not know what she was without it. That she would not be able to continue without Jem was also clear. She was not naïve enough to think that she could manage without him. He was the physical strength Ara needed to maintain her position.

Jem was forcing her to realize she would have to make a break from her world as captain and become the wife and mother she was destined to be. Her heart ached. She had pushed the idea from her mind.

Celeste interrupted her thoughts of last night's meeting.

"Out with you," she said, holding a towel ready for her. "I must dress you wonderfully today. You will look as good during the day as you do at night. Yes?"

She rubbed her vigorously. "We will impress this husband, no? He will not be thinking of anything but you, my *cherie*."

While Celeste helped her dress, she thought of Theo. She was eager to see him today. "Where is my husband? Do you know what he is doing?"

"He left early. He went with Mister Jem to the old mill. They talked of fixing it." She nudged her towards her dressing table. "We will do your hair. A braid, I think, but on the side. We must look a little stylish, yes?"

Arabella did not want to wait to see Theo. "I think I will ride out and bring them a picnic."

Celeste paused while working her hair. "You want your riding clothes?"

"No. My skirt will do. If I go, I will make it work. I haven't time to change again."

Celeste frowned. "He will think you unmannered." She gave her braid a tug but softened her rebuke with a smile. "But you want to see him today and that is a good thing."

Arabella's cheeks warmed. She did want to see him. Mostly she wanted to touch him to see if the magic was still there in the daylight.

Chapter Thirteen

Arabella secured the basket onto her horse. She led it to the mounting block. Jamie assisted her into the saddle. She tucked her skirts discretely around her legs. At Harwood she often rode astride. It was safer and handier for her when surveying the land.

The mill was across the field and down a sharp hill into a draw. Its wheels rotated on a stream that cut through her pastures on its journey to the sea. It had not been operational for years. The lane that had once been worn by constant traffic to and from the old mill, was now overgrown and grassy from disuse. It would be a boon to see the mill running once more.

Arabella let her horse walk as her mind wandered to Theo. She thought of his blue and gold eyes boring into her as his hands roamed her. She could not seem to stop thinking about it. It was wonderful.

The lane to the mill was a favorite of hers. It meandered down the hill in a series of lazy turns to the creek. From there, a small bridge led to the other side of the draw and up the gulley to the heights of Bergen's Point.

She closed her eyes, threw her head back, and let the sun warm her face. The steady rhythm of the horse beneath her rocked her in the saddle. The birds sang from the trees that lined each side of the weathered road. It was good to be alive.

Her thoughts wandered again to Theo. She loved his laugh. He was still a mystery to her; one that she looked forward to exploring. She remembered his words about being thankful for this match. This morning she was thankful too.

An image of Theo naked, as he stood beside her bed, floated into her mind. His sex had stood erect and ominous on his lean muscular body. She had been so afraid. She smiled at the memory. She felt his hot breath on her neck and his hands squeezing her breasts. And his tongue. Oh god. She groaned aloud. She felt his mouth on her as surely as if he were beside her. To her surprise, her stomach tightened, and a rush of dampness filled her nether regions. The press of her lower body against the saddle and the steady beat of the horse only made it worse. By the time she had made the turn around a bluff of thick bushes and reached the mill, she was filled with an overpowering aching need.

These were dangerous thoughts indeed. She slid from her horse by the stream's edge. Theo and Jem walked towards her. She was sure her cheeks were flushed. In a panic, she knew that surely, they would notice her aroused state. And she wanted Theo. She wanted him desperately.

"I brought a picnic lunch," she said as they approached. "Jem, I wonder if you could set it up. I must...I absolutely must show Theo the lily I have seen."

She grabbed Theo by the hand and pulled him back

down the trail towards the bushes. She knew it made no sense but didn't care.

Theo opened his mouth to speak but before he could she was running towards the bluff, her hand gripping his. She did not turn around or pause until they were safely behind the shrubbery.

She looked at him at last. He wore his signature half smile. He tilted his head curiously and waited for her to speak. She could not. Now that he was near her, she could only look at him. She felt her cheeks burn. She watched his face lose the playful grin, as his eyes bored into hers.

Finally, she stepped close to him and put her hand on his pants between his legs. She felt his organ swell and jerk at her touch. She gently squeezed him, hearing his answering deep groan. He put his hands on both sides of her head and kissed her roughly. She kissed him back, frantically sucking his tongue in a parody of sexual thrusts. She rubbed him as he pulled her to the ground. He yanked her skirts up and his hand found her. She was wet and slippery. He groaned again and made a choking sound that was half laugh, half strangled shout. He pressed his body against her. She could feel his erection through his pants as he moved.

She closed her eyes and savored the feel of it. The rough material chaffed her, sending delicious shock waves through her body. The tip of him was able to penetrate her slightly despite the pants. It teased her and she wetted it in return. Her heart pounded in her chest. Her body ached, arching against him with a desperation she had never felt. Reaching down she tugged at his belt, attempting to release him. She wanted him now.

He left her to free himself from his trousers. She reached out for him, unable to control her whimpers, until he was back in her arms. He plunged into her. He was only able to move one quick stroke before she felt her body explode in wave after wave of ecstasy. She opened herself to him, pulling him as deeply as she could take him. His organ throbbed and burst inside her. She opened her mouth to scream. He put his mouth on hers, smothering the sound as her body lurched and trembled its flood of release.

"Oh, my god. Oh, my god." He gasped, before collapsing on top of her.

For a few minutes, there was nothing. She thought she may have passed out. When she opened her eyes and returned to reality, Theo was above her, braced up on an elbow. He looked into her eyes and gifted her with a slow lazy smile. She returned it.

"The French call it the little death," he told her in a low drawl. He traced her lips with his fingers and pushed his hips forward. He was still inside her. He leaned down and kissed her ever so gently. She felt him twitch and move. She was warm and wet.

"My god, but you are marvelous. You are a wonder, a goddess, and mine." He kissed her lips.

She slowly became aware of their surroundings. Tall grass, green and lush, hid them from view. She looked to the side and saw an overgrown honeysuckle bush. The buzzing of bees at their work gathering nectar mixed with the summer sounds of grasshoppers and filled her senses. A clear blue sky framed Theo above her.

She felt a part of it all. It was as though she belonged. She and Theo were a piece of all of this. Their bodies coming together was as natural as this field.

She looked at his gold flecked eyes and smiled at him. He would be her lifelong mate. She thought of sharing this with him. It made her giggle. He would think she was silly at best. She laughed again. She felt a rush of pure happiness.

"I feel so good. I feel natural as though this is meant to be," she blurted out.

He laughed his loud exuberant laugh, and she knew he felt as she did; happy to be here and happy to be alive.

He stood and arranged his trousers. Reaching out to her to help her up, he said, "Come on. We want to get back. The idea of Jem coming to find us gives me the shivers."

He helped her adjust her skirts and picked a blade of grass from her hair. Pulling her close, he gave her a peck on the cheek before offering his arm.

"You are perfect," he said.

Jem had spread out a picnic blanket and sat uncomfortably on it. The basket sat unopened beside him. His arms were crossed.

"Was it a lily worth seeing then?" he asked, his weathered face impassive.

"It was," Theo said. "It was truly the most beautiful lily I have ever encountered."

He grinned at Arabella.

Jem grunted, reaching for the picnic basket.

They ate in silence. Arabella occasionally stole a glance at Theo, smiling when their eyes met. Jem seemed unaware. He kept his eyes on his food. Arabella was happy she had packed extra, remembering Jem's voracious appetite.

When the meal was finished, Jem pulled a piece of dry grass to pick his teeth. "The mill is fixable. I will be hiring some boys from the village to mend her. When I go up north this week, I will find a miller. He'll not make much this year, but there's the promise of a good living in the future. I heard the miller up the coast has an apprentice that is eager for a place of his own."

"That is great news!" Arabella said.

Jem nodded. "There will be plenty of work for carpenters here. The millhouse will need an update." He paused. "The cottage along the draw needs a new roof. If I bring in the livestock next week, we will need a hand living here along the draw to tend them. I will find a man for that too."

"You are bringing in livestock?" Theo asked curiously. It was a strategy he too had concluded would benefit the estate.

"Sixty head of sheep. They'll range along the draw as they did in the past. It'll be good to see these rocky hills in use again." He gave Theo a hard look. "That is if your money comes in to pay the quarterly wages. We've the money for one or the other."

Theo was about to ask what money he was speaking of. The accounts were drained. Until he transferred funds, there was nothing to be had, yet Jem would be purchasing an entire herd of sheep and fixing the mill. Then he knew. He decided now was not the time to bring up the subject.

"The money will be in. I will go up to London this week to transfer funds."

Jem uttered a satisfied grunt.

"It is so exciting." Arabella gave Jem an appreciative look. "Aran will be much surprised and pleased." She shared Theo's plan to bring in a crew from the village, and the farmers who would soon be arriving. Jem nodded his approval.

She started to pack up the picnic lunch. She smiled to herself. Just as her grandmother had suggested, her marriage had been the answer to her many problems. Theo loaded the basket and helped her mount. It had been a glorious picnic.

As she climbed the winding gully road toward home, she

thought of the week to come. Theo would be off to London. She should have been pleased with the opportunity to make a quick run to the continent. Instead, she felt confused. Jem was clearly hesitant and would have to be convinced to go with her.

And worse, she was beginning to enjoy the company of her husband.

For the first time Arabella seriously considered a life without her persona of Captain Ara. It was too frightening to think about. She had worked hard to build her image. Unlike other captains, she had always been forced to prove her worth. Her first battles had been with her crew. The secret of her gender was soon known. Only after she had shown over and over her superior skill had they accepted her at the helm. Without Jem it would have been impossible.

And then she had forged a reputation and a role in the smuggling community. To earn the respect of the other captains had been an even greater challenge. But she had accomplished it. She had been meaner and tougher than any of them. For the first time she acknowledged Captain Ara was not just about earning the money she needed for her estate. Captain Ara was her life, her passion, and her victory. To give it all up now seemed impossible.

With the money from her marriage and Theo as her husband her role as captain was no longer a necessity. Even Jem expected her to simply give it up. She was just not sure she could do it.

She sighed. Having a husband was a more complicated enterprise than she had anticipated.

Chapter Fourteen

When Arabella had been mounted and on her way home, Theo turned back towards the mill. Jem stood beside the creek as if giving it his final appraisal. In the last few minutes, he had heard him speak more than he ever had. It was clear to him that Jem was a solid overseer. It was clear to him too, the money he had spoken of came from smuggling profits. There had not been significant money from this estate for some time. Even now, there would not be a steady source of income here until fall, and then only if they found renters for the holdings.

He wondered how Jem would feel about him forbidding the illegal trade. He did not know if he had an enemy or an ally. He hoped it was the latter.

It was time to find out.

He walked up to Jem and stood beside him, feeling dwarfed by his massive height. His stomach twisted with apprehension. He had no interest in being crushed this afternoon.

He blurted out, "I know about the smuggling."

Jem was immobile for long seconds before he turned slowly towards Theo and looked down at him. His scarred face was serious as his cold eyes bored into him.

Theo was sure he was dead. Feeling like an errant schoolboy, he concentrated on not shuffling his feet while he met his gaze. "I found a letter from Aran which made it all abundantly clear. I, ah, I have not talked to her, to Arabella about it."

His voice sounded high-pitched to him.

He cleared his throat and tried again. "I want it to stop. I have found my wife and I have decided I want to keep her."

Despite his attempts to hold himself still, he found himself taking a quick step back.

"Do ye now?" Jem asked.

"Safe," Theo stuttered. "I need to keep her safe. If she is taken at sea, I don't know if I can help her. You must agree it is all too much for her? I understand the past. I've read the accounts. I saw the state of this place two years ago and I have some sense of what it took to bring it back. But that is over now."

Jem remained silent; his rough face impassive. Only a glint in his steely eyes indicated he had registered Theo's words at all.

Theo felt himself becoming desperate and took a calming breath. "She is mine. I would look after her," he said earnestly. He met the man's eyes. "I might need your help in this."

Jem turned back to the mill. He cleared his throat. "She and her brother have been mine to care for since their father left this world. The smuggling, there was no other way to keep what was theirs. I supported it."

Theo waited long minutes before Jem continued. "I've told her it's done. I'll support ye with this."

He walked off towards the mill. It was clear he had no more to say on the matter.

At supper that night, Theo found himself seated at the head of the long oaken table. He looked around as he waited for Arabella. Again, the room was dark. He scowled at the heavy mahogany paneled walls. The sole window was covered with thick damask curtains. Ornate wall sconces provided the only light. A sideboard lurked in the shadows next to a swinging door which he assumed led to the kitchens. The elaborate candelabra hung unlit above the table, its holders barren. He detested this room.

He walked to the windows and pulled back the heavy curtains. The evening twilight helped relieve some of the gloom.

Better, he thought as he looked back towards the table. The lighting showed the faded carpet to disadvantage, but the room was now far superior to the shadowy cave it had been. At least it was clean. Arabella had taken his advice and brought in a housekeeper and maid to help with the place.

He picked up the place setting at the far end of the table, balancing the cutlery, glasses, and napkin on the plate, and moved it to the left of his place. He arranged it carefully and looked at it with satisfaction. Even better.

He looked at the cold fireplace to his right and frowned. He wanted the room to be perfect. Tonight, he needed to convince his lovely wife to come with him to London. It was a couple of days' journey just to get to town. A week alone here next to the sea was too dangerous for Arabella. She could well go on a run. Indeed, with him gone, it would be the perfect opportunity for her. He thought of the arrogant masked captain he had seen at The Meadows three months ago. The cutters would relish her capture. He would not allow it.

He had not confronted her with his knowledge of her double life. And he wouldn't until she was safely in London.

Arnold came through the swinging door with a decanter of wine. Theo sat down in his chair and examined him. He looked as though he had struggled to fit into livery. His gloveless hands shook as he poured the wine.

"I wonder, Arnold, if you could light the fire."

"I could. I could, sir." Arnold set the wine down on the table with a *thunk* and turned to the fire. It was obvious he preferred that task. He concluded Arnold was new to this work. Probably a better sailor than a footman, he thought grimly.

The lad had a blaze going in no time and stood back to admire it.

"There ye go." He turned to Theo with a triumphant smile. "I'll see about supper for you then."

Forgetting about the wine, he strode to the kitchen, with large clumping strides. *Yes, definitely a better sailor than footman*, thought Theo with a wry smile.

When Arabella entered the room, Theo's breath caught. Her hair was piled high upon her head. She wore a shimmering red gown that clung to her body. It was cut low, with a long slash between her breasts. When she moved, the outline of her slender hips and legs was obvious.

He stood and took her hand. "You are breathtaking, my dear."

She smiled her impish grin. "It is in the modern style—

to be worn without petticoats. It is called the body move-ment." She let go of his hand, doing a twirl. The curve of her hips was evident. "Do you like it? I love it. It feels wonderful to be so free."

There was a refreshing exuberance about her.

His eyes travelled the length of her body. Both the gown and her stance were now blatantly sexual. When he met her eyes, they danced with mischief. She clearly knew how enticing she was and relished the idea of teasing him. His body tightened.

"I do," he said, "though I am not sure I would want anyone but me to see you in it. I think you might create a scandal should you wear it in town."

She laughed, childishly delighted with his response. It was a joyful easy sound. She was happy. It pleased him.

She looked at the neat arrangement of place settings at the end of the table and smiled at him. "We will be able to speak without shouting tonight. How civilized."

"I thought it might be a refreshing change."

They enjoyed a congenial meal. He purposely kept the conversation light. He discussed the food, the wine, his grandmother, and hers. Finally, the evening was coming to an end. He poured them a glass of sweet madeira.

Leaning back in his chair and swirling his madeira around in his glass, he contemplated the best way to bring up the trip to town. He had promised her he would not take her from Harwood, but this was just a short trip. He decided to simply come out with it.

"I have to go to London to transfer funds. I need you to be with me."

He watched her carefully. She looked down, considering the idea. Her hands twisted in her lap. He thought about the Arabella of Harwood Place. Here, she roamed the estate without barriers. She had spent years doing as she pleased. She had been allowed to be part woman, part hoyden. Suddenly he knew her attempts to avoid town life were more than just a desire to be on the sea. The strictures in the world of high society would be like a prison to her. He watched the emotions play on her face.

This too would be a problem for her. She had none of the sly duplicity required to survive in society. She was too blatantly honest. The women of his world would eat her alive.

"I could for a week or two. Now would be a suitable time for me, but..." When she looked at him again, her eyes were wide. Their black depths reflected the glow of the fire.

Oh god. When she looks at me like this, I can deny her nothing. I must hold firm.

"I so wanted to get to know you here. Where I am comfortable." She reached over and took his hand. "I am not my best in town. I feel out of place. It is not for me."

Her fingers gripped his.

"A week or two. It would be a honeymoon trip. And besides," he said, "this time you will be with me. You cannot be out of place when your place is with me."

She sighed. He hoped he would not be forced to demand it. He knew he would hog-tie her and haul her there if he had to.

She looked up with an impish grin. "I will go with you for at least two weeks if you will spend this week here with me."

Theo leapt at the bargain. "Deal."

He expelled a breath. For three weeks at least she was safe with him.

That evening began ten days of a romp in Yorkshire with his beautiful wife. They spent every minute of it together. At first, she was interested solely in the discovery of her sexuality. Her enthusiasm was contagious. At every opportunity, they made love. And he found that he could not resist her; with her, he was insatiable. It was the strangest thing. He had had many lovers, but never had he been so obsessed with a woman.

One morning after a night spent with her in his arms, a night which should have left him drained and sated, they had ridden to the mill to check the progress being made on its repairs. No one was about. She leaned against the open doorframe and waited for him as he looped the reins of his horse to the fence. When he went to walk by her, he paused and looked at her beautiful wind-blown face.

She gifted him with a slow sexy smile. It was enough. He could not resist pulling her into his arms for a kiss. The kiss, which had begun as perfunctory, became a passionate embrace. He wrapped his arms around her and kissed her, losing himself in the taste and feel of her. She tugged on his shirt, her hands finding his bare skin, then running the length of his back.

He pulled up her skirts and felt her. She was wet and ready for him. He groaned against her mouth, unable to resist sliding his fingers into her. When she shifted and eagerly met his touch, wiggling her body to accommodate him, it was too much. He loosened his pants and drove into her.

She wrapped her legs around him and hung on to his shoulders. And he took Arabella there, braced up in the doorframe. He pounded into her, desperate and savage, unable to control the unquenchable desire that she could instill in him. He felt her explode into her climax, and pushed powerfully, forcing her body up the rough wooden frame, and shouting his release.

After, he could only rest his head against the curve of her shoulder and pant against her neck. Her legs released him, and she slid to her feet. He pulled away from her and looked at her face. Her eyes were dark and mysterious.

Once again, she gave her slow sexy smile. He felt his body twitch in response.

My god, he thought, can I ever get enough of this woman? His need for her disturbed him. He stepped back from her and adjusted his clothing.

"I am afraid I have splinters." She laughed. "You will be in charge of removing them."

"That I can do," he said with a smile.

When they returned to the house to change, he discovered she did indeed have splinters. He spent half an hour with tweezers working over her bare bum. Ultimately, he found himself with his face nestled between her thighs, tasting her sweetness. Again, they made love, this time slowly and gently.

And still that night when he held her in his arms, he wanted her. Finally, she curled up against him and slept.

He looked at her face in the amber glow of the lantern. She was the picture of innocence. Again, he tried to impose the face of the ragged smuggling captain on her. It was impossible to align the two images. This woman by his side was as youthful and exuberant as a child. While it was true, she rode the estate like a man, astride, involved in every decision which affected her beloved Harwood, as a wife and a woman she was guileless and loving. The Captain Ara he had met at The Meadows had been arrogant and hard. He had exuded power, with his crew standing beside him in a show of loyalty and respect. Theo shook his head to dispel the scene.

And yet he knew it to be true. Every night he experienced a moment of dread, wondering if this night would be the one she did not come to sleep in his room. He dreaded she would claim a headache or illness in order to have the privacy to sneak away to her ship. Sometimes in the dead of night, she would stir. He would be instantly awake, waiting for her to steal away from his bed. It tormented him.

With each day together, he liked and enjoyed her more. And with each day, his anxiety grew. He loved to be with her on her wild Yorkshire home, but he yearned for the relief of taking her safely inland, where she would not have the persistent draw of the Bella, docked only a mile away, rocking menacingly in the waves, waiting for her.

Chapter Fifteen

For ten days, there had been nothing but Theo. It had gone by too quicky for her. He had given her the week she had asked for. Then for three days more, she had found a reason to delay their departure. She had run out of excuses. She leaned back in the tub, closing her eyes. Even now she could hear Celeste bustling about, packing her things.

She wondered about town life with Theo. She had always felt painfully shy at the soirees and dancehalls of London. It all seemed foreign to her. She was much more comfortable aboard a ship or roaming the rocky land at Harwood. But perhaps he was right, and it would be different this time.

He told her that his friends were in town. His best friend, Ambrose, had a new wife too. That she was a dress designer who had probably done her red gown interested her. Women in business were rare, especially married women. This friend of Theo's must be an unusual person indeed. She sighed. She would try, but she had had little luck making friends with women.

Overall, despite her misgivings, a trip to London now was good timing for her. The village men were fishing. She and Jem had often taken the Bella out to fish, but he was away transporting the goods they had stashed at Tremble Point and exchanging it for livestock. This time even their stake would be spent. It meant there would be no money from smuggling left to invest in trade goods. She squeezed her eyes shut to avoid the thought. She would think of it later.

The revenue boys were frustrated. Boat after boat had been searched to no avail. No one along their rocky coast was moving goods at sea.

Jamie reported that if the boats went out before dawn as they often did, signal lights could sometimes be seen from the rise above the village aimed towards the cliffs above Bergen's Point. That the signals were then transmitted out to sea beyond the point was clear, but to date they had been unable to find the spotter.

They had tested them out. The signals would only flash if a boat went out with a heavy crew instead of the two or three men needed to fish. If a boat did not load nets or traps it was sure to be boarded and searched. Especially if it headed out around Bergen's Point towards the channel. It was clear the boats were carefully watched. If the culprits were not discovered before she came home, Arabella knew she would take a more active role in the investigation, starting with the Vicar, scoundrel that he was.

Arabella's thoughts turned to Theo. He had been a wonder and a joy. Oddly, she found she had not missed Captain Ara. She had been busy learning about her husband and her new role as wife. She was beginning to think she could accomplish this transition to being the wife he wanted. For two days, they had not left the bedroom.

Outside of Celeste who had laughed as she changed their sheets and ran their bath, they had seen no one. Their food had been left at the door.

On the third day, they had roused themselves enough to take a ride through the fields. Upon arriving home, they had raced up the stairs, discarding their clothing and screeching with laughter in a mad dash to reach the privacy of the bedroom. She had no idea what the servants thought of her, and she did not care. By the fourth day, they had ventured further afield, even doing formal suppers. They went for a ride each morning after that.

They twice had taken out the Bella. Arabella had had the chance to relish her other passion. It had been a perfect honeymoon.

After supper, they tried to spend time getting to know each other. She had always begun her sedate evenings with her grandmother by playing several compositions on the piano. To her surprise, when she performed for Theo, he joined her on the keyboard. Together they would play rousing duets, often ending in laughter with the joy of their synchronicity.

Like her brother Aran, Theo loved poetry. He had found several books of poems which he read to entertain her. Shakespeare's sonnets were his favorite, and he chose a new one for her each day. She began to relish the time spent with him.

And not once had she considered finding a way to send him on his way to London without her. Each time the conflict of her life in the past as a captain nagged at her, she dismissed it. She would deal with the problem later. For now, she only wanted to be near Theo and enjoy him. Though initially she had worried about the trip to London, today she was thankful she had agreed.

At times, Theo asked her questions about the Bella or her time at sea. Arabella always managed to skirt the subject. She did not want to lie to Theo, but she could not tell him the truth. And then Theo would look at her strangely. Sometimes, she almost felt as though he suspected something, and her stomach would churn.

Jem had insisted she give up her role of captain. She was trying, and so far, her role of wife had more than distracted her from that vocation.

She debated telling Theo, but she had her crew to protect. It was her responsibility to keep them safe. She was not sure what his reaction would be. She only knew keeping secrets had been a habit long instilled in her. It was the only way when discovery had its hard consequences.

And now she must try to enter his world.

Chapter Sixteen

Theo tucked the new trinket he had purchased in his pocket. It was a diamond bracelet for Arabella. He thought of her childish glee when receiving a gift. Nothing made her happier than a surprise. He wanted to spoil her.

It had been three weeks now since their arrival in London, and almost six since he had married and still, she dominated his every waking moment. He had done all he could to make her happy.

He had purchased a new mare for her. Each morning, they were able to ride in the park. Keeping her indoors was inconceivable when she was used to the wilds of Yorkshire.

He had also insisted she enhance her wardrobe. Fortunately, she and Kate, Ambrose's wife, had become fast friends. For days, they had pored over sketches and talked of nothing but silk, puffed sleeves, and laced bodices. Nothing could have made him more pleased. If he could keep her engaged, she might be convinced to stay a little longer.

And he had discovered Arabella liked the opera. Four times they had caught shows. She was enthralled by the music. Her love of the glitter and the glamour was a surprise to him. She oohed and aahed over the wardrobe and jewels worn by the wealthy patrons. Before each performance, they people watched. She was eager to know which ladies were of the courtesan variety and which were ladies of the town.

"But how can you tell?" she had asked as she ogled them through her opera glasses.

"One knows these things," he had answered. And she had swatted him with her fan.

"Oh, dear. I get the feeling you may know this too well," she had said. But she had laughed, and he had been relieved she did not deny him his past.

Once he pointed out the monstrously obese Lady Cargill. He told her the funny story about her falling into a trash barrel in the lobby of the opera house.

"It had taken three orderlies to pull her wedged body free. And I, like everyone present at the opera that night, still struggle to wipe the image of those massive red petti-coats from my mind." She laughed. Nothing pleased her more than a disparaging story about the elite. He thought it helped her to be more comfortable in their presence. He gifted her with as many of those tales as he could.

Theo was satisfied with the job he had done thus far keeping her in town. Today she had happily gone out to tea with Kate, who would be introducing her to several ladies from town. It was precisely the situation he hoped for.

He smiled as he walked into his club to meet Ambrose. He found him at his usual table near the fireplace.

"Ah, Theo." Ambrose looked at his watch. "You are late. I had almost given up on you."

"I had to buy my wife a little gift. I thought diamonds

might suit her." He proudly pulled the box from his pocket and, opening it, laid it on the table.

Ambrose looked at it and gave a soft whistle of appreciation. "More treasure for your little pirate?" He chuckled.

Theo looked at him suspiciously, snapped the lid closed, and left the box on the table. He shrugged. "I want to keep her happy."

The waiter arrived. They both ordered a brandy.

When it was served, Ambrose raised his glass to the light and swirled the drink before taking a sip. "It is good brandy, but not to the caliber that can be found on the Yorkshire coast. One hears tales that good French stock is in abundance there."

Theo stared at him. "You know."

"Of course, I know." Ambrose set down his glass and sighed. "I had been wracking my brain trying to remember where I had seen her before. After all, those eyes are hard to forget. The whole encounter is etched in my mind. And then she said something about a lugger and the sea. It all fell into place. She was at the Meadows the night we came for the codes." Ambrose shook his head. "It boggles the mind to think you found the only female pirate in existence and married her." Serious, he looked at Theo. "What the hell are you going to do?"

Theo let out a long breath. "For now, I am keeping her from the sea. Every day she is here with me, she is safe. I live in terror of her slipping away some night." Theo brushed a lock of hair back from his forehead. His mouth twisted into his usual half grin. "And it is worse than that. I love her desperately. She has somehow become the center of my world. I have to protect her, and I don't know how."

"Forbid her to go out. For god's sake, Theo, if she refuses, move her inland permanently." Ambrose leaned forward and glared at him. "Do you have the slightest idea of what could happen to her if she were caught? I have been in the navy. If they discover she is a woman, all hell will break loose. They will use her roughly. And the revenue boys? My god, Theo, they'd be worse."

Theo sat back up and groaned. "It's not as simple as that." He told him about the letter and what he knew of her brother's work for Admiral Hews. He added, "She doesn't know I know. I had hoped she would confide in me, that she would learn to trust me."

"Theo, you must confront her. You are married. You will need to deal with this together." Ambrose slapped his hand on the table. "She cannot expect to have a marriage and be a bloody pirate."

"She is a smuggler, not a bloody pirate." Theo realized he had raised his voice. He looked around to see if he had been heard. Several men were looking at him curiously. He swore under his breath. When he next spoke, he lowered his voice. "But I agree. It's time. She has agreed to stay another three days. Then it is back to Harwood. Once home, we will deal with it."

"I remember the arrogant captain we met that night at the Meadows. Surrounded by her crew, she had been formidable. I would confront her now while she is on your territory." He sounded like the military man he had once been.

"It is not a war, Ambrose, for god's sake."

Ambrose shrugged. "I think it is. Take it from me, marriage is a constant battle to stay in command." He placed a finger on the velvet box on the table. "Besides, you already have your peace offering."

Theo considered the idea. He looked at Ambrose with

some distress. "I find it hard to win battles with my Arabella. She only has to look at me and I am done."

"Buck up, man." Ambrose snorted. "You must begin as you intend to continue. As a commander, I know these things. Arabella will be a tough one to direct, it is true. But trust me, every battle lost is ground never regained. Heaven knows I have begun to learn this the hard way."

Theo decided that Ambrose's advice was worthy. The timing was right. Tonight, for the first time in days, they had no plans for the evening.

It was time to confront her.

Chapter Seventeen

He knew Arabella anticipated a night of making love. At supper, she wore the red dress which had so enthralled him at Harwood. It clung to her body. She sat close to him, taking every opportunity to touch his shoulder or stroke his hand. She smiled, joked, and entertained him.

"Shall we retire early?" he suggested when they finished dessert.

"What a wonderful idea." Arabella replied, rising to take his arm as they left the dining room. She cuddled against him on the way to the stairs. He tried to enjoy Arabella's antics but found himself distracted by the battle ahead.

Theo led her to her room and went through their adjoining door to change and to think about the argument he and Arabella were sure to have. Setting his peace offering on his dressing table, he wrapped the belt of his robe more tightly around him. Taking a deep, fortifying breath, he opened her door.

Arabella stood at her mirror wearing a shimmering silk

nightgown. It was almost transparent, extending to just past her thighs. When she turned to him, he could see her dark nipples standing rigidly at attention. Lower on her body, the material clung to her in all the right places. Dark shadows where her thighs met enticed him.

She ran her hand down her body. Smiling mischievously, she said, "Do you like it? Kate had it made for me."

He grimaced. This was going to be more difficult than he had thought. "Sit down, Arabella. We need to talk."

She sat at her dressing table and looked at him with her dark innocent eyes. He tried to concentrate on the scarfed captain he had once met. He ran his hand through his hair and leaned against their adjoining door. It was impossible. She looked young and beautiful. There was nothing resembling the arrogant captain in Arabella tonight.

Taking a deep breath, he decided to begin the battle. "I know about the smuggling. I know about your forays as Captain Ara."

His words fell like a bomb into the room.

Her mouth dropped in shock. She met his eyes. For long moments, they just stared at each other.

She got up from her chair and paced the room. When she paused to look at him, her dark eyes were hard and glittered ominously in the lamp light. "How did you find out?"

"I watched you go out when we were at Harwood. There must have been a meeting of some sort. Before you returned, I searched your room."

She flinched.

"I found your letter from Aran."

"How dare you? How could you go through my things!" Her face flushed. "My room is private. You have no right!"

"I have every right!" All his frustration erupted in a fury.

"For god's sake, you are my wife! Or have you forgotten that uncomfortable truth?"

"Am I to have no privacy then? Is that it?" She ripped a tie from her hair and flung it onto her dressing table. She tossed her head; her hair swirled around her.

Looking at her now, with her faced flushed and her black eyes glittering, he thought she had never looked so beautiful.

His voice remained firm. "No, you do not. Do not speak of rights. You do not have the right to risk yourself at sea. And you had no right to keep this secret from me."

"Secrets! You lied to me! All this time you knew. You made love to me. You pretended to care for me." She snatched up a water glass from her dressing table and threw it at him. He stepped aside and it shattered against the wall.

Theo looked down at the shards of glass on the floor. He brushed a broken chunk away from him with his foot.

"Lied to you! My god, woman, no one has been more duplicitous than you. You dare to accuse me of lying?" he said, stepping towards her. He raised his voice. "It is over. Done. I forbid you to even think about it. You will never make a run again."

"You forbid me! You cannot order me about as if I am your servant girl." She put her hands on her hips and glared at him. Using the deep voice she had mastered at sea, she growled at him, "I am a captain and a damn good one. Ye'll not be giving me orders now or ever."

It was a direct challenge.

Theo threw back his head and laughed. This time it was a bitter sound. She had mistaken his pampering and generosity for weakness. White hot rage washed over him.

"It seems that you have forgotten who you're speaking to," he said, his voice dangerously soft. He walked over to her and stared down at her. "I am your husband. I will have you remember that."

He grabbed her nightgown just above her breasts. In one quick jerk, he ripped the material in two. It lay in pieces at her feet.

"Theo!" Her mouth dropped in an expression of outrage.

He picked her up and tossed her nude body onto the bed.

She stared at him open-mouthed as he removed his robe.

"You cannot... you cannot be thinking to do this now, Theo," she stuttered, looking up at him wide-eyed once more.

"I am and we will. Two reasons." He crawled in beside her and put his hands on her breasts. He cupped one breast in each hand, using his thumbs to rub her dark nipples. He watched them swell to his touch. Bending over her, he sucked each one and nibbled it before raising his head to blow softly on them. He looked at her confused face and laughed again.

"First and most importantly, I would have you remember just who I am." He slid his hands across her taunt belly and grabbed her roughly between her thighs. He squeezed her hard, lifting her hips with his one hand, before relaxing his grip and gently stoking her. To his amazement, a flush of welcoming dampness met his fingers. He looked at Arabella, feeling the tension leave his body and kissed her gently. "I am your husband. I am not one of your crew."

He slid down her body and forced her legs apart by nuzzling his head between them. He kissed and licked her tender parts. She moaned and he raised his eyes to look at her. Her slender dark body lay writhing before him on the white sheets.

"And second," he said, "there is no purpose in spatting at each other like a pair of alley cats. We understand each other quite well in this bed. Now, tell me you want me, Arabella."

"I want you, Theo," she said in a quiet voice.

He moved on top of her and pushed himself into her wetness. He ground himself against her until he filled her completely. When she arched against him, he used his hips to slam his body against hers in a brutal thrust. Grabbing her hips, he held her there, pressed against his body until she squirmed. Her muscles gripped him, squeezing him in rhythmic spasms, willing him to stroke her.

She whimpered; soft little sounds that always drove him wild. Groaning, she wrapped her arms and legs around him.

"Oh god, Theo, I love you so much."

His mind reeled before he began making mad passionate love to her.

Arabella slept with her head resting on his chest. He shifted her carefully onto her pillow and tucked the sheet around her. He looked at her for a long time. As always, she was innocent and childlike in her sleep. Yet never had he been with a more passionate woman. He smiled wryly. His wife was a contradiction. She was passionate and fierce, a talented and fearless captain, but in the ways of love and relationships she had a refreshing honesty.

She stirred in her sleep and pulled the sheet down below her breasts. He smiled. He loved her small breasts. He cupped his hand around one. It was firm and tight. Somehow, her breasts seemed fuller than they had that day in the gazebo. He leaned over and examined her more closely.

The area around her nipples had darkened. And yes, he thought, these breasts are swollen and larger. He wondered if the new duties of a wife could change her in this way.

Theo slid the sheet down to examine her body. She was slim and muscular. He could find no noticeable differences there. If he were to choose the animal, she most resembled, it would be a panther, lean and black.

He let his hands roam her, gently examining every part of her. Her woman's belly was rounded but firm and tight as always. He could not resist gently holding her between her thighs and he left his hand there as he slid his body back alongside her. To his surprise, he felt himself swell and fill with need. He wondered if the wanting of her would ever stop.

Theo lay against her, breathing her feminine scent. He thought about her words tonight. She had said she loved him. He knew she loved him. With sudden insight, he realized she had loved him for a long time.

But through all the gift-giving and pampering, the teasing and the time spent together, she had never uttered a word of love. And tonight, he thought in confusion, after a raging battle, she tells me she loves me.

He shook his head. Her words had been only passion. She probably would not remember saying them. It would take a while for him to help her understand what they had together. He could be patient.

He felt his organ begin to throb and ache. Unconsciously, he had pressed himself into her belly. Moving his hips slightly against her brought new agonies, and he groaned.

He looked at her. She looked back at him with sleepy eyes and a soft smile. She opened her arms and he turned into her. He slid inside her. She was wet and so warm. His hips moved slowly, easing himself back and forth inside her. He wanted her to retain her sleepy half-awake state. And so, he rocked her and whispered quietly to her of dreams while he took her. Very gently, very tenderly he made love to her.

She kept her eyes closed and her body completely relaxed. She purred softly. He felt her body ripple, her lips parted, and she moaned as she found her woman's pleasure but softly and delicately this time. She was snug against him, wet and slippery from her release. He felt his organ burst inside her. He held her carefully while his own body spasmed. Then he rolled them slowly to their sides. He smiled to see she was sound asleep once more. He eased himself from her and pulled the sheet up over her.

In the morning, they would speak about the whole issue of smuggling.

Chapter Eighteen

Arabella heard Theo place the breakfast tray on the bedside table. Then he went into her dressing room where she could hear him rummaging around. She shook herself awake and sat up, pulling the sheet around her.

When he came back into the room, he tossed a heavy cotton nightgown at her.

"Put it on," he said. "We have some things we need to talk about. I do not want any distractions."

His voice brooked no argument. She obediently pulled the nightgown over her head and past her hips and legs. It was old. It had long sleeves and a high collar. Where he had found it, she had no idea. Celeste would have shuddered.

He nodded as if satisfied and dragged a chair up to the side table. She swung her legs to the floor and pulled her gown down discretely covering her legs. She scowled at him. He was completely dressed and at ease, while she felt itchy and vulnerable in this old nightie.

Theo looked at her and laughed. "Have some tea. You'll feel better."

He poured them both a cup and handed one to her. Holding her cup with both hands she blew on it, before taking a sip. She set it down and tried to run her fingers through her tangled hair. Giving up, she looked at him and waited for him to begin his talk.

Theo meticulously smeared his toast with jelly, seeming nonchalant, yet carefully avoiding her eyes. Thinking of last night's argument made her stomach turn. She picked up her tea but found she could hardly swallow with his eyes on her.

She remembered telling Theo she loved him last night and felt her cheeks flame. In a horrible flash of insight, she knew it to be true. Odd that she could only recognize this love when she was in danger of losing it.

Her heart raced. Maybe he had already decided his new wife was not for him. He was an earl. He would not want to be tied to a smuggler of all things. Bile rose in her throat. She tried to swallow but could not fight the nausea.

Arabella leapt up and ran to her dressing room. Hanging over her basin, she vomited over and over until she was coughing and weak. Theo's arms reached around her waist and held her. She felt a moment of gratitude before she began again. She heaved until there was nothing left in her stomach. And still Theo held her, his hands tight on her belly.

Leaning against him, she took a moment to catch her breath. After she had recovered, she pulled his hands from her and said, "I am fine now. I need a minute to clean up. Please."

She did not want to look at him or have him see her face.

She washed her face and cleaned her teeth. Remarkably, she felt fine. It was as though the whole incident had not happened. Sighing with relief, she decided to brush out her hair as well. She set the offending basin down and covered it with a towel, then began to make some headway on her unruly mess of hair.

When she returned to the room, she felt completely herself. She was hungry and helped herself to breakfast. And all the while, Theo watched her, at first with concern and then his beautiful half smile returned. When she had eaten her fill, she leaned back and enjoyed her tea.

"Feeling better, I take it," he said.

"I am. I don't know what came over me, but whatever it was, I am quite fine now."

"Good. We will begin our little talk." Theo paused and watched her leerily as though he half expected her to jump up and return to the dressing room. When she remained where she was, looking fit, he seemed to sigh with relief.

She smiled. In some strange way, his discomfort was endearing. She felt more at ease. He had held her belly while she was sick. She was sure he would not have done it if he planned to walk out on her this morning. It was a panic attack, she thought. An unnecessary one. She placed her hands on her lap and waited for him to proceed.

"Now then." He cleared his throat. "Last night, I told you, your smuggling days were over. They are. It is too dangerous for you. Think about the trouble should you be caught. It is a needless risk now."

"I agree."

"If you are caught, the revenue boys will tear you apart. I have tried to understand and believe I do, but I will not—"

"I agree. I will end it," she interrupted.

"You will end it?"

"Yes. Jem has already forbidden it. I would not go on a run without him. But more than that I understand my role as your wife would make it impossible." Her words took even her by surprise. In her heart, Arabella had always known that she could not be Captain Ara forever. She had avoided reality for as long as she could.

The time had come.

Theo looked at her with confusion. She realized he had expected an argument. He had obviously prepared a lecture. He looked so disappointed and dumbfounded, she found herself bursting into laughter.

He did not laugh with her.

She cleared her throat and looked at him more seriously. "There is one favor I would ask of you in return."

He nodded, relieved, as though he had suspected the issue would not be resolved as quickly as it had and antici-pated a tough bargain.

"I am loyal to my crew. And more than that, I care about my village and the coastal people of my home. I know you may not understand life on our coast. It is different there. The folks at home have made their living by smuggling goods from the mainland for two hundred years. It is not wrong or even illegal in their mind. It is only their life." She sighed. "Our people would be hard pressed to survive without it. A man makes more from one night than he would with a month of wages. Everyone is aware of it, and almost everyone has a hand in it at some point."

She took a breath and looked at him. He was listening.

She continued, "Even the farmers benefit. Rather than selling wool almost at cost here in England, a trader will give them three times the price and more."

Theo smirked. "I am not sure you will convince me of the righteousness of the trade, but I do understand your argument."

"Yes, well. We have a problem. There is a ring of thieves operating in our midst."

Theo threw back his head and laughed wholeheartedly. "You don't say," he choked out.

"What is so funny? It's hardly a laughable matter." She glared at him.

He chuckled. "I am sorry. It's just..." He looked at her irritated expression. Carefully composing his face into more serious lines and waving away his earlier comment, he added, "Never mind. Go on."

"Anyway..." She looked him, waiting until he regained a more serious countenance. "There is a revenue cutter, the one who searched us on our cruise, who is taking down our boats and stealing the cargo."

"What do you mean?"

"If he catches a smuggler, he steals the load. He swears the crews to secrecy on pain of death and heads off with the spoils. I have his name. It's Captain Berg. The captain who searched our ship on our wedding day."

"Whew." Theo gave a soft whistle. "You are sure?"

She frowned. "Of course, I am sure. And what is worse, he has someone on the shore signaling him when the boats go out to sea, especially without nets or with the larger crew needed to cross the channel and load goods. Smuggling is always a risk, but for the men of our village, losing their cargo has become more certain than not."

She explained to him their theory about the signals and Bergen's Point.

"The man would be making a tidy fortune. Huh!" He grimaced. "Quite the enterprise."

She explained her thoughts on the involvement of the Vicar with his shared name and the attempts to find the signal man on the point.

"Who owns the land on the cliffs?" Theo asked.

"The new man, Mr. Sheffeld, lives on the point, but I do not know if he owns or rents. He was at our wedding. The big fellow in short pants and tights. A disagreeable looking sort."

"Easy enough to find out. We can check the land titles office here in town. It will all be there."

"I want to uncover these culprits. I would like your help, but I would be satisfied with at least your indulgence while I help to solve the problem." She looked at him and waited anxiously for his response. "It would be my last action as a captain."

"Hmmm. And this is your favor?" He looked at her earnestly. "In exchange for ending your career as a smuggler?"

"Yes."

"This time I have a condition. After all, you have told me you had planned to stop smuggling in any case." He reached for her hand. "I want your honesty. I do not want secrets between us."

He held her hands and squeezed them. "We both have our pasts. I will keep mine and you may have yours."

"It depends on your past. You know mine but I know nothing of yours."

He shrugged. "I have not lived so wild as you." He gave her a smile. "But there have been many lovers. These things I would not want to share."

She felt her face redden. She did not want him to share that part of his life with her either, but there was one thing she had to know. "Do you have a lover now?"

He gave a bark of laughter. "I could not keep a lover even if I wanted to. You are all I can handle, I am afraid." He leaned forward and kissed her, a peck on the lips. "So, no. I ended my last affair before I came to you. I will not have another unless you cast me aside."

"It is a deal. I give you my word as a captain—"

He looked at her and raised his brows.

"And as a wife," she added, "I will be honest with you. No more secrets."

"Hmmm. We have made another bargain then." He rose and paced the floor. "There are two things we can do while we are here in town. First, I will check the land titles office and find out what I can about Bergen's Point. If you are correct, and messages are being relayed, then whoever is up there must have access and familiarity with the property. The Vicar may be involved but he seemed a dull man to me. Our Mr. Sheffeld is another story. And while I am there, I will check for any public records on the Bergs."

He paused, looking speculatively at her. "And second, Admiral Hews is hosting a party tonight. Kate's aunt is serving as hostess. The place will be crawling with navy boys. I had thought to spare you an evening mingling with your enemies, but if you agree, I think we should go. We might be able to find out something about your Captain Berg." He grinned at her. "Do you think you can manage to consort with the troops for one evening?"

"Oh, perfect!" She clapped her hands together. "I would so love to end Berg's little game in our village."

"We will try, my dear, but it will be a serious business. Tonight, at the party, you must let me do all the inquiries. You will be surrounded by the King's men." He scowled at her. "So, for god's sake, say nothing of luggers or sailing."

She laughed happily and flew into his lap. "I will not. I will say nothing to anyone but you." She gave him an impish grin. "And now please tell me that I can get out of this horrible gown."

"Let me help you." He yanked the nightgown up past her hips and pulled it over her head, flinging it into the corner in one motion. Looking down at her, he drawled, "Is there a better way to start the day than having a naked Arabella in my lap?"

She looked at him with eyes that sparkled with mischief while running her tongue lightly across her lower lip. Shifting in his lap, she put a leg on each side of his and, facing him, she smiled. "I do not think so, my lord."

"Well, let's hope the day ends just as well. I have to admit I feel a little uneasy about bringing my warrior wife into a room full of her enemies."

She leaned against his chest and said in her most innocent voice, "But I am the picture of the gentile wife. What could possibly go wrong?"

Chapter Nineteen

Hours later, Arabella was awakened to the sounds of Celeste bustling about in her room. She must have fallen back asleep. Lately, it seemed she could sleep forever.

It is all the lovemaking, she thought with a grin. She sat up and, stretching, yawned loudly. It would be another glorious day. She was in love. She pictured her Theo with his half smile, his blond hair swept back from his forehead, and hugged herself with pleasure.

She was shook from her reverie by the image of Celeste at the end of her bed. One hand was on her hip. The other held the basin, a towel still discretely draped across it.

"What is this?"

Arabella flushed. "I was sick this morning."

Celeste looked at her and paled.

Arabella quickly added, "But I am fine now. Really, I am. I was sick and then everything was back to normal. I am quite fit."

Celeste could be a terror when Arabella showed the slightest signs of illness.

Celeste slowly set the basin on her dressing table and sat down dejectedly on the edge of her bed. "Aye, yi yi. There is always such a price to pay for a little fun. Yes? I had hoped you would have more time. But no. Mon Dieu. It must have been immediate."

She shook her head sadly.

Arabella rose from her bed and pulled on her dressing gown. "Celeste, whatever is the matter? Look." She spread her arms wide and smiled. "I feel wonderful!"

"No, no, my *cherie*. You have not bled." She got up and put her hand on Arabella's belly, giving it a little shake. "You have a babe here, my girl. I hoped you were just late. A little more time to play for you. But no. So soon. *C'est dommage.*"

Arabella's mouth dropped. She whirled and stood in front of the mirror, holding the lapels of her dressing gown wide, and stared at herself. She looked the same. Her breasts had ached lately, and she put her hands on them. They felt sore. But her belly was flat as usual.

"It cannot be. I look the same, Celeste." A strange panic flooded her body. "But I am not ready to be a mother. I had not thought...It cannot be true."

She turned to Celeste, hoping somehow, she could tell her it was all a terrible mistake.

She did not. Instead, she patted her on the shoulder. "It is early days, my sweet. Do not worry over much. It is what happens when you are young and healthy, yes?"

Arabella hung her head to hide the tears that had formed in her eyes.

Celeste put a hand under her chin. She lifted Arabella's head and brushed away her tears. "Smile, *cherie*. There is nothing to do about it now. You will be a fine young mother."

Arabella managed a wobbly smile, before she burst into tears. She held on to Celeste and sobbed until she felt drained and numb. She spent the rest of the afternoon in her bedroom, feeling desolate and depressed. Celeste brought her meals and urged her to eat. She nibbled a bit but found she had little appetite. When Celeste cheerfully reminded her, she must now eat for two, she glared at her.

It was late when she finally put on some day clothes and went downstairs. She was thankful to discover Theo was still away, beginning his investigations. He was to blame for all this after all. She wanted no part of him.

She paced the town house. It was an elaborate mausoleum, with its lofty ceilings and hard tile floors. Theo's home was formal and starkly bare of anything to warm it into a comfortable atmosphere, unlike her beloved Harwood. Arabella pulled the drapes aside in the sitting room to view the garden. She looked at it and loathed its carefully manicured lawn and precise beds of flowers. It was caged by a thick hedge, beyond which the walls of a neighboring town house rose up blocking the view. There were no wilds of Yorkshire here.

She stood at the window and envisioned the sea near her home. She heard the roar of the surf and felt the icy cold spray of water on her face. She envisioned herself upon the rail and saw the vast expanse of sea before her. She gripped the folds of her dress. She wanted the freedom of her trousers. She wanted to go back to the time before Theo. She wanted the Bella. But it was all gone. This new life inside her proved her to be a woman and a wife. She tried to reason that she had made this decision before she realized her body had betrayed her, but it was no use. She felt emotional and brittle. And angry.

The garden had darkened into twilight when she heard Theo behind her.

"There you are." Theo stood in the doorway and looked at her curiously. "You're not dressed for the party."

He pulled out his watch from his pocket and glanced at it. "You will have to hurry, my dear."

She shrugged. "I will." She walked to the door where he stood and paused in front of him. "I need to go home, Theo. I want to go home tomorrow."

He put his hands on her shoulders and looked into her eyes. She held herself rigid and stared blankly at him.

"Tomorrow, Theo," she repeated.

He nodded. He kept his eyes on her hers and answered slowly, "If it is what you want." Then he squeezed her shoulders and, smiling at her with exaggerated cheerfulness, said, "I searched the land titles office. It seems we will have to go to Scarborough in the north to find the titles. But tonight, we might make some headway."

He tilted his head in his endearing way and looked at her.

She was not moved by his attempts to charm her. "Later, Theo." She sighed. "Now, I must get dressed."

He leaned in to kiss her lips, but she turned away. He kissed her pale cheek instead.

Chapter Twenty

The ball was a crush. As Theo had predicted, the room was littered with officers. The brilliant kaleidoscope of glimmering gowns was accented by the blue uniforms of the navy. Each time Theo looked at Arabella to gage her reaction, she seemed distracted. He was convinced the presence of so many of the King's men must have intimidated her—she stood stoically by his side for most of the evening. The only time she was the least bit animated was when Kate joined them. And even then, she was quiet and pensive.

Theo scanned the crowd watching as the admiral headed for the card room. The time might be right to have a conversation with him.

He turned to Ambrose. "Could you look out for Arabella? I think I will check out the card room."

Ambrose followed his gaze. "Be careful, Theo. The admiral is not the jolly country gentleman he so well portrays. He is wily. He will measure every word you say. He may even store it for future use. And lord only knows what he will do if he catches word of your wife's escapades."

"I know. I will take care." Theo was aware he must take every precaution around the admiral.

Today, while searching titles, he had thought about the possibility of informing the admiral of the wayward revenue captain. He had quickly dismissed the idea. There would be too many questions about how he had come by this inside information. The admiral would be suspicious. It would not take the man long to look at Theo's connections in Yorkshire. And that could only be his wife and her family. It would be another danger for her.

And then, even if the admiral believed him, there was little even he could do without hard evidence.

"Theo, what is it you are up to?" Ambrose asked with a frown.

"I need a word with Admiral Hews. It's...there is something I hope to find out."

Ambrose sighed and said, "Fine. I will take Arabella for a turn around the dance floor but for the love of god, man, take care." Theo nodded and hurried after the admiral.

Standing in the doorway, Theo surveyed the card room. Seated around several tables were clusters of guests, mostly male but also a smattering of females, who had gathered to play whist. Gambling at house parties had become the fashion; fortunes were won and lost in these sedate settings.

A bar stood at the side of the room, where footmen loaded trays of champagne to be carried to the party. Another servant filled drinks of brandy or gin for the players in the room.

He found the admiral on a stool at the bar enjoying a reprieve from the noise of the ballroom. He was in luck. He would get a word alone with him after all.

"Admiral Hews," Theo said as he approached, "an excellent party, sir."

He reached out and shook his hand.

"Ah, Theo. Yes, it has gone rather well." The admiral beamed at him. "Sit down, sit down and tell me your news. I hear you are recently married."

He wagged his bushy eyebrows at him. "I saw her across the room. Lovely girl. I knew her father, you know."

Theo smiled at him. He did indeed look like the country gentleman Ambrose had described him as. Tonight, he wore tuxedo jacket and trousers. But he looked uncomfortable as though the suit was a little too snug and a little too formal for him. His wide sideburns, bushy eyebrows, and generous pot belly gave him a jocular appearance. He looked like a much-loved grandfather.

Theo was not fooled.

"Yes. I am pleased with her. I did hear that her father had been a military man," Theo answered politely.

"Yes, well, sad story that one. The last I heard, the corporal's daughter was tucked away along the Yorkshire coast somewhere. How ever did you find her?"

"My grandmother set up the match. She has long known the family."

He nodded. "The Lady Osbourne, of course. Well, it is good to see you have brought the young woman to town. Show her off a little." He chuckled.

Theo was struck by the amount of knowledge this man carried. He guessed there was no one who tracked the activities in society more than him. But then, it all made sense; he was head of the Home Office.

"I spent the first few weeks of my marriage out on the coast at my wife's estate. We go back tomorrow. Beautiful country. I had a chance to take a few sails off the coast there."

"Did you? I now leave sailing to the young. Having

spent too many years on the ocean, I find that I enjoy my feet firmly on the ground these days."

Theo laughed. "Hard to believe. Oh, and I met an employee of yours. A Captain Berg."

Theo tried to appear nonchalant.

"Did you?" The admiral's face remained kindly, but Theo noticed a sharp gleam in his eyes. Tread carefully, he silently reminded himself.

Theo chuckled. "He boarded us and searched our boat. I think he was sad to discover we were just a pair of newly-weds on a cruise."

"It is good to know someone is out there doing their job. I hope you were not too disturbed?"

"Oh no. It was interesting. We had a little conversation, and all was well. He told me he was new to the area, and just getting to know that part of the coast."

"Yes. Well, we shuffled him down from North of Scarborough. He had been posted up at Saltburn. Thankfully, it was quiet there."

It was time to change the subject. He had gotten Berg's former posting and that was enough. He would not get more. If he tried, he would raise the Admiral's suspicion. Theo sighed. "Well, from what I can see, it is quiet close to Harwood too. Not much in the way of entertainment there sadly."

The admiral laughed. "You have a beautiful new wife. It should be enough to keep you entertained for a while at least."

Theo grinned. "You are right. She has me entertained indeed. And I better get back to her. It has been a pleasure to talk to you, sir."

Theo walked back into the main room, weaving his way through the crowds towards Arabella. Catching a glimpse of her, he was relieved to see her laugh at something Kate said to her.

It had been a disturbing evening. Arabella was strangely distant and withdrawn. When he left this morning, all had been well. They had fought hard last night but from his point of view everything had gone well. She had agreed to withdraw from smuggling with a grace which surprised him. She had been loving and playful. He could not understand what had happened to bring about this change in her.

She was so distant and cold. Had it been any other woman but her, he would have suspected she played with his emotions. But this was Arabella. She was above all spontaneous and exuberant. She could not mask her feelings. This dreadful blankness was impossible to endure. Whatever had happened, he had to find its cause.

And he had to take her home. She was homesick. He was surprised she had survived in town as long as she had.

"Ah, Theo, back at last." Ambrose clapped him on the shoulder. "You must help me entertain these lovely ladies."

"Theo, Arabella tells me you leave for home tomorrow. I had hoped we could spend more time together." Kate looked at him and smiled.

He liked Kate. She was perfect for his friend Ambrose. These past weeks, she had helped him entertain Arabella for which he would be forever grateful. Once they had settled in his country home, he would invite them for a visit.

Though Arabella's face was pale, she was stunning tonight. She wore a shimmering gown of pale pink with embroidered sequins which caught the light. Her black hair was piled upon her head in an elaborate coiffure with stylish curls adorning her face.

He smiled at her. "Yes, my lovely wife has had enough of town life."

"I think we will be leaving town soon as well. I purchased a horse here in town and I am eager to see her safely home," said Ambrose.

The orchestra began to play a Viennese waltz.

"Ah, my Katherine," Ambrose said as he took his wife's arm. "We must dance this waltz."

Theo was left facing Arabella. He was about to ask her to dance as well when he saw Dierdra bearing down on them.

"Oh god," he groaned. Before he could make his escape, Dierdra had grabbed his arm and was pulling him against her.

"My Theo. What a surprise. I heard you had married a Spaniard and disappeared into the wilds of Yorkshire. But here you are." She gave him a syrupy smile. "Tired of her already, darling?"

She gave Arabella a smug glance before leaning intimately into him and brushing her bountiful breasts against him. Her dress was cut so low, the dark rim of her nipples peeked out from her tightly laced bodice when she moved.

Theo tried to pull himself free of her grip, but she held firmly to his jacket.

"Dierdra, I would like you to meet my wife, Arabella, Countess Pembroke," he said, looking at Arabella as he struggled to free himself. His use of Arabella's new title seemed to inspire Dierdra to hang on to him with even greater determination.

Arabella's eyes blackened with a dangerous glint. Spots of color appeared on her cheeks. Theo attempted to shift his body between the women, cursing Dierdra silently.

Dierdra tittered. "Oh, I so apologize, my dear. I had no idea."

It was clear to Theo that the opposite was true. Dierdra

had every intention of insulting Arabella. She nudged Theo aside, while looking at Arabella with disdain. She was here to take jealous revenge on the woman who had usurped her position, taking easily what she had for so long strived for.

"But you mustn't be allowed to keep my Theo all to yourself." she said, reaching up to lay her hand on Theo's cheek.

He slapped her hand away. Dierdra gave a brittle laugh but was not deterred. Her hand wandered to his chest, and she splayed her fingers wide in a blatant display of familiarity and possessiveness.

Arabella took a step forward using her superior height to force Dierdra to look up to meet her gaze.

"Enough," she commanded. It was her captain's voice, but ominous in its dangerous intensity. Her eyes had turned a deadly black.

Dierdra's eyes widened in surprise and fear. Arabella leaned closer. Dierdra was forced to sway back from Arabella's intimidating stance.

"If you put your hands on my man again, I will break each of your fat little fingers." Arabella punctuated each word with lethal intent. Her lips curled into a snarl. She leaned even further into Dierdra's face, forcing the woman to arch back uncomfortably, and growled, "And I will do it slowly, enjoying the snap and crackle of each one."

Dierdra stumbled backwards, only just keeping herself from falling. She hustled away, turning only once to give Arabella a look of terror before disappearing into the crowd.

Theo took a moment to recover. Arabella's dark intensity had even frightened him. He had glimpsed the renegade she could be. His mouth was open, and he snapped it shut. His Arabella was indeed the panther he had thought last night.

My god, she even growled, he thought with amazement.

Well, so much for his worries about her being eaten alive by the town's ladies.

Her face was still flushed with anger, and he was relieved to see her more herself. Somehow, that he would be relieved to see her in such a state, and consider it, 'more herself' struck him as humorous.

He laughed loudly and took her arm. "Come, my lovely countess. I think it is time we left. Clearly the evening has become a dead bore."

Tomorrow, he would take her home to Harwood Place. Tonight, he longed to hold her against him in their bed, and somehow discover what had made her so pale and distant.

Chapter Twenty-One

For the first time since his marriage, Theo slept alone in his own room. Arabella had asked for privacy. He had only nodded and kissed her lightly on her cheek. But lying alone in his wide bed left him desolate and depressed. It was impossible to sleep without her slender body beside him.

Still sleepless after what seemed like hours, he decided that sleeping apart was not what he wanted in this marriage. Though it was the standard here in town, he was not going to tolerate it. He was determined to set down some ground rules. If she was angry with him, then so be it. The bed was wide enough for her to ignore him.

He thought of Ambrose's words at the club. If marriage was a war, then he was determined to win at least a few battles. When he finally slept, he did not wake up until late in the morning.

It was a loud crash which had startled him awake. Jumping up, and pulling on his robe, he rushed to Arabella's room. When he swung the door open, he saw only her empty rumpled bed. A decanter lay broken on the floor, with water spreading in a dark pool on the carpet around it. And then he heard it. She was vomiting again.

He stepped into her dressing room and held her as he had yesterday morning. As she heaved and choked, he tightened his grip on her belly to steady her. When she finally stilled, she began to sob, great loud gulps that wrenched at his heart. He twisted her around and held her against him.

"It is not going away," she cried.

He felt helpless. He simply rubbed her back and let her cry. Gradually, her sobbing waned until there were only a few discordant hiccups.

"I need to clean up. Please, Theo."

He took that as his cue to give her some privacy and quietly left the room.

Sitting on the edge of her bed, he waited impatiently for her to return. Something was very wrong. This was the second time she had spent her morning over the basin desperately ill. He had no idea what it could be. He had thought her first illness had been the result of nerves, a reaction to having to face his knowledge of her escapades as a smuggler.

Celeste came into the room carrying a breakfast tray. She set it on the end table.

"I brought for two." She smiled, pleased with herself. "Where is my girl?"

"She has been sick again, Celeste." He could not keep his worry from his voice.

She looked at Theo's anxious face and laughed with delight. It seemed to please her to see him so concerned.

"Ah, that is good. She will be hungry now."

Theo looked at her with an expression of horror.

She laughed again and patted him on the back. "Oh, you are a good man. Too good, I think." She looked meaningfully at his lap and cackled. "It will all be better soon. A month or two of this and that is all. Then it is all just here. Yes?"

She rubbed her belly and laughed again before bustling out of the room.

"Oh, my word, she's pregnant," Theo thought aloud.

He was not sure how to feel. It certainly explained the last twenty-four hours. He wanted to be happy. It was why he had married. His heir might be on the way. But Arabella's misery dampened his enthusiasm.

He thought about his little smuggler of a wife. There had been too many changes for her. First, marriage, then she had been forced to give up her life at sea, and now this. He wished he had never brought her to town. She was homesick; that was another problem. Today he would take her home.

Uncertain what to do, he walked back to his room and grabbed his appeasement gift. He thought perhaps he could make her smile. He sat on the chair at her mirror and waited. His thoughts turned to this new child growing in her body. It was already making its appearance felt. Joy surged through him at the image of his future family.

He only hoped his beautiful Arabella would feel better soon.

When Arabella came into the room, he opened his arms wide. To his surprise she brushed by him and sat on the edge of the bed.

Looking into her pale and forlorn face, he said, "Today we start for home. You will be back on that rocky ground in two days." He said trying to cheer her. "It is really just one more sleep away from Harwood."

She smiled at him. It was not her usual impish grin, but it was a start.

"Come on." He nudged her knees and smiled, "We have breakfast. Let's see what Celeste has brought us."

To his surprise, she ate heartily. When she was sipping her tea, he handed her the boxed bracelet.

"It is a gift. I bought it for you to thank you for coming to town with me."

She held the box in her hands and rubbed the embossed lettering in its lid with her thumbs. "Theo, I have been angry with you."

She looked down then slowly raised her head to look at him. A glint of anger flashed in her eyes.

"And it is your fault." She set his gift unopened on the side table. "I don't think I can accept a gift from you right now. I am feeling too unhappy and bitter to enjoy it."

She looked at him with wide eyes, the eyes he so loved. His stomach flipped.

"I don't even know what I need from you." She sobbed and covered her face with her hands.

Pulling her into his arms, he held her while she cried. It was all very confusing—he had always assumed his wife would be thrilled with the news of a pregnancy. This was not what he had envisioned at all. He had no idea what he could do to help her.

Chapter Twenty-Two

Theo's family coach had been prepared for their trip home. Arabella settled herself on the seat, then sniffed the air. Some over-zealous servant had scrubbed the interior with a disinfectant laced with lye. A wave of nausea overwhelmed her. To make matters the coach swayed as it began to move along the lane. Her stomach began to protest. Fighting the urge to vomit she tried unsuccessfully to swallow, attempting to forestall the inevitable. It was not working. Pulling back the coach window, she thrust out her head and gulped the fresh air.

"Stop the coach. I need out," she gasped.

Theo rapped on the sliding door to the coachman. The coach lurched to a halt. Before it even came to a stop, Arabella scrambled out. She began to retch. Celeste held back her hair as she emptied her stomach.

When Arabella was finished, her stomach sore and empty, Celeste handed her a cloth. She wiped her face, looking around her for the first time. Theo stood helplessly by the step of the coach. On the street, a cluster of people paused to watch the display. She felt her cheeks redden. Angry tears filled her eyes. She brushed past Theo and attempted to climb back into the carriage to hide from all the prying eyes.

As soon as she entered the coach and took a breath, she reared back, stepping back into the street. Theo reached to assist her.

She slapped his hands away. "I am not getting back into that coach."

"You have to. Here, let me be of help." He tried to lift her into the carriage, but she squirmed away and punched him hard on the shoulder. Theo could only gape at her.

"But you have to, Arabella. We are going home." He glanced at Celeste, but she only shrugged. There was nothing she could do to help.

"I cannot ride in that stinking thing, and I won't!" Arabella backed away from the carriage and stood with her hands on her hips.

He stared at her; she stood resolute.

Finally, he walked to the baggage wagon. Her new mare and his horse were attached with leading ropes. He looked at the driver. "Get down here, young man, and help me saddle the horses."

Without a word, he led the horse to her and helped her mount. She rode as she did at home, astride, tucking her skirts in around her, not caring at this point that she was a countess, in a gown not a riding habit, or that her behavior would be considered scandalous.

She glanced at Theo after he too had mounted.

"Better?" he asked.

"Much better," she replied.

Not another word was spoken until they had ridden for several hours.

"You are looking pale again, Arabella," he said, concerned.

"My back is aching, Theo."

Theo halted the wagons. "This time you will listen to me, Arabella. I want you off your horse and up on the seat with the coachman."

"I will be all right, Theo. I will."

He narrowed his eyes. "Off," was all he said, lifting his arms to assist her.

She slid off her horse and allowed him to help her up onto the driver's seat. She was feeling miserable. Her back ached.

She scowled at him. "You are a very stubborn man, Theo. I had not noticed it before. It's a character flaw."

He snorted at her. "Someone here is stubborn, and I don't think it's me."

It was her turn to snort.

He rode beside the carriage, attempting to converse with her, but she answered him only in monosyllables until he gave up. She was feeling miserable, and no amount of playful bantering could relieve her.

When they reached the inn, she was stiff and sore. She wanted to go to bed, but Celeste demanded she eat. She helped her with her clothes.

"Celeste, my back is aching so. I just need to sleep."

"This is not good, *cherie*. I will talk to your *monsieur*."

Arabella was quick to object. "Please don't mention my problem, Celeste. I don't want him to know just yet."

Two spots of color appeared on Celeste's cheeks. She abruptly turned to the door and mumbled, "I will only tell him you must rest."

After Celeste left, Arabella fell into a deep sleep.

The only reprieve from misery had been that Theo held

her through the night, then helped her survive the morning ritual of vomiting which she had begun to dread. Her back still ached. Theo decided that they would spend another day at the inn, where she could rest, and he could search for a second coach to hire, so she could travel comfortably.

She thought it odd Theo had not commented on her illness, but she was thankful. She found she could not talk about a child inside her that she still fought to acknowledge herself. This pregnancy made her future clear. It solidified the decision to lose captain Ara forever. She would now be the Countess of Pembroke. All her work and achievements on the sea would soon be a distant memory. It was too much.

She resented Theo. If he had not been so deliciously attractive, none of this would have happened. On some level, she knew she was being unreasonable. But for now, she held on to her anger.

She spent the day resting. Celeste had somewhere found a tattered penny dreadful for her to read. She had laughed at the gruesome tale of a villainous smuggler and his murderous exploits. Only coming down for supper, she slept soundly again, with Theo's arm wrapped protectively around her. She was relieved too when he had made no demands on her. Again, when he came to bed, he only held her. He slid his hand down to her belly and kept it there. Arabella lay on her side with her back against Theo's warm body and slept.

Morning found her seated in the hired coach with Theo. Celeste had chosen to ride in the more comfortable family coach, quite happy to be feeling pampered.

Theo smiled at Arabella. "I have been thinking about your thieves. I thought we could discuss our plan of action before arriving home." He leaned back against the seat.

"I've not had the opportunity to tell you about my success with the Admiral."

He raised his chin, obviously proud of his achievements. "I have our surly captain's last posting. He had been working out of Saltburn. I thought I might stop there while I'm in the north checking the land titles. Find out what I can."

For the first time in days, her eyes sparkled with enthusiasm. "That is wonderful, Theo. Yesterday afternoon I gave it some thought too. I know you want to go up north to find those land titles, but I also had the idea we might invite the Bergs for supper."

Theo looked at her with surprise. "That surly captain? I think not."

"No, Theo. The Vicar and his wife. Only think of it. If you are going up north anyway, think of what we might discover if you knew their former village and could do a little snooping. If they are involved, the evidence is sure to be there." She raised her brows. "Why else would they have moved? Perhaps they were found out."

"There are any number of reasons why they might take a new posting, Arabella. Their motivation may not involve smuggling at all."

"But it could," she insisted. "Besides, I need to know. If they are not involved, their lives might be in danger anyway. It is only a matter of time before the boys get impatient with attempting to find the accomplice and take them out."

"Take them out? You do not think they would kill them, do you? Not a Vicar, surely?" Theo asked.

"Of course, they'll kill them. And worse if they become frustrated enough. The Yorkshire men are not squeamish when it comes to retribution. It has only been a few years since the incident at Robin Hood's Bay where they captured and slaughtered the revenue boys in the most gruesome of ways." She looked at him earnestly. "There is no law to protect them. They have their own justice."

"My god." He leaned back and considered for a moment. "Then yes, I think we might want to try to find out what we can about the Vicar and his wife. If they are innocent, they will need to be warned and your brutes will have to be called off."

"They are not brutes, Theo. And they are not mine."

Theo sighed. "My worry, Arabella, is you are not a spy. You have a great deal of difficulty not expressing every emotion that comes to mind. Only think of the scene you made at the Admiral's ball."

Arabella glared at him. "It might be best if you did not mention that topic, Theo. Your little lady friend—oh, my mistake, your chubby lady friend—was lucky to have survived. I still regret I did not have my cutlas so I could slit her nose."

She used her hand as a mock cutlas and gestured as if she were doing that very thing.

Theo laughed. "You have just proved my point. How can I expect you to be secretive and surreptitious when you cannot control yourself?"

"Theo, the incident at the ball was different," she protested. "The woman was challenging me, and you know it. The Vicar and his wife will have no idea what is going on. The local gentry are expected to invite them to supper. And it would only be natural to ask about their last posting."

"Hmmm. I will think about it."

"I am going to invite them as soon as I get home." She looked at him and crossed her arms. "I will have them there for tomorrow night. You may argue with me about whether or not I interrogate them, but you will not argue with me about whether, as a young wife, I am allowed to invite the Vicar and his wife to be our first dinner guests."

"Arabella, this has nothing to do with your budding talents as a hostess and you know it."

"Hmm. You cannot know that." She smiled at him mischievously and was pleased to hear his loud laughter.

She looked at him curiously. He was a strange man. Nothing seemed to make him happier than a rousing argument with her.

He finally said, "I will agree only if you let me do any questioning. I would think I would have more luck with the Vicar than you might have with his silent wife."

She agreed, but secretly she knew if the opportunity to get a little information about their last parish was there, she would take it. If their former post were Saltburn, or anywhere near it, she would have the connection she needed. The Vicar and the captain shared a last name. Both were new to the area. It was too much of a coincidence.

Their discussion had distracted her from her former misery. They continued the journey in comfortable conversation. Theo described to her his home out of London. She was interested to know he had a place on the sea. For the first time, she contemplated what life might be like there for her.

He even had a sailboat, though he admitted it was no match for the Bella. At the mention of his paltry boat a flood of despair washed over her. This child inside her made it painfully obvious that her life as she knew it was over. She looked at Theo again, her heart filled with resentment.

He seemed to note her change in mood when he described his small sailboat and quickly returned to views of the sea from the estate, but it was too late. Arabella was filled with a sense of loss.

Arabella admitted grimly to herself that she did not want to think about leaving her beloved Yorkshire. And if she squashed any thought of her pregnancy, she was less angry with Theo. Yet she continued to feel the festering core of resentment inside her. It burned. Only planning an investigation into the renegade revenue captain helped to temporarily relieve the bitterness.

The day passed quickly. In no time at all, they were climbing the steep hill to Harwood Place. She smiled to see its gray stone walls in the distance and the overgrown trees and hedges which lined the drive.

Harwood was a large manor house. It was two stories with wings stretching out at least fifty feet from each side of the entry. The building itself was in the popular Queen Anne style, symmetrical and welcoming with its tall windows adorning the façade. From a distance, the exterior was still elaborate, giving no hint of the impoverished struggle within to maintain at least the illusion of wealth and prestige. Arabella and Aran had long since closed off one side of the house. It was both unnecessary and too expensive for them to maintain.

Near the house, it was clear the front gardens had been neglected. Weeds and wild shrubs had sprouted along the foundation. Arabella only cared she was home. She hurried up the steps to be welcomed by Grimes, their elderly butler, and gloried in her return.

They ate early. Arabella had sent her invitation to the Vicar and received a positive reply before at last retiring to her bedroom. She was tired again. She had just washed up when Theo came in, comfortably dressed in his robe, and began peeling it off to climb into bed.

"What are you doing?" she asked, watching him pull back the sheets.

"Going to bed," he replied without the slightest sense he might be invading her private domain. To her astonishment, he crawled completely naked into her bed.

"Not here, Theo. You cannot sleep here. You know I need my privacy."

"No."

"That is it? No?" She stood and waited for some explanation. She grabbed her robe thinking she would simply move to his room. He leapt up stark naked and snatched her arm.

He raised his voice. "Do not even think about it. If you move to my room, I will simply follow. If you find another room, I will be there too. If you sleep on the floor then dammit, I will be beside you."

Arabella closed her eyes to block out his presence. She had no energy to fight tonight.

"Theo, you can't." She sighed and opened her eyes. "In the morning I will be sick. What if I am sick during the night? Do you really want that? I cannot have you holding my retching stomach eternally. You cannot appreciate it."

"I do." He raised his voice again. "You married me, Arabella, and this is the bloody price. I will have it no other way. If I wish to be here to watch you puke your guts out every god damn morning, then that is what I shall do."

He leaned forward and spoke more quietly, directly into her face. "Indeed, there is nothing I like more than hearing you retch. And I will hold your bloody stomach for a lifetime if I bloody well want to." With his hands on his naked hips he glared, daring her to disagree.

Suddenly the whole scene seemed humorous to Arabella. She looked at him and laughed. His words and indeed the whole situation was ridiculous. Seeing his disgruntled face only made her laugh harder.

"Fine," she sputtered, "but I swear I will come to you without cleaning my mouth and with vomit smeared in my hair."

"Perfect. I will look forward to it." His demeaner changed completely with his victory. He reached over and patted her bottom with a pleased smile. "I knew you would see it my way," he said, looking completely proud of himself and beaming as though he had won a major race at sea.

She felt her heart swell. For the first time in days, she wanted his touch.

He returned to bed. She pulled her nightgown off over her head and joined him. The first thing he did was turn her away from him and attempt to hold her from behind as he had for days. She had to twist herself back to face him. Even then, he tried to pull her in for a hug rather than make love to her.

She pressed her body against him. She could feel him swollen against her belly. She squirmed and rubbed against him, all actions she knew he loved, but he held her, trying to still her with his hands by holding her hips in place. He seemed to fight her. Something was bothering him. It was apparent he was determined to only hold her.

She leaned back to look at his face. He was clearly struggling. With a slow sexy smile, she moved slowly up and down against him and watched him catch his breath. Theo watched her. He seemed confused and even slightly panicked.

She rolled on top of him. His chest was hard. She took his nipples and worked them the way he had done to her so many times. She nibbled them, blew on them, and smiled when they hardened and swelled.

She used her tongue and hands to love his smooth chest, working her way to the downy hair which ran from his belly button to his groin. He groaned and gripped her shoulders. She felt him hot and throbbing between her breasts and grinned at him.

Slowly, with her eyes on him, she felt his silky organ. She held him in her hand and stroked him up and down. She slid down further and put its tip into her mouth. She held her lips around it sucking, licking, then taking him fully in her mouth and moving slowly up and down the length of him. One hand still held him at his base and the other gripped the hair of his lower belly, gently pumping him to the rhythm he had taught her.

All the while she watched him. He moaned and gripped her shoulders, holding her firmly in place. He gasped and muttered her name. When he writhed and called out with a sound which was almost agonizing, she took her mouth from him and looked at him with wonder. She held him at his base and relished the surge of power she felt.

A sheen of clear jelly had pooled at the tip of his organ. She leaned close to him, willing him to watch while she used only her tongue to taste him. He was salty and tangy. She smiled again, feeling her power as she used her lips with exaggerated motions to suck the sticky wetness from him. He groaned again, a long, tortured sound.

She rose up, bracing herself above him, to take him inside her. He had shown her how to ride him and she was ready to have him.

He sat up quickly and tried to stop her.

"No, Arabella." His voice was hoarse as though the words pained him. "I'll not hurt you. "

She only smiled at him and placed him inside her. She rode him with her feet at his hips, pumping him hard. She felt him jerk inside her. Only then did she let herself find her pleasure. She leaned back, feeling each burst and shiver from him. And then, like he had done so many times, she collapsed on top of him. She slowly straightened her legs laying her head upon his chest, listening to his breathing slow.

He rolled her to her side. Holding her beneath her chin, he looked into her eyes. "Arabella, have I hurt you?"

His voice was quiet, but his eyes pierced hers.

He knew. She smiled at him but this time it was wobbly and nervous. "Theo, I do not think you can hurt me in this way. At least not yet."

For a terrible moment, she felt her eyes fill with tears and she buried her head into his neck. She had been able for a few minutes to forget her pregnancy. Now it all came rushing back to her.

She took his hand and placed it on her flat belly. She wanted to talk to him about it but could not. She did not have the words. So instead, she pressed his hand into her tummy hard. With his other arm, he pulled her close and held her.

"I would have you happier about this, my love," he whispered into her ear.

She whispered back, "I am not ready, Theo. Not yet."

Arabella lay awake listening to the sounds of Theo breathing deeply as he slept beside her. She squeezed her eyes shut to attempt to block all thoughts of her pregnancy, forcing her mind to contemplate instead the supper tomorrow with the Vicar and his wife. She was determined to get the proof she needed that the Vicar was conspiring with the revenue men. Tomorrow would be the first step in bringing down the arrogant Captain Berg.

Chapter Twenty-Three

Arabella took great care to be sure all was ready to host her guests. She wanted them to feel relaxed and comfortable. Maybe then they would share a little too much information. She had searched the cellars for the best wines and brandy, planning to serve them at every opportunity. She had even had the cook prepare a dessert laced with liqueur.

She dressed carefully, foregoing anything Theo had purchased for her in town and going with a high-necked day dress. Standing in front of her mirror, Arabella was satisfied with her conservative appearance. Her hair was split in the middle and pulled back into a plain bun. The dress was a shade of mauve which washed out her skin tones. Her only jewelry was a lovely brooch her grandmother had given her. After all, she must look as though she was trying to impress.

"*Mon Dieu*," Celeste complained, "you look like a baker's wife."

"Good," Arabella said with a laugh. "I want to play a young wife nervous to entertain for the first time."

And that is exactly what I am, she thought with a grin.

When all was ready, she paced between the receiving room and the dining area. Theo had the servants convert a small sitting room into a makeshift dining area, insisting the formal dining area was too dark and forbidding. He had the fires lit in both rooms. Like her, he wanted a homey atmosphere.

She was thankful she had the help of her new housekeeper and downstairs maid. The old furniture had been polished to a glowing sheen; the carpets cleaned. She had laid the table with roses from the patio.

She was impressed with the effect. It was comfortable, with just a hint of the prestige they might expect to find when dining with an earl.

At the last minute, she had gone to the kitchens and asked the cook to make up a fruit punch which disguised a healthy dose of added gin.

"Not too much gin," she cautioned, "If she is not a drinker, we do not want her dizzy with it."

Supper was an awkward affair. The only redeeming quality was the food, which the Vicar enjoyed with enthusiasm. He was a heavy man. His wool jacket hung open, revealing a vest whose buttons strained to hold back an expansive belly. His pale face was square and stoic. When he did speak, he did so in biblical quotes, which he delivered with staunch righteousness and much shaking of jowls.

Theo tried to engage him but was having some difficulty. He finally chose the topic of their recent marriage.

"I believe we are rubbing along rather well." He smiled at Arabella. "We have had only a few disputes thus far."

The Vicar nodded sagely. "Edith and I often refer to the words of the Lord in this matter."

He cleared his throat, raised his chin, and said sagely, "'With all humility and gentleness, with patience bearing with one another in love, eager to maintain the unity of the spirit in the bond of peace.'" He looked from Theo to Arabella as though expecting a rebuttal before adding, "Ephesians."

Satisfied, he returned to devouring his meal.

"Yes. Well, we certainly have made a few peace bonds." Theo watched the man eat as though debating his next mode of attack.

Arabella smiled sympathetically at Theo from across the table. She too was struggling. At least Theo had been able to get the man to look up. She could not seem to get the Vicar's wife to do even that. Edith Berg sat huddled over her food. Her thin fingers clutched her cutlery as if she expected someone might rip it away from her at any time. Like her husband, she ate as though she had not been fed in a long while.

She looked hopefully at Edith's empty glass. When she had offered wine, the Vicar had declared that his wife did not touch alcohol of any kind and Arabella had happily offered the punch.

"Arnold, bring more punch for Mrs. Berg, please." asked Arabella.

The Vicar's wife raised her head and nodded slightly, muttering a quiet thank you.

Theo tried again. "We have been engaged in bringing back the land here. Even now, our overseer is off buying livestock. Being new here I have made some plans for the future."

The Vicar looked at Theo, chewing a mouthful of pheasant and swallowing before saying, "'For I know the plans I have for you,' declares the Lord, 'plans to prosper you and not to harm you, plans to give you hope and a future.'"

Theo ignored his response. "And what of you and your wife? I am sure you must have plans for your flock down in the village?"

The Vicar raised his bulky head about to give his solemn reply.

Arnold interrupted, as he refilled Edith's glass, "Should I bring in the dessert now, ma'am? Cook says it's all ready."

"Yes, Arnold, that would be lovely."

Dessert was eaten quietly. Theo had given up all attempts to make conversation. Arabella smiled with satisfaction as she watched the Vicar's wife help herself to a second heaping dessert. For a small woman, she had a voracious appetite. Arabella was pleased with the brandied chocolate fudge she had chosen. It was extremely sweet. She could not have been more delighted to see the woman empty her punch glass as she ate.

She motioned for Arnold to refill it. There was hope for the evening yet.

When she announced, "I believe it is time for the men to withdraw for their cigars," Theo shot her such a pained expression, she had to bite her lip to restrain a giggle.

Once settled in the receiving room with the Vicar's wife, she said, "I think we will stick with the punch."

Normally, a hostess would have served a sweet madeira or coffee.

To her surprise, Edith had lifted her head and replied, "Yes. It's very good," with a smile which seemed to crumple up her small face.

"So, tell me, Edith, how do you like it here in our small village? I know it can be rather quiet most days." She noticed Edith's glass was empty again and motioned to Arnold once more before Edith raised her head.

Edith held out her glass for Arnold to fill it. When he

tried to withdraw, she said, "Wait, wait," took a deep swig of her drink, and held it out once more for Arnold to top it off. She settled back against the chesterfield. Arabella noticed her feet did not quite reach the floor.

"It is the same as most places. This time I have a garden and a view." Her voice was sweet, like a child's, and Arabella smiled at the sound of it.

"Have you lived in many places then?"

The gin had done its job. Maybe too well. Edith leaned back, looking relaxed.

"Oh, I have, I have. Henry takes me where he will," she said in her high-pitched voice, gesturing wildly with the hand holding her punch.

Arabella winced, thinking she might spill it, but she held tight to it and managed another swig before she continued.

"It is much the same here as our last place in Saltburn." She sighed. "And before that, Bulbous."

She tried to set her glass down on the side table but missed. The glass fell and shattered.

She leaned forward crying, "Oh goodness, oh goodness," then attempted to rise from the sofa to clean it.

"No, my dear, it is quite all right," Arabella said. "Arnold will get it."

Arnold hurried forward and brushed the shards of glass into a little pail.

"Arnold, I think you better bring us a coffee after all," she said, feeling her heart beating in her chest. With no effort at all, the Vicar's wife had given her what she needed. Now her problem was going to be the challenge of sobering her up before the Vicar returned. She did not think he would take kindly to his wife in this condition.

The coffee seemed to help. To her surprise, Edith continued to chatter happily. In fact, she hardly took a breath between tales of her life in the various communities where they had resided.

"... and they had the most marvelous oysters there. If nothing else, I learned well how to prepare them. At first, plenty of women would come by to show me new dishes, but then…" She sighed and looked at Arabella with a sad face. "Like everywhere else, the visits dwindled. It is always just me and Henry after a while. Now in Saltburn we had some lovely rose bushes. They bloomed yellow; can you imagine?"

Arabella tried to keep her drinking coffee. She offered Edith biscuits which she nibbled between descriptions of the churches and villages she had lived in along the English coast. And always along the coast.

"Have you ever lived inland?" she asked Edith.

"Never. Henry likes it by the sea. Always the sea. I must say I tire of the smell of fish. I grew up inland, you know. My father was a vicar too, but unlike Henry, he liked to stay in one place. I miss my home. Henry assures me I will be allowed to visit someday, but the visit never comes. My sister came once to see me in Saltburn…"

Gradually, Edith began to calm a little. Arabella sighed with relief. She was shocked by both Edith's childish interpretations and her girlish voice. She even felt a little sorry for her. If she were not so deeply suspicious of the Vicar, Arabella knew she would invite Edith up to the house again. But everything the woman had told her supported the theory of the vicar as the rat they had thought him.

Edith leaned forward and patted her hand, saying, "You did a lovely job with supper. I am so honored to be your first guest."

When the men returned, Edith quickly shifted to the edge of her seat and hunched her shoulders once more.

The Vicar gave his wife's bowed head a stern look and announced, "We must take our leave."

Edith stood and hustled to his side, her back hunched and her head down. She seemed to have shrunk to an even smaller frame.

"So soon?" Arabella protested politely.

"I have a sermon to write. There is always much work to be done for the Lord." He cleared his throat and added, "And we know that in all things God works for the good of those who love him, who have been called according to his purpose... Romans."

When they had seen their guests out the door, Theo collapsed onto the sofa and let out a pained groan.

"That was a long, long evening. And hardly worth it." He looked at Arabella and grimaced. "All I could get out of him was endless passages from the scriptures. It was most annoying and god-awful boring. And I am sure the slimy bastard was doing it to avoid any real conversation. I got nothing from the man."

Arabella sat across from him in a chair and smiled triumphantly. "How disappointing for you." She leaned forward, preening with her success. "I, on the other hand, was able to get all we need and more."

"What? How?" He sat up.

"Well, it appears I am an expert at espionage, after all. I will expect you to eat your earlier words concerning my abilities as a spy."

"What have you found out?" he demanded, ignoring her comments about her expertise.

"The Vicar and his wife were last at Saltburn. Quite the coincidence, is it not? Wasn't it Saltburn the admiral said was captain Berg's last posting? And before that, Bulbous down the coast." She snorted. "I expect we will find the captain worked the Bulbous area as well."

Theo looked at her curiously. "How in the world did you get that silent woman to tell you all of that? I did not hear her speak a word all evening."

She was tempted to give him a story which hi-lighted her skills at interrogation but decided against it. She shrugged and admitted the truth. "I think it was the gin, actually."

"The gin?"

"I laced the punch with gin. It was a delicious concoction. Cook and I were able to put together a fruity recipe which disguised the alcohol content nicely. Edith could not seem to get enough of it."

"You what?" He looked at her and laughed. "That is marvelous! And it worked. I take it all back. You have done an excellent piece of espionage tonight."

Arabella smiled. "I did. I think we can safely assume the captain and the Vicar are related. Likely brothers."

"Yes, I think you are right. It is too coincidental to think they would follow each other along the coast. Now if we could only discover the third man in this operation." He rubbed his chin thoughtfully. "I cannot help but think your third man is tied to the land at Bergen's Point. I wonder about Sheffeld. That he should appear in such a prime location at this time is another uncomfortable coincidence."

"It is. I think he may well be our man. I would like to prove it. It would be interesting to see if he too had some connection to the revenue captain." Arabella smiled to herself, pleased with the progress they had made.

"I think I will stop at Saltburn and try to discover what I can. Especially if the land titles prove what I suspect," Theo said.

"What is it you suspect?"

"I am beginning to think the land may be owned by the captain. If I am right, then we indeed have a connection between Sheffeld, the Vicar, and the captain." He looked at her with some concern. "You do realize that even if we find the connection, it is still not enough to have the trio brought up on charges and convicted? Even the admiral would be loath to take any action on the connection alone."

She snorted. "It is enough evidence for me and the boys. I have no intentions of waiting for the admiral's justice." She narrowed her eyes and jutted out her chin. "We will do our own justice."

Theo stood up abruptly. "No, you will not. When I agreed to help you with this plan, I had no intention of being an accomplice to murder."

"It is only right those thieves get what they deserve!" She too rose from her seat and glared at him. "How else can we possibly find a way to stop those crooks?"

"Arabella." He took her firmly by the shoulders and gave her a little shake to get her complete attention. When her eyes were on his he continued, "You will promise me you will not say a word about our discoveries to the smugglers or anyone else for now."

She looked at him, with her lips pressed together stubbornly. She had planned from the start to share their discoveries with the captains as soon as she could get word to them.

"Arabella, I am warning you. I will not proceed another step until I have your word on this matter. And if I withdraw, you may well get the Vicar, who is a sitting duck down at the village, but you will never get the captain and his coconspirator."

She shot him a resentful look and pulled away from

him. "How will we ever get enough on them to get your brand of justice? It is not fair, Theo."

He sighed. "We will find a way. One step at a time, Arabella. First, we will prove our theories concerning who is involved. Once that is accomplished, we can concoct a plan to catch them. For instance, the captain must store his loot somewhere. We may never catch him at sea, where he has only his crew and the smuggler's words on his actions, but we could well catch him on land. If we can find his hoard." He took her hands, "Your word Arabella. I'll not proceed at all without it."

After a moment's stubborn hesitation she huffed, "Oh, all right. We will do it your way."

"We will, and though it may take some time, we'll catch the culprits."

Arabella looked at him with interest. "Do you think it is possible? To catch him red-handed as it were?"

"Arabella, we will find an honest method of dealing with him. If we can find where he keeps the goods, we can bring the magistrate into this." He smiled grimly. "From what I have heard, the law around here is strongly biased on the side of the free traders anyway. I am sure the magistrate will be more than eager to put these thieves away. You must trust me in this."

He narrowed his eyes at her. "You must not forget you have promised to leave your smuggling days behind you. And that includes whatever gruesome revenge you may have planned for these thieves."

She sighed. "I've not planned anything. I just assumed turning our information over to the captains would be our only hope for fair play in this."

He put his arms around her. "You are a countess now, Arabella. My countess. Your allegiance is to me and not to the smuggling captains. From now on, all your dealings will have to be on the right side of the law."

"I suppose you're right," she admitted grudgingly. Secretly, she believed him to be wrong. The captain in her protested this method.

"What we find out is between us only. I'll not have the blood of these revenue boys on my hands," Theo said.

Arabella gave another long-suffering sigh. It appeared she would have to trust Theo's assurance justice would be done in the traditional method. Much to her chagrin, she knew she would be forced to do things his way. First, they must be sure of their suspicions and then they must find a way to expose them. It seemed an arduous process to her.

"Yes, Theo," she said at last, "you have my word, I will remain mum on this matter."

"Good." He smiled at her. "You will be my conservative little countess yet," he teased.

She rolled her eyes at him, and he laughed.

"Now, then." He took her hands and led her to the sofa to sit beside him. "We must make our plans. I hope to leave tomorrow. I don't want to be away from you too long. One night at the most would suit me. I thought, since I am visiting coastal towns, you might let me take the Bella. If I go by land, the journey along the twisting roads of York-shire would take over a week. It only makes sense to go by sea."

"An excellent idea. I could come along." She smiled happily.

"No, I want you to stay here and relax. We have only just returned from a difficult journey from London." He looked at her with concern. "You are pale. You need your rest."

She reluctantly agreed. It would be nice to enjoy the comfort of her own bed for a few days.

"Do you think you could put a crew together for me? I would ask Jem, but he's not back yet. And I don't want Arnold or Jamie. I would leave you with a few servants for your comfort while I am gone."

She laughed. "You are much more observant than I thought." She gave him an appreciative glance. It surprised her that he had been able to identify her crew so easily. "Yes, I will put a crew together. I wish Jem were here. Then I could send him with you to keep you safe."

"He will be arriving any day. And I would rather he was here with you." He pulled her close.

The two of them made plans for him to first visit Scarborough to find the public record on the ownership of the point. Then he would proceed to Saltburn where he would snoop around for information on the activities of the Vicar and possibly Sheffeld and the captain.

"There is a pub on the waterfront at Saltburn called the Eagle's Nest. In it, you may find a captain by the name of Moreland. I know him, or rather, Captain Ara knows him. I did a favor for him once and he owes me," she said in her firm captain's voice.

Theo looked at her with interest. That she could change her voice so, was startling. This time she had done so unconsciously.

Arabella continued in the same tone, "Remind him Ara was pleased to load the silks. That way he will know you come from me. Then if he knows anything about the shenanigans of our thieves, he will be sure to share it with you."

Theo contemplated her words. Arabella as a force amongst the smuggling community was a concept which was only beginning to take shape in his mind. With a sinking feeling, he realized becoming a wife and mother would be a hard transformation for her. He knew too, despite her promises and efforts, she had only just begun to learn how to live her life as his countess.

He pulled her close and kissed her on the forehead, before tucking her into his shoulder. "Thank you, Ara. Your advice will come in handy indeed."

With luck, in a day or two, he would have the information to begin phase two of their plans. He only hoped Arabella could resist the temptation to begin her rough justice. One thing was certain; he would not have to worry about her making a run—he had her ship.

What possible trouble could she get into on land?

Chapter Twenty-Four

Theo pulled Arabella into his arms and soundly kissed her goodbye before leaving her warm bed.

"It will only be one night," he assured her. "I plan to reach Scarborough early. I will search the records and head to Saltburn before the day is done. Hopefully tomorrow I'll have all I need before noon and be back to you before you know it."

The trip by sea was uneventful. They had to fight a head wind but other than that all had progressed as planned.

The land titles office was manned by an elderly man in wire framed glasses. Theo gave him his name and title. That he was an earl impressed the man. He was as helpful as he could, finding the maps of their township for him and then looking up the titles. Being an earl had its benefits.

"Ah, here it is then," the man said, running his finger down a massive ledger. "It's Bergen's Point you wanted, is it not?"

Theo leaned over and looked at the spot the fellow had

indicated with his palsied fingers. "Yes," he said with some excitement when he saw the land location. "That is it."

"We'll have a more complete file here," the man said, tottering over to a massive cabinet and pulling out a drawer.

The drawer was stuffed tight with neatly numbered files. The old man went back to the ledger and read the number on the entry once again before returning to his files and pulling out the one they needed.

"Here it is." He smiled and laid the file open on the table, covering the ledger. "This can give you a few more details of the sale. It'll all be here."

Theo studied the document. He had been right. The land had been purchased recently by Captain John Berg. It was all there.

He took a deep breath and addressed the old gentleman. "Are there copies of this document? I may need a copy."

The gentleman pulled the page down to reveal a second copy beneath it. "We do not like to give these out. If I loan it to you, it must be returned promptly."

Theo assured him he would have it returned to him before the month was out. He hoped he could deliver on the promise. The fellow took down his name and particulars.

Satisfied with what he had gleaned from the office, he hurried back to his ship. Now he had only to investigate the coastal town of the revenue man's last post.

Arriving in Saltburn ahead of schedule, he was hopeful he could get some information here and perhaps be home tonight. Once they had anchored and secured the ship, he hurried down the dock and began to look for the pub Arabella had told him about.

It was nearing twilight. The boats were tied up in rows. But for the screaming of seagulls, all was quiet along the shore. The village, like many along the coast, was situated in a cove; sandwiched between the sea and the highlands behind it. At the end of the dock, planks separated the village from the rocky shore. He walked along this makeshift wharf. It was high tide. Occasionally, a heavy wave would hit the rock below and spray him with a salty mist.

Further along, he was assaulted by the smell of rotting fish. Beside him was the cleaning shack: a long building, its roof held up with stout wooden pillars leaving the work area open to the air. Inside, heavy tables were being scraped clean by a lad. Two other boys were edging a barrel of fish guts to a waiting wagon.

There must have been a good catch today, Theo thought, wrinkling his nose at the odor.

He had only walked a few more steps when he saw the faded sign of The Eagle's Nest. Pushing aside the heavy oak door, he strode inside. As he took a moment to let his eyes adjust to the dark gloom of its low ceilings, he noticed the once raucous noise of the pub gradually quieting.

Once his eyes had adjusted to the dim light, he noted the place was packed with the men who worked the sea. And every one of them was staring at him silently. He realized he was overdressed. Theo looked like the earl he was. Though his title had been such a boon to him at the land titles office, with the proprietor helping him in every conceivable way, it was of no help here. Here it would be a hindrance.

Every eye in the house watched him with deep suspicion. It was unnerving. His hair stood up on the back of his neck as he walked across the planked floors to a bar at the rear of the building. Waiting by the bar, he cursed his stupidity. He should have borrowed the clothes of a crew member for this task. These rough seafarers likely thought him a government man, here to cause them trouble.

The bartender walked over to him and stared. There was no offer of a drink.

Theo cleared his throat deciding to play the only card he had. He tried to tone down his upper-class accent and said, "Captain Ara of the Bella sent me here. I am here for business with Captain Moreland. Can you point me in his direction?"

The bartender stared at him a long time before answering. He finally grunted. "He is not to be found here tonight. You'll catch him in the morning if you're here early enough. Takes his breakfast here, he does."

Theo thanked him and with some relief left the intimidating atmosphere of the pub. His hopes of returning home tonight and surprising Arabella were dashed. He would sleep aboard the Bella tonight. Tomorrow, he would dress more appropriately and hopefully get some information.

Chapter Twenty-Five

Arabella spent a luxurious morning in bed. There was something to be said about having the place to herself. She enjoyed a day checking the household accounts. She even spent some time in her garden, planning her improvements and envisioning its return to its former glory. Cook had made her a favorite meal and she had lingered over supper, eating far too much.

After supper, she decided to bring her new mare a treat. She went through the kitchens, finding an apple and a handful of carrots, before heading for the stables.

When she entered the stables, she found Jamie propped up against a bale of hay. His face was contorted in pain.

"Jamie, what has happened?" she said with some concern.

"Good day, mistress. I was a fool, is what happened. Got in the way and had my foot trampled on by one of the coach horses."

Arabella crouched down to examine him. Together, they

carefully removed the boot, then his heavy woolen sock. The foot was red and swollen.

"Take a few breaths, Jamie," Arabella said. "I'll check to see if it's broken."

She ran her fingers along his foot, careful to feel for any breaks. She looked at his face and gently twisted the foot from side to side. He had not shouted in pain, and she smiled in relief.

"Bend your toes, Jamie," she said. "Let's see if you can move it."

Jamie turned his toes up and down and twirled his ankle hesitantly. "Everything seems to be working."

He grinned with relief.

"It is bruised badly, and very swollen. You will not be walking on this foot for a day or two at least."

"Oh aye, and that's a problem." He looked at her with some alarm. "It's my turn to be up the cliffs tonight. I said I would sit and watch for a flash or two from the Vicarage. We're sure it's him, the bloody knave. We have him pegged. The lights come from the Vicar for sure, but we agreed to find the second traitor. And Captain Barr was going to take out his boat with a full crew and no nets, to give me a chance to spot him. And now this."

He gestured to his foot.

Arabella let her mind race. This was a perfect opportunity for her. She could take his place. Her face flushed with excitement. She would have to go as Captain Ara. A woman could not be wandering the point alone at night. This was her one last chance to take on her other persona.

She would not be betraying Theo. She had only promised him not to go to sea. She was not going to sea. It would be a simple night's work. It was unlikely he would ever hear of it. Indeed, there was no need for him to know. If this was her last chance, she was determined to take it.

She cleared her throat and declared in her captain voice, "I'll be taking that shift for you, Jamie."

"But Ara, what would your man have to say? Or Jem? I'm like to be skinned alive by both." He looked a little panicked.

She patted him on the shoulder and spoke again in her captain's voice. "Not to worry, lad. I'll be home before either of them. It's only a little jaunt to Bergen's Point. There's no harm in it. Besides, it grows late. There's no time to find a replacement. I'm sure ye'll not want to face the wrath of Captain Barr, who'll have gone through much trouble to set the bait."

"Aye, there is that," he replied.

It was settled. She hurried to the house to change into her captain's gear.

"*Mon Dieu cherie!*" Celeste said when Arabella informed her of her plans. "You cannot. It is not right that you should be running about like this. *Merde!* Your Theo will be much angry! Yes? *Non, non,* my dear. Think of your babe. This cannot be good."

Arabella ignored her protests. She was excited to be off.

"Help me with this sash," she said.

Celeste complied, muttering her disapproval.

In no time, Arabella was mounted. She carried a lantern with a swiveled lid so she could adjust its light if she needed to. Her cutlas hung by her side. As she rode out of Harwood, she smiled to herself. It had been too long since she last rode as Captain Ara. For a moment, she wished she were on her way to the Bella. All in good time, she thought to herself. Maybe she could convince Jem to come with her on another run. She laughed aloud. It was not the high-pitched giggle of Arabella, but a low masculine sound.

Arabella decided to take the old mill road. She would leave her horse at the mill and walk up the rise to the height of the land. The sky was darkening fast. She would be able to reach a suitable location on the hills just in time to catch a signal, should there be one. Urging her horse to a gallop, she soon reached the end of the trail and then walked up the other side, her horse safely tied to the gate at the mill.

The night was warm and eerily quiet. Her stomach clenched with excitement. It was so good to wear her trousers once more. She put her hand on her cutlas and smiled. For one more night, she was Ara, tough and strong.

Remembering Theo's suspicions, she deliberately chose a hiding place close to Sheffeld manor. She found a safe location, where she could see both the dim lights of the village and the dark and looming out-buildings of the Sheffeld manor house, with the sea beyond it. She was encased by the shrubs around her when she squatted down. She sat on the ground and made furrows through the shrubbery to give her a clear line of vision, while she made herself comfortable. It might be a long night.

The last vestiges of sunset had begun to fade. It was cloudy with no moon or stars to lighten the night. Soon it was so inky dark nothing but the village lights and a pale orange light from the Sheffeld house were able to give her the lay of the land. An owl hooted, its eerie call making her jump.

For at least an hour, the owl's call was the only event. She had just decided this had been the most boring and fruitless evening ever when a flash from the village alerted her senses. It was followed by several more in quick succession.

She turned inland to look for a response. Her brow furrowed. The problem was whoever received the message would not likely return it in the same direction for all the village to see. No, they would turn to the sea and signal Captain Berg. She would not see the flashes unless she was around the front of the point, facing the Sheffeld property. It was probably the reason the boys had had no luck finding the spotter. They were expecting a man along the point but not one from as far as the Sheffeld estate.

She was sure Theo was correct and Sheffeld was involved. What she needed to do was move quickly around the perimeter to face his buildings, where she could see his transmissions out to sea.

She glanced back to the village. Another flash lit up the sky. She decided to make a run across the clearing and change her angle. Closing her eyes, she envisioned the layout of the farm as she had seen it when she first reached her hiding spot. Remembering a bluff of trees at the perimeter, she smiled. It would be the perfect location to intercept his signal.

Awkwardly holding her lantern across her chest so it would not clang, she made a mad dash across the clearing. Her run was only just over a hundred yards but felt like miles. By the time she reached the trees, her heart was beating frantically in her breast as much from fear as exertion. Resting against the trunk of a tree as she caught her breath, she waited with dread for a shout or movement from the house. To her relief, all was quiet.

Working her way through the trees, she aimed for the distant edge of the bluff where she would have a clear view. There was blackness all around her. She had to stretch out her arms and feel her way through the brush. She tried to do this as silently as possible, but it was difficult when her feet constantly fought the deadfall on the forest floor.

Her arms bumped into a solid object. It was a shed of some sort. She walked forward, resting her left hand against it. There was no twigs or dead wood for her feet to struggle against here, allowing her to move smoothly to the building's far corner.

She had her view of the sea. To her right, she could see the soft amber lighting in the manor house. It was an excellent location. Now she had only to wait for a signal flash. Long minutes passed. She leaned against the building and caught her breath. Sure she had been too long making her way to the edge of the bluff, her heart sank.

Then it happened. A bright lantern flashed from the dark upper windows of the manor house. It flashed again and she smiled in the darkness.

Got you, she thought, satisfied with her discovery.

She turned to the sea. A series of flashes, vague in the distance, but discernable, answered the signals. She let out a long breath. Theo had been correct. Sheffeld was the third man.

Now the hard part would come. Now they would have to prove it.

Leaning back, she took a deep breath and closed her eyes. It had been a productive night's work. She could go home the way she had come.

Her head and back rested against the building. She touched the wall tentatively. What was this building hidden here in the grove? It was far from the house. What purpose could it possibly serve?

Her heart began to beat hard in her chest. Could this hidden shed be the warehouse for their hoard? She had to know. If it were true, then they had them. They could wait here with the magistrate after a shipment had been seized and catch them red-handed. And if the shed even now held contraband, Sheffeld would be hard pressed to explain it. She envisioned the captain and Sheffeld being hauled away in chains and smiled to herself. Perhaps Theo was right. Maybe it was possible to get their justice his way.

Arabella slid around the corner and worked her way to the door. She found a handle and pushed it gently. It shifted and rolled forward. The building had sliding doors like those that could be found on a stable. This would allow the doors to slide to almost the width of the building. Handy to back in a wagon and unload.

She pushed the door forward until she had created an opening wide enough for her to squeeze through. Her heart pounded in her chest as she slipped inside. In her eagerness, she neglected to pull the door closed behind her. It was even blacker inside than it had been amongst the trees.

She sat down and worked her lantern. Once lit, she held it high.

The entire back of the room was packed from floor to ceiling with tubs of what she assumed was brandy and gin. To the left, long narrow crates which she knew to be silk were stacked almost to the roof. She walked forward into the room, trying to do a count on the tubs of brandy. When she had a solid estimate of the goods, she smiled to herself.

She had found it! She had found the stash. She wanted to shout with joy. Theo would be surprised and pleased with her. They were well on their way to catching the bloody thieves. And the captains! The smuggling crews would celebrate her success. She almost laughed aloud.

"Captain Ara, I assume. What a pleasure to welcome you to our little treasure house."

All her exuberance drained from her with the sound of that voice. Her stomach churned.

Arabella turned slowly with a sickening dread. Her heart sank. Sheffeld stood with a pistol aimed at her guts. She felt a wave of panic and squashed it. It would not help her now. She might have only seconds to live. Her only hope was to buy some time and wait for an opportunity. An opportunity when a pistol was not aimed at her with deadly certainty.

For a split second, she thought of Theo and the little baby nestled in her tummy. It gave her the courage she needed. She had no choice but to do all she could to survive. She was life itself to her child.

Taking a calming breath, she answered Sheffeld with all the bravado she could muster. "Good day, sir. It is a fine stash indeed. I do not believe I have seen better. My healthy storehouse is meager compared to this. You are to be commended."

Breathing careful, slow breaths, she stilled her pounding heart. If ever she had played the adventurous, devil-may-care Ara well, she would have to do so now.

"Set the lantern down and keep your hands where I can see them."

Arabella slowly set the lantern down and held out her gloved hands. "I too have a treasure, you know. Not as grand as this," she said, twirling her gloved hand, "but substantial."

She shrugged and smiled beneath her mask.

"Is that so?"

Arabella felt a wave of fresh hope. He was interested. Murdering Captain Ara without draining him of his treasure would be a foolish move. But she could not count on him recognizing this.

"I must say, I am quite jealous of this bounty." She talked slowly, keeping her voice low and watching his every move.

Be calm, she told herself. She wanted her captor to be relaxed and feel in control. For him to panic now would be her death. If he was smart, he might negotiate with her. Captain Ara was a worthy prize for him. But only if he was alive.

"Even I, who as you know am a legend in this business, have not managed to pile it up this high."

Sheffeld looked at her speculatively. "I might be interested in this bounty. But then again, I might not. I might consider it boon enough to shoot the famous Captain Ara."

He sneered.

Arabella shrugged. "You could, but I would bargain with you. Even without my stash, I am a prize my crew would pay dearly for. And as for me, how much of my stash might I pay for my life? It could be a good deal for both of us."

Sheffeld laughed. It was a grating sound. But he looked at Arabella with renewed interest.

"Aye, it could be a good deal for both of us," he mimicked her and laughed again. "It surely would. And one of the best for you, eh?"

He raised a hand to stroke his heavy red beard as he contemplated.

Arabella smiled beneath her mask. She gestured with her hands as if to say take it or leave it, disguising as best she could her horrible anticipation. She had enticed him with possible rewards as well as she could. His next words would be her life or her death.

He strolled to a rack beside the door and pulled down a

roll of rope. "I will have to consult my partners on this. This deal will have to jell and set a while."

Tension flowed from her body. Her knees weakened and she bit the inside of her mouth, using the pain to help her focus on not sinking to the floor in relief. She would live, at least for now.

He walked towards her with his pistol in one hand and a coil of thick rope in the other. "Sit down very slowly. Hold your hands above your head."

Arabella eased onto the ground. She kept her arms raised.

"Clutch those hands together. I want to get a nice solid knot on them."

Arabella did as she was told. He stepped behind her. The rope tugged tightly around her wrists. Sheffeld grabbed her cutlas from her belt and tossed it towards the door.

"Now stick out your legs. And keep those arms up where I can see them." Keeping the gun trained on her, he looped the rope around her booted ankles and pulled it tight. He put his gun down and finished the job. When he was done, he stood back and admired his handywork.

Curiosity crossed his face, and he reached for her scarf. She tossed her head and smiled beneath her mask.

"Touch it." She laughed, a deep, low sound. "Because it is wet leprosy. You will have a special gift from me which will last a lifetime."

Sheffeld pulled his hand back and she laughed again.

"It is a gift I would love to give you." Arabella thanked the sordid rumors about her ugly disease. They had always served her well, even more so now.

He scowled at her. "You will have a long wait, I am afraid. My man will be busy until tomorrow. Even then, it might be late afternoon at least. But he will come and then you will have a chance to show us your famous stash. Have a good sleep, Captain Ara. It has been a pleasure."

He laughed as he walked across the room and hung her lantern on a wired hook by the door. He snatched up her cutlas. With only a smiling glance in her direction, he left, pulling the door tight behind him. The lock clicked into place.

After a few minutes, the unmistakable clangs of chains being slung through its handles could be heard. Sheffeld was going to guarantee there would be no possibility of escape. Her reputation had its uses but, in this case, it had not served her well.

She hung her head and fought back the cursed tears that threatened to overwhelm her.

She had made a dreadful mistake when she had not pulled the door shut behind her. A ribbon of light across the grounds would have alerted him. Stupid, stupid, stupid. Her eagerness to find the stash and her bloody ego had cost her dearly. She had been so wrapped up in her triumph, she had made a child's error.

She knew the excise men hoped to ransom her. What they wanted was her stash of goods. There was no stash. Jem would have sold it all to purchase the herd. Normally they would have held back funds to purchase trade goods for the next run, but there was to be no next run. This time all of it would have been spent on livestock. If Sheffeld and Captain Berg discovered this, her life was worthless. Already she was sure Sheffeld itched to murder her. She had no choice but to find a way out of this mess before negotiations began.

Arabella cursed her mistake once more. Looking up at the lantern, she scowled. Perhaps he had made a mistake too.

The Smuggler

She would only need to find it.

Chapter Twenty-Six

Theo crawled into the narrow bunk in the ship's cabin. He thought of Arabella soft and warm in her bed. He was relieved she had stayed behind, safely at Harwood. A day of rest would be good for her, and maybe just what she needed to help her feel better about this baby.

His thoughts turned to his task tomorrow. The bartender had said Captain Moreland would be early. Nothing could suit him more. He wanted to get what information he could, then board the Bella and hopefully be home by noon. A morning's sail if the winds were favorable would easily have him down the coast and docked before lunch.

He smiled at his anticipated reunion with his renegade wife. Strange how one night without her seemed so long. With a vision of her luminous black eyes in his mind, he fell asleep.

Theo awoke at dawn. He took some care with his apparel, borrowing a soft woolen sweater with the signature rolled collar of the sailor from his crew. His trousers were oiled denim and belled over his boots. Satisfied with his appearance, he made his way back to the Eagle's Nest just as the sun was rising on the sea's horizon. Thinking he had arrived too early; he was surprised when the door to the ale house opened easily.

The only customer was seated alone next to a massive stone fireplace. He was a burly man, with massive shoulders and straggly black hair, half of which was pulled back from his face and tied, the other half hung in twisted fronds around his weathered face. He attacked a breakfast of eggs and sausage with gusto, not looking up to see who had entered the room.

Theo walked to the familiar man behind the heavy oak counter. "Captain Moreland, I assume?" he asked, indicating the intimidating figure at his meal.

"Aye."

"Bring me a breakfast. I will be joining the man." He tossed a coin onto the bar, walked over to the captain's table, pulled out a chair, and sat.

The smuggling captain did not look up. Instead, he wiped yolk from his pewter plate with a piece of loaf and stuffed the whole of it into his mouth.

"I am here from Captain Ara," Theo said. Only then did the man acknowledge him, looking at him with narrowed pale eyes while chewing his bread.

The bartender slapped a plate of food in front of Theo.

The captain handed the man his plate and growled. "I'll have another, Tom." He wiped his mouth on his sleeve and stared at Theo, assessing the possibility of his connection to Ara with skepticism. Theo realized even his clothes did not disguise the obvious truth that he was out of his element here. How Arabella had managed her persona with this crowd was a mystery to him.

"Ara said to mention he was pleased to load the silks. He needs a favor." Theo was careful to use the masculine pronoun.

"Oh, aye." The pronouncement relaxed the man at once.

Theo let out a breath he had not been aware he was holding. Twice now he had been forced to use Arabella's name. It was clear Arabella had a formidable reputation. To accomplish that with these characters must have been a feat indeed.

The captain looked at him and said, "Well, get on with it then. What can I do for the man?"

Theo decided to be blunt. "It is information we need. We have a new revenue cutter stealing cargoes. Captain Berg is the name. He has at least two accomplices, a Vicar and we think a fellow named Sheffeld. What might you know about that?"

"Dirty thieving whores!" The captain picked up the crust of a loaf and shook it at Theo. "The bastard did the same here. And Sheffeld, well, that scurvy knave would be his first mate, or at least he was when they were here. Ran the bastards off, we did."

Theo ate his breakfast while he listened to the angry tales of abuse the locals had suffered. The incidents were the same, except during the time they had spent at Saltburn, Sheffeld had worked the cutter at Captain Berg's side.

"As for the Vicar," Captain Moreland said, "by the time we went to hang the bastard, he was gone. Packed up in the night he did."

Theo thanked him for his information.

"It's glad I'll be when I hear Ara and the southern boys have strung them up. Send him my best. If there is aught else that can be done from here, tell the wiry lad we're ready to loan a hand."

"I'll do that," Theo replied. He was beginning to realize the scope of Arabella's reputation as a captain. He had known she worked the sea but seeing the respect the other captains had for her was a revelation. He began to understand the sacrifices and changes she was making to her life.

It was time to leave. He had what he needed. He boarded the Bella, the sails were raised, and he was on his way to Harwood.

He smiled with satisfaction at the progress he had made today. Arabella would be pleased. Now they would have to search the countryside to find the captain's stash. He contemplated the problem. They would have to find his loading zone and follow the man back to his lair. It would be hard but not impossible. He would show Arabella all could be done within the law.

But first he would come home to her. He frowned, thinking that even now she might be sick with no one to hold her heaving belly. At least she was safe at home, getting some much-needed rest. He felt the steady north breeze.

"Tie the sail to the bowsprit," he hollered, "full speed ahead."

Chapter Twenty-Seven

Arabella looked up at the lantern. It was too high for her to access even if she were able to roll her way to it. A wave of panic washed over. She would die here with her little one still tucked inside her belly. She pushed her knotted hands into her belly and tried to calm herself.

She closed her eyes and pictured her little son. He looked like Theo with his soft curly locks and blue and gold eyes. She envisioned him as a young man. To her surprise, he took on the persona of a young warrior. He turned to her and gave her a half smile, filled with the confidence she needed. The image whirled and she saw a young girl with equally gold flecked blue eyes and black hair. There were two!

"Faith," the girl whispered to her before fading off into her dreams.

Her stomach settled. She rubbed her hands lovingly across her lower belly. Her babies were confident she could survive. She would not disappoint them. Or Theo. Her beautiful, loving Theo.

All this time, she had been mourning the loss of Ara, instead of celebrating Theo, and the babies inside her. She was able now to rank her priorities. She was determined to live through this ordeal.

And when I do, I will be the wife, mother, and countess he needs. I have been so wrong.

Breathe, she told herself, and think.

She began to move her wrists attempting to loosen the cords which held them in place. For an hour, she worked her hands to no avail. Even when she had chaffed her wrists bloody, the ropes could not be moved. Sheffeld was a sailor. Above all, he knew how to tie knots. She expelled a breath and looked down to her feet. He had tied his rope around her boots. It was a mistake. If she could pull off a boot, she might have enough slack to free her legs.

Using her wrists and working her feet, she was able to slide the rope high enough to wriggle her foot free of the boot. It had taken precious time. She estimated she had worked her feet for two long hours. It was only her dogged determination which kept her at her painstaking task. But she had done it. Once the boot was off, it was short work to free her feet. She worked her boot back on and stood.

Pacing the room to stretch out her limbs, Arabella contemplated her next move. A wave of frustration and fear washed over her. It was hopeless. Her hands were tied too tightly. Even if she rubbed them against the corner of the silk crates, it would take hours or even days to fray the ropes enough to break their hold. She hung her head as hot tears filled her eyes.

She pressed her bloody wrists against her belly and took from her babies a renewed strength. She would not let them down. She held their lives, and she would keep them safe. No matter what the journey.

She stood beneath the lantern, looking at it with longing. If she could access it, she could burn the ropes from her hands. She tried to hold her hands up to the lantern but could not reach the flame that way. The sides of the lantern were warm, but not warm enough to burn the rope. If she could get it down, and perhaps use her mouth to pull back the cover, she would reach the open flames.

But first she would have to reach it. She looked around the shed. There was nothing. No chair or desk, no furniture at all. She fought back the nagging sense of hopelessness. "By god, I will find a way!" she swore, allowing herself to become angry.

She turned back to look at the stash. The tubs were awkward. She would not be able to balance on one even if she could get it to the lantern. But the crates of silk were perfect. They were at least a foot thick, perhaps more. If she could hop up on one, its height would be enough for her to reach the lantern's wire handle with her teeth. The problem was they were stacked high. She would have to climb without her hands to the top of an eight-foot stack and, squeezing between the stack and the roof, force one of the crates down with her legs.

She had her plan. Climbing up the stack would be difficult, but not impossible. The packers had not taken care to pile them evenly. The protruding edges would allow her narrow ledges for her feet. Again and again, she attempted the climb. Each time her body swayed outward and without her hands to hold her against the stack, she fell back to the floor. Her body bruised and ached with each attempt.

A band of daylight appeared between the eaves and walls of the shed. The night had passed too quickly. If Sheffeld decided to check on her this morning, all would be lost. Arabella's stomach turned with the possibility. She quickly dismissed the concern as beyond the realm of her ability to control and attacked the wall of silk again.

This time, she used her teeth and chin to grip the edges of the crates and hold her body tight against them. It worked. Gradually, she made her way up the barrier. At last, she was able to squirm into the narrow hold above the pile. She thanked her slender body as she twisted around to force the three-foot long crate forward and down to the floor.

It hit the floor with a resounding crash. She peered through the crack between the eaves and walls to see if the noise had alerted Sheffeld to her activity. She froze. Sheffeld was coming down the stairs of his home, a bowler hat on his head and a riding crop in one hand. He paused and looked toward the shed. From this distance, she could not see his expression, but she was sure he smiled. To her relief, he headed for his stables. She stared for an eternity at the stable door. When Sheffeld finally came out, he was atop a mare. He trotted towards the shed.

Arabella held her breath, sure that this time she was defeated, but he only looked at the locked doors with chains wrapped securely around its handles from his saddle, and smiling, wheeled his horse about. He galloped back up past the house and down his lane. He was off to bring back the revenue captain.

It will buy me a little time, an hour perhaps, maybe more, she thought. But there was much to be done to give her even the chance of survival.

Chapter Twenty-Eight

Jamie and Arnold conferred quietly in the stables.

"I don't know what's to be done." Arnold looked at Jamie, his face filled with worry after a sleepless night. "I'm wishing Jem were here. He was supposed to be here yesterday, but something's held him up."

"She has been caught for sure. There is no denying it now. It grows later and later and still no sign of her. I went up to the mill and found her horse. She is up at the point still," Arnold said in a despondent voice. "There is only you and I here who can help her."

He scowled at Jamie's foot with disgust. "And you're gimped up and not much use."

"Aye." Jamie kicked out with his good foot, hitting the gate of an empty stall.

"I don't know. We're stymied for sure. We can't wait for Jem or the master. We have to move now, or she'll be lost." Arnold's shoulders slumped as he added, "If she ain't done for already."

Arnold considered silently for a minute. When he

glanced back at Jamie, he had his plan. "I have to go to the village. Find the captains and stir them up to help us find her. Searching for this accomplice was their plan. They'll need to help us now."

Jamie looked at him with renewed hope. "Aye. It won't take much to stir them up. Their patience with this business is thin."

"I hope you have the right of it. I'll hustle down there. You stay here and wait for Jem or the master."

Arnold rode down to the village. He found the captains where he thought they would be—in the ale house arguing about their plans to stop the new revenue cutter. Emotions were high. It seemed Captain Barr had been searched last night. Even worse, word had reached them of another smuggler from down the coast who had had his load stolen just two days ago. They yelled their outrage, slamming their pewter mugs against the tables with zeal. The place was packed with not just the captains and their crews but villagers, eager for the latest news.

Arnold tried in vain to get the attention of the captains, but he was just a working sailor and not to be acknowledged in this crowd. He could not be heard. Finally, in desperation, he stood upon the bar and let loose a loud whistle. The room quieted and all eyes turned toward him.

"I have important news," he shouted. He had their attention now. The last of the conversations died down. "The bloody bastards took Ara last night."

The room erupted into chaos with everyone shouting and swearing.

Arnold was forced to whistle again. When the room quieted down, he added, "He went up to the land above the point last night to catch our third man and has not returned. Jem's away. We need some help to fetch him back." He looked around the room. "If he still lives."

The room exploded. It took several minutes before the crowd was still enough for the captains to talk and hatch a plan. Arnold frowned when it was decided their best line of attack was the Vicar. The Vicar was a known participant in this business and would be sure to know the fate of Ara.

"But is there time?" Arnold hollered. "Ara could even now be facing his death."

No one heeded his shouts.

They had been eager to get at the Vicar for a long time. Their patience was worn thin. This was the opportunity they had waited for, and they would not be denied.

Shouts of, "Hang him!" and "tar and feather him!" filled the pub. The people spilled out into the street and headed up the hill. More villagers joined them as they progressed to the Vicarage. Someone had loaded warm pitch onto a cart and followed the mob. Several women ran into their homes to grab their feather ticks and join the unruly crowd. Soon the entire village had become a part of the noisy throng. Arnold followed along, pushed forward by the angry mob.

The Vicar stood on his front porch surveying the approaching crowd with confusion. By the time he realized he was the target of their angst, it was too late. He ran to his gate, managing to open it, and charged down the lane a few meters before he was tackled to the ground.

Two men grabbed him by the shoulders. He was forced to stand before the screaming crowd and take a panoply of abuse and charges. Someone threw a rock at him. His forehead bled where the rock made contact.

Finally, three captains—Peasley, Barr, and Gorge— emerged from the crowd to question him.

"It seems ye have one of our boys, ya dirty thieving scoundrel. You'll give up where he is or face the pitch." Captain Gorge flung his arm back to indicate the barrel that was even now being unloaded onto the lane. His hawk face turned to the Vicar, and he scowled.

The Vicar shouted, "'Cease from anger and forsake wrath. Do not fret, it leads only to evildoing'... Psalms."

"I say we hang him and be done with him!" someone yelled from the crowd, ignoring his biblical appeal.

The mob roared its approval.

"Where is he now?" Barr leaned in close.

The Vicar could only stutter his response. "I... I don't know who you speak of. There is no one here, I swear."

"It's Captain Ara and we'll have him back, before we run you out of town on a rail." Barr grabbed him by his shirt front and shook him. "Where is he then?"

"I don't know! I don't know, I tell you!" The Vicar was becoming desperate. He shouted, "'He is exalted in power. And he will do no violence to justice and abundant right-eousness'...Proverbs."

Again, his words were ignored. The village women had hauled their feather ticks to the front. A lad was busy slicing them open to reveal the mounds of feathers within.

The Vicar began to scream. It was a high-pitched terrible sound. Instead of moving the mob to pity, it spurred them on to even greater violence. Rocks and curses were thrown his way with deadly intent.

"I don't know an Ara," he muttered. "Please have mercy. I have no knowledge of this."

"Ah, but you have knowledge of the loot you've stolen, that we know for sure. And we have had enough of the likes of you. What special verse do ye have for traitors and thieves?" Captain Peasley looked to the men holding him. "Strip him. We'll tar him up."

"Wait!" Arnold yelled, pushing himself through the crowd. "Ye must question him again. He knows. I'm sure of it."

His voice drowned in the roars of the mob.

The men ripped the Vicar's shirt and jacket from his body. The crowd gave a collective roar of applause. They mercifully left him his trousers and boots. He was dragged to the barrel where a few men tried to paint his squirming white body with the pitch. They gave up, instead grabbing and lifting him screaming to be dunked into the heated barrel. The Vicar flailed about, while the villagers stormed in with a frenzy to push his body beneath the steaming tar.

And then the whole thing toppled over. Barrel and tar and man rolled into the dusty street. At first the crowd leapt back. But then they came again. This time with feathers. Handfuls of them were swatted on him sticking obscenely to his body. He was eventually thrown into a feather tick and further pushed and prodded. The Vicar's screams had turned to whimpers.

Two men came forward with a long pole and tossed it on the ground next to the moaning Vicar. A group of villagers rushed forward to tie his feathered limbs to the pole. The Vicar offered no resistance.

"Out of town! Out of town!" the mob chanted.

And so, it was done. He was carried past the town limits and tossed into the ditch. He was left there for his family to attend. In this case, his wife, who had stood upon her porch and watched the whole ordeal with her fists pressed against her crumpled face and her shoulders hunched.

The captains stood in a little huddle at the scene of the

crime. They had not followed the crowd to the outskirts of town. They had other matters to discuss.

The mob had its fill. The people, subdued and quiet now, wandered in twos and threes back to their homes. They muttered amongst themselves that the Vicar was lucky to escape with his life. And indeed, he was.

Arnold let them pass him in a daze. He slumped, turning slowly toward Harwood. He had failed to get the help he needed. The Vicar's gruesome plight was no benefit to their search for Arabella. Much time had been wasted to no avail. He and Jamie were on their own. Somehow, they would need to find a way to rescue their captain.

Chapter Twenty-Nine

Theo was enjoying the crisp north wind upon his face. With such favorable winds, they had made the journey in record time. The village appeared on the horizon ahead and he smiled. In no time, they were docked. Theo helped the crew secure the boat before proceeding to the stables to fetch his horse.

The village was oddly quiet. There was no one moving about. He frowned at the strangeness of it. The wharf was deserted as were the village streets.

When he came to the stables, again, no one was around. He hollered but got no response. He shrugged. There must be an event of some kind taking place. Looking around, he found his saddle resting on a wooden rail. Theo saddled up his horse himself, deciding he would have to settle with the proprietor later. He was eager to be on his way. There was much to discuss with Arabella.

Once on the road, he met clusters of villagers returning to their homes. Ahead, three men stood in the center of the road. A black puddle of tar pooled in the dust before them.

Scatterings of feathers blew across the lane and were caught up in the ditches or clung to gates.

Theo stopped his horse. "What has happened here?"

"The Vicar met his justice," the tallest man answered. He was long and lean with a face which was sharp featured like a hawk. "He got a tarring and it's less than he deserved."

Theo shivered. "Did you kill him?"

"Nah, he'll live and more's the pity," a burly fellow in a faded bandana answered. He squinted up at Theo. "You're from on top of the hill at Harwood? We are needing to go up the old mill road. Not a problem for ya, is it?"

"I don't think so," Theo answered slowly.

Something was happening. He scanned the faces of the men on the road. He was not likely to get any further information here. He tipped his hat and hurried on his way.

He was more likely to get his news from Arabella and her crew. He started to feel uneasy. Things had heated up in the brief time he had been away. He thought of Arabella and his stomach rolled. He had to get home and be sure she had avoided this fray.

He spurred his horse to a gallop, passing the little crowd at the town limits without a glance in his rush to return home.

He brought his horse into the stable. Jem was standing with Jamic. They appeared to be in a heated debate. Both went silent as he led his horse to its stall. They looked at him with fearful expressions.

His heart sank. Something terrible had happened involving Arabella. Standing wordlessly, he waited for their dreaded news.

Jem cleared his throat. "I just rode up. It seems there has been a spot of trouble whilst we've been away." He looked

Theo steadily in the eyes. "Arabella went up to the point last night to take a turn at watching for the spotter. She's not come back."

Theo felt his world spin. He leaned against his horse. Then in a burst of energy he tried to mount her. He intended to ride hard to the point immediately, to find Arabella and bring her home.

Jem stopped him with a firm hand on his shoulder. "No," he said in a calm calculating voice. "You will do her no good if you ride in and get yourself shot. And you might be the death of her."

He firmly turned Theo's body away from the horse. "We will need a plan."

"Sweet Jesus, they might have killed her." Theo's mind was reeling. He gasped for breath.

"No, they will not," Jem said. "Ara is worth good coin to them. She knows it as well as they do. These boyos are in it for a profit. They will try to ransom her."

When Theo had regained his breath and stilled his rolling stomach, Jem nudged him forward and pushed him down hard onto a hay bale. "Sit and listen. If we want to get her back safe, we have to think this through."

Theo nodded, still dazed.

"Now then, it is sure that she has been discovered," Jem said. "Jamie tells me she is dressed as Captain Ara. If they caught her, she'll try to bargain. She's more capable than you think in these matters. And she's a recognizable prize. They'll not shoot her outright. She has no bounty on her head, but she's a captain and worth gold to her crew. They'll know that."

Theo interjected, "She will be up at the Sheffeld place. We shared our suspicions about the man. From the information I learned up north, he is our man." Theo gave Jem and Jamie a quick overview of his discoveries.

"Aye. Well, we have our man for sure then. And you can bet he has her up there somewhere. This is good. We'll go on up, watch the place, find her, and bring her out." He shot Theo a warning look. "It must be done with care. We cannot have a shootout. I'll not risk her to that."

"I want the magistrate summoned," Theo demanded. "I want them arrested. We will head up there, Jem and me. But I want Jamie sent to bring in the magistrate."

The magistrate was stationed in the next village. It would take some time for Jamie to ride to summon him and more time to bring him back to Sheffeld manor. But it must be done.

Jem and Jamie looked at him with identical expressions of horror.

"You can't be serious, man?" Jem looked rattled for the first time. "We handle our own justice here."

"Not this time." Theo was firm.

The sailors looked at each other as though certain Theo had lost his mind.

"We are smugglers. We can't summon the magistrate," Jamie objected.

Theo raised his voice. "She is the Countess of Pembroke whether she is dressed as a bloody pirate or not." He pointed at Jamie and narrowed his eyes. "And you will tell him that. Sheffeld is holding the countess against her will and he will pay the price."

Jem raised his brows, looking at Theo with interest.

"Aye." He nodded, his expression sly. "You have a point. And the magistrate is a good Yorkshire man. He'll know what to do with the renegade revenue boys.

It was settled. Jem and Theo would ride down the old mill road and make their way up the draw to Sheffeld manor. Once there, they would do surveillance, hoping to find where Captain Berg and Sheffeld had Arabella. Their aim would be to free her without confronting Sheffeld or any of the men he may have there. Jamie would ride for the magistrate.

When Jem and Theo approached the mill, they were surprised to find more than a half a dozen horses and men milling about. The captains had joined them. They would have help.

For now, he would think of nothing but her rescue. Each time his mind tried to go to a negative scenario, he pushed the thoughts away. He would get his Arabella back, one way or another.

Chapter Thirty

Arabella managed to skid the crate across the floor by shoving it with her feet. She hopped on top of the box and smiled when she realized her teeth would indeed reach the lantern's handle hooked upon its wire holder.

She was able to free it without much trouble. For once, she was thankful for the scarf that covered her cheek. It protected her from being burned from the lantern's heated sides.

Burning the rope was another matter. She winced and gritted her teeth as the flames scalded her wrists, which were already coated in dried blood. Tears ran down her cheeks as she fought the pain with deep calming breaths, forcing herself to hold her bindings over the fire and watching the rope begin to char. When she could tolerate it no longer, she rubbed out the flames against her legs. The rope was frayed and burned thin. Shifting back to the crate she began to work the ropes back and forth against the corner of the wooden box. After only half a dozen strong swipes the rope gave way.

She sat on the floor, assessing her damaged wrists. They had begun to blister. There was nothing she could do except to ignore them. She had freed her body. She longed for her cutlas. When they pulled back the doors, whoever was first to step inside would have had her blade at their unsuspecting throat. It would have been her freedom.

She needed a weapon. She looked grimly around the room, but there was nothing. She thought about the silk crates. She could use a piece of board to smash the first man to enter the building in the head, and possibly leave him incapable, but that would do her no good. She was sure Sheffeld had gone to get the captain. He had told her that. If there were at least two of them, the second man would have her. She might even be shot.

She touched her hands to her belly and closed her eyes. Her babies rested there. She felt a wave of nausea and fought it off. She had to survive. There were three of them in this room and she was their captain. Besides which, Theo would never forgive her if she failed. Even if she were dead, he would forever blame her for this disaster.

She looked at the boxes of silk. She could burn and smooth a piece of wood to make a weapon, but it would be unlikely to be effective. Wood did not make a good blade. She glanced down at the lantern again. It held the only metal in the room. The rotating shield consisted of a series of metal segments designed to allow its user to adjust the intensity of light needed or even to direct a flash of light. It was metal, thin, and thus easily swiveled between the lantern's cap and a groove close to its base. A segment of that would make a sound and deadly blade. She smiled.

Removing the lantern's cap and freeing a segment took only minutes. She looked at her weapon appreciably. Its edges were thin and jagged. Perfect. She laughed when she realized that its blade was so sharp, she would have to create a hand hold. Using bits of wood and silk to hold the hilt in place, she completed the task. Turning her weapon in her hand, she tested its balance. It was not her cutlas, but it would slice a throat easily.

She turned down the lantern light to dim. Let them lose a second while their eyes adjusted to the light. She needed every advantage.

It had been a long and busy night. Now all she had to do was watch and wait. She climbed up her stack of silks. This time the journey was an easy one. She pushed down several crates to make herself a seat from which she could peer between the crack at the eaves with ease.

There was a chance now to defeat her captors. Arabella balanced her makeshift knife in her hand, visualizing what she must do when they entered. She prayed the element of surprise would be enough to help her overcome the strength of the men. If the first to pull the sliding door open was the captain, she would have him by the throat and negotiate her freedom. If it was Sheffield, who was taller and heavier, she might not be able to have the knife at his throat before he overpowered her.

Chapter Thirty-One

Theo sat amongst the shrubbery which surrounded the Sheffeld place. Jem was beside him. Poor Jem had to hunch his massive body to allow the shrubs to shield him from view.

All along the perimeter of the estate, the smugglers sat silently. They waited patiently for some movement or sign which might indicate Ara's presence. Thus far, there had been nothing. It did not look as though there were even servants about the place. All was still.

Theo thought about Arabella as he waited. He tried not to consider the possibility she had not survived the night. He controlled his fear by thinking about how he could punish her when she was safe. If she were not pregnant, he could beat her. He smiled at the thought of holding her bare butt on his lap and slapping it until it was a nice stinging red. This time, she had pushed the limits too far. He would not do her any damage and by god, she deserved it. She had sworn to give up her life as a smuggler and he was determined to see that she do it.

If she lived. He pushed the thought away as he had done a thousand times since he had discovered her gone. Concentrate on your retribution, he reminded himself.

Jem was sure she would survive intact, and she bloody well better. He looked at the big man beside him. It seemed as though Jem had not once considered the possibility she had not survived or that they would be unsuccessful. His quiet assurance gave him confidence. Jem was a rock. Nothing could deter him from his goal. Theo would take his lead from him.

The bushes began to shift and rustle on either side of him. The smugglers were becoming impatient. It had been over an hour since they had squatted down to watch and wait. And almost two since they had come together for their makeshift meeting at the mill, before beginning their trek up the draw.

Gathered at the mill, the captains' biggest concern had been who would be the leader of the group. Theo had tried to take charge, but they had dismissed his claim quickly. He could hardly argue he had the right as Captain Ara's husband, thus he had been forced to remain silent.

Captain Barr had shouted, "I am the oldest and the senior captain here. I claim the right."

His pronouncement had been met with a chorus of protests. Each of the burly captains had hollered their qualifications.

Theo was about to yell that they did not need a leader; they just needed to get on with it. He was becoming more and more frustrated with this ridiculous competition. They were wasting valuable time.

It was finally Jem who put an end to the debate. "As Ara's first mate, I claim the role," he said in his quiet voice.

Theo had been surprised to see the captains pause and

listen to his words. It was apparent Jem commanded some respect of his own. Besides, he was not a part of the rivalry between the captains.

Jem had continued firmly, "I am the leader of this posse and will hear no further arguments on this matter."

And so, they now waited for his command.

Theo was about to break the silence and share with Jem his concerns about the restlessness of the men, when the sound of hoof beats interrupted his thoughts. Two horses, coming at a gallop. To his surprise, they trotted past the house, heading instead to the bluffs across the grounds. As they passed where he was hidden, Theo saw with satisfaction that it was Captain Berg and his cohort, Sheffeld.

They stopped at the bluff and dismounted. Theo looked more carefully at the grove of trees and saw what appeared to be a corner of a building peeking out from the thick brush. He had missed that. There was a rustling sound amongst the shrubs as three telescopes extended for a closer look.

The grating screech of a sliding door preceded the captain and Sheffeld's disappearance into the shed.

It was time to move.

Chapter Thirty-Two

Arabella watched as the riders approached. It was time. She hopped down from the crates and took her place beside the door. She pressed her back solidly against the wall, holding her weapon ready. This time, it was not just fear that pulled her belly tight, but anticipation. She relished the idea of slitting the captain's throat but dismissed this thought. She needed his life as a bargaining chip to buy her freedom.

She heard them work the lock on the door. The chains rattled as they slid between the handles.

Sheffeld's voice could be heard saying, "He is tied up right and tight."

"Ah well," the voice of the captain said. "You did good. We will get a pretty penny for him and more if what he said about his hoard is true."

The captain stepped into the room. In a flash, Arabella flung her arm about him and had him by the throat. She allowed her blade to slice just a little into his throat before she pulled him back.

She felt him still beneath her grasp and smiled. "Don't

235

move," she snarled into his ear. She gave her hand another jerk to slice his neck once more. "And tell your man to drop his pistol. Before his bullet kills me, my last action will be to cut your scrawny throat."

"Sheffeld," the captain said, his voice a high-pitched squeaking sound, "drop your weapon. The man means business."

"And do it slowly. Then you can step inside and lay with your hands above your head," Ara instructed. She pulled the captain back and to the side.

She watched Sheffeld's every move. When he was situated as she wanted him, she used her free hand to reach down and grab the captain's pistol, which she flung high. It landed on the crates with a plunk.

She forced the captain to the door. Using her foot, she gave the door a solid shove. It slid open easily.

Her eyes widened in shock. Lined up along the open doorway were smugglers. They looked a fearless lot. Each held a weapon leveled and ready. Several held both cutlas and pistol. She spotted Jem and Theo amongst the crew. Their mouths were open in shock. They had expected a battle, but instead the fight was over. Ara had defeated the revenue men before they could provide any assistance. She smiled at them beneath her ragged mask.

"You're just in time to help me bind them up, boys," she said in the voice of Ara. "There's rope hung on the wall to your right."

Her voice shook them out of their frozen positions. The room burst into a hub of activity. Captain Gorge grabbed Berg from her and flung him to the ground. He held his foot firmly on his neck, while others rushed to tie his hands behind his back and secure his legs. In only minutes, both men were firmly tied up and braced against the tubs. To add further insult, Captain Peasley had ripped strips from his grimy shirt which were used to gag them.

She looked at Theo and her stomach turned. He made to walk towards her, but she shook her head. He stopped dead in his tracks. His lips tightened and he stared at her, his face a mask of anger.

But if he came near her now, she would fall into his arms and let him hug her. It would not do. Not here in front of all the captains. She glared at him, willing him to understand. She looked meaningfully at the captains and slowly shook her head once more.

Jem walked between them. He put a hand on Theo's shoulder.

"Leave her this," he murmured to Theo. "You'll have her alone soon enough."

Her eyes followed Theo as he withdrew and leaned against the door frame, glowering at her from across the room.

Then all eyes turned to the doors at the sound of horses approaching. Jamie had arrived with the magistrate and three of the constable's men.

A chorus of curses filled the room. "Bloody hell. I just finished doing a count on these tubs. I had the loot divided and we'd have seen a tidy reward for this day's work."

"Ah, the bastards," Captain Gorge growled, "always there to take away the prize from the working blokes."

"I want no part of this," Peasley muttered. "I'll be heading out and leave the sorting of this mess to the likes of the earl here."

He looked over at Ara. "You're a fine legend, to be sure. I'll have a few good stories to tell of this day."

"Aye." Captain Barr chuckled. "You hardly needed us.

My only sadness is that we didn't get to string 'em up before the law got here."

The boys packed up to go. When Captain Gorge passed Theo, who was still braced against the door frame, he pointed a finger directly into his face. Looking down at him with his hawk face close and intimidating, he said, "It's you who must see to finishing the job here. We all expect to hear the tales of these villains hanging from the gallows."

The smugglers left, melting back into the shrubbery to head down the draw and back to their waiting horses.

Theo strode across the room and grabbed Arabella. He yanked her scarf down around her chin and searched her face. Then he pulled her tight against his body and held her there, squeezing her hard.

"Theo, you are crushing me."

He arched back, still holding her firmly, and pulled the tattered hat from her head, flinging it to the ground in disgust. Her braid tumbled down her chest. He arranged it neatly, before meeting her eyes.

"I am all right, Theo. Really, I am."

He did not respond but gazed down at her belly.

"And they are fine too," she said.

He went to take her arm as the magistrate approached. When he saw the burnt blisters and the blood upon her wrists, he glared wordlessly at her. Letting her hand drop, he slid his arm around her waist instead, ready to give a statement to the magistrate.

When the magistrate had all the evidence he needed to arrest Captain Berg and Sheffeld, he informed Theo he would be coming to Harwood to take his formal statement later in the day. It felt as though only minutes had passed when Arabella, Jem, and Theo were walking down the trail to the mill. Theo kept his arm firmly around her until they reached their horses.

She realized Theo had not spoken a word to her when he finally broke his silence and said, "No," as she attempted to mount her horse. "You will ride with me."

He tied her horse's reins to his saddle horn and boosted her up. Then he mounted up behind her, taking the reins.

Jem too remained silent. He rode beside them, and though she glanced at him hoping to appeal to him for help with Theo, he stubbornly refused to even look at her.

She sighed. Everyone was angry with her. She could not understand why. She had gone up the draw and had been captured but all had ended well. Even now, the captain and Sheffeld were tied to a horse and on their way to prison. The ring of thieves had been broken up. Theo had even gotten his way; the scoundrels arrested, instead of hung as the captains had so wanted.

It was going to be another long night if Theo wanted to argue with her. She was exhausted. She leaned back against Theo and let her eyes close.

She awakened in Theo's arms as he carried her into the receiving room and laid her on the sofa. She vaguely heard Celeste's voice raised in alarm, chattering in rapid French. And then Jem was tending her wrists. As a batsman, Jem had treated a variety of wounds on the battlefield. She trusted him, yet she had to close her eyes and could not seem to hold her wrists out to him while he tried to clean her wounds. Theo eventually had to hold her arms, so that Jem could finish cleaning, then apply his stinging ointment before bandaging them up for her.

"I will come by and change these bandages tomorrow. Keep them dry. You have some nasty bruising, but the rest of you will heal fine," Jem said. He laid a huge hand on the top of her head and patted her once before leaving.

She felt abandoned. She closed her eyes tight to fight back the tears that threatened to run down her cheeks. She did not succeed.

Then, though she protested she could walk, Theo scooped her up and carried her up the stairs to the bedroom. Celeste helped her get into a warm soft nightie and she fell asleep instantly.

She awoke only once more as she felt Theo's arm slide around her and pull her back against his warm body.

Chapter Thirty-Three

Theo lay in bed and stared at the ceiling. Beside him lay his wife, her face a picture of innocence in sleep. A wave of hopelessness washed over him. Today she had risked both her life and the life of the child she held in her womb. He was not angry. This was beyond anger. There seemed to be no solution.

I will forever be second to this persona. She cannot give it up, not for me and not for any future family we may have. Today was proof enough.

She had been close to death these past few days. She could not continue to be Captain Ara without ultimately facing the horrendous consequences of that choice. It was only a matter of time before she would be caught. Next time, she would be killed. But all of this seemed to have no impact on her. There was nothing else to offer her. Everything he was, and all he had, was not enough.

He could think of no way forward. He rubbed his hand over his face.

Where do we go from here? How can I even speak to her tomor-

row? What is there to say? All these questions plagued him. The realization that he could not bear to face the morning washed over him. He was nauseous.

Carefully, he pulled his arm away from her warm belly. He slipped from the bed, looking down at her.

I cannot do it, Arabella. I cannot stand by while you risk your life, and everything we have together.

He gently tucked the sheets around her and retreated to his room, where he packed a few clothes. Minutes later, he was quietly shutting his door.

He saddled his horse and led it from the stables at a walk, so as not to wake or alarm the household. He thought of the four of them doing the same the other night and laughed bitterly at his naivety. They would have no need to hide their activities now.

"I will leave them to it," he said aloud.

———————

When Arabella awoke in the late morning, Theo was gone. At first, she thought he had found some activity to occupy himself. His horse was not in the stables. Because Jem had brought the sheep, she assumed Theo was in the gully fencing the pasture with him. But that was not the case. Jem returned to change her bandages having not seen or heard from Theo.

When he did not join her for supper, she began to panic. She ran up to his room. His case was missing. His closet was in disarray, as though he had rooted through it.

He had left her. She was sure of it.

She staggered back to her room and fell into bed. And she cried. She cried until there were no more tears left. She cursed herself for heading up the draw that fateful night.

She wished he had given her the chance to explain her feelings towards him and the babies. As a prisoner, when everything was hopeless, she had discovered just how much her new family meant to her. It was the babies she carried in her belly, and Theo, which had given her the strength to survive. She longed to tell him that when she needed it most, her strength had come from her little family and not Captain Ara.

She cursed her stubborn stupidity. She had tried to hang on to what was, instead of looking to the future. She had had it all and let it slip away.

And worst of all, she admitted it had been her monstrous ego which had driven her to the choices she had made. It seemed as though she had always been in competition, starting with Aran and her need to surpass him in all their endeavors. Had she had a mother, things might not have progressed to the point they had. But she had grown up wild here in Yorkshire, with only men as her role models and only their pursuits had seemed of value.

But she enjoyed the competition. Her exploits at the Sheffeld place had gained her the respect of the smugglers. She had secured forever her legend as Captain Ara. Yet she had lost.

She was ready now to give up all that was Captain Ara. She was ready now to be the countess that Theo wanted. But it was too late. She was not sure how she would even live without him. She had to press her belly to remind herself, she would somehow go on. It was a long time before she was able to set aside her misery and fall asleep.

In the morning, she was nauseous once more. The babies had given her only two short days of release from the morning's agonies. She ran to her dressing room and the basin which awaited her. She retched until there was nothing left in her to retch.

She wandered back to bed feeling numb. There was no point in getting up at all. Breakfast and dinner trays came and went.

After two days, Celeste made a determined attempt to rouse her.

"Up, *cherie*. You must get up. It is time to dress." She pulled at her hand. "Come, my girl, enough of bed. You need to face the day. The sun is shining."

Arabella only rolled over, pulling the pillow over her head to block the sound of Celeste's cajoling.

She roused herself to eat a little food each day. Unfortunately, most of it was immediately vomited. As the days passed, she found she had little energy to do anything other than sleep. And she thought of nothing. It was too painful to consider Theo or the babies. It was so much better just to sleep.

Then Jem arrived. He simply scooped her up and carried her outside.

"It is time for a little fresh air, Arabella." He took her down to the garden patio and plopped her down on a wooden chair. Celeste wrapped a blanket around her, as she was still in her nightgown. Arnold brought her a tray of fruit.

Jem pulled a chair up beside her. "Missy, your Harwood is here waiting for you. I'll give you a day to eat and regain your strength. Then you'll ride with me to check the progress on the homesteads. There are decisions to be made." He handed her a piece of apple. "Eat."

She ate. This time, she was able to keep it down.

Jem buttered a biscuit and handed it to her. "We've repaired the shepherd's cabin," he said. "The new man is living comfortably and happy for employment. His boy has gone north to purchase a couple of dogs. He insists the job cannot be done without them. I know little about the matter of sheep, but if a sheepdog is required, then so be it." Jem chuckled.

Arabella looked at him, giving him the ghost of her smile. It was the most she had heard him talk in a long while.

Jem handed her another biscuit, then carried on. "The millhouse is ready. Theo was right to bring in the crews. The work is being completed quickly."

At the mention of Theo's name, she began to cry. Great wrenching sobs wracked her body. "I have lost Theo, Jem, and it hurts so bad."

Jem stood and held her shoulders, letting her cry. When she eased, Celeste handed him a handkerchief. He pushed it into Arabella's hand. She mopped her face and blew her nose.

"There." Jem patted her. "Don't be worrying about Theo. He'll be back. The man can't keep from you, and this I know. Give him a little time, love."

"Do you think so, Jem?"

"I'm sure of it." He helped her to her feet. "But for now, today, you'll dress. And you'll spend the day outside."

Arabella did as she was told. To her surprise, she found she was able to move through the day. She ate a meal for supper. That night she fell into a natural dreamless sleep. For the first time, she felt as though she might survive.

One morning after more than a week, Celeste arrived with a piece of mail for her. She looked at the envelope. Theo's handwriting was scrawled across its face. Her heart leapt. She snatched the letter from Celeste. Her first impulse was to rip it open.

She paused. What if the letter was a goodbye? Or perhaps he had just relayed instructions for their continued existence apart, with no personal input at all; that would be worse.

Her stomach heaved. Grabbing the letter, she hurried to the basin in her dressing room. She kept the letter beside her, propped up on the pitcher while she was sick. Each time she glanced at it, her stomach turned.

"It will have to be read," she whispered aloud. She could not face it yet.

Chapter Thirty-Four

Theo rode through the night, haunted by the image of her face. Each time her luminous eyes appealed to him; he crushed the thought. She had made her choice clear.

After twelve hours in the saddle, he stopped at an inn. He slept. The morning saw him back on the road. By habit, he found he was on the way to London. It is just as good a destination as any.

He arrived in his townhouse and roamed the silent rooms, his boots echoing on the tiled floors. Arabella was right; the place was a mausoleum. The well-trained servants were invisible, except when required for direct service. He had never felt alone in his city home, yet now his loneliness plagued him.

He spent a week getting drunk daily in his club. There was no reprieve there for him either. As the days passed, he only found himself more weary and sick from the excessive amounts of brandy. And still the image of his beautiful wife haunted him. The one outcome of his drunken presence must have been to alert the gossips. He received an unwelcome visitor on the eighth day.

"A guest to see you, sir." His footman stood at the library door. "A Madame Dierdra Barum."

"Tell her I am not receiving," Theo responded, pouring himself a brandy.

Dierdra brushed past his butler and entered the room. "Theo, you cannot hide from me. When I heard you were in town, and alone this time, I knew I had to see you."

She strolled into the room, removing her shawl, and tossing it into a chair.

She had obviously spent a great deal of time on her appearance. Her hair was elaborately coiled around her head. Her makeup was liberally applied; her lips glowed bright red. He glanced down at her and noticed she wore a neckline so low, her ample bosom threatened to spill out. The bodice of her gown was embroidered over sheer lace, leaving little to the imagination.

He got up from his desk, walked around the front of it, and leaned back against it. Dierdra was here for one thing. Maybe two, he thought grimly. She might want him, but he was sure part of her motivation was revenge on Arabella. He looked at her. Maybe she would be able to dull the pain he felt.

She sauntered to his desk. Her gown hinted at her body beneath it. It was clear she wore nothing under those skirts. She came up to him, close enough for him to reach out and touch her, if it was what he desired. She took a deep breath, arching her back to emphasize the red orbs peeking through her revealing bodice. Dierdra had dressed for her role.

He took a drink of brandy, watching her listlessly. "What is it you want, Dierdra?"

His lips twisted into a humorless grin.

"I think you need a little comfort, darling," she purred. "I came as soon as I heard you were in town."

She reached down and slid her hand into his partially opened shirt. She let her fingers trail across his body. Smiling at what she considered his acquiescence, she used her other hand to undo the buttons on his shirt. He let her. She pulled his shirt wide and examined his bare chest.

"The wild cat you call wife does not know how to manage you." She said, purring softly. "You must remember how good we were together."

She leaned forward to kiss his bared skin while her arms slipped around him to run up and down his back.

Theo stood absolutely still while she licked and stroked him. She began to unclasp his belt. Her perfume was sweet and cloying, filling his senses. He looked down at her long-painted nails as they worked the buttons on his fly, swallowing the bile in his throat. The thought of making love to Dierdra was too much for him to bear.

She gave a throaty chuckle, reaching into his open trousers to grasp him.

He reached down and grabbed her hand, stilling her progress. Slowly, he put her hand back on the desk beside him and stood erect. Wordlessly, he redid his belt, then his shirt. She took a step back and watched him.

With his clothing readjusted, he looked at her. Addressing her in a flat, emotionless voice, he said, "Dierdra, you need to leave. I do not want you, nor can I foresee a future where I ever will."

Dierdra eased herself away from his desk. Her eyes flashed with an angry glitter. She walked across the room and picked up her shawl. Draping it over her shoulder, she shrugged. "It is your loss, Theo. I have other fish to fry."

"Then I will leave you to it, Dierdra. Close the door on your way out."

Dierdra strutted to the door. She glared at him a final time.

"Not a problem!" She sneered, before slamming the door with a crash.

Theo returned to sit at his desk. He breathed a long, drawn-out sigh. He wished he had wanted Dierdra, that he could take her with the abandon he had felt not so long ago. But he could not. Arabella had entered his mind and nothing, it seemed, could exorcise her.

He could not indulge in another day of drunkenness. He flung his glass into the fireplace, feeling a sense of satisfaction when it shattered. Living without Arabella was too painful. There was no reprieve. Drunk or sober, she possessed him.

On a whim, he went to his room and packed his case. He was going to visit Ambrose. Maybe there he would find a solution to this agony.

———

Five hours later, he rode his horse into the stables at The Meadows. He arrived in time for their evening meal.

Kate took his arm at the door. "I do not know what brings you here, Theo, but I am so pleased with the visit. We were just sitting down to supper. Won't you join us?" She turned to the footman. "Take his things to the green room, Ned."

She patted Theo's arm and gave him a toothy smile. "I will give you a few minutes to freshen up, but then I expect you to join us in the dining room. We will wait supper for you."

"Thank you, Kate. It is just what I need. It was a rather grueling ride. I won't keep you waiting too long." He glanced at his best friend who had joined them in the entry and nodded his greeting. "Ambrose."

Ambrose looked at him with concern. Theo realized he must make a sorry sight. He was dusty from the ride, with eyes that itched from lack of sleep. "Theo, this is an unexpected visit," Ambrose said reaching out to shake his hand, "but a welcome one."

"Yes," he said shaking Ambrose's hand, "It was a...an impulsive decision Ambrose. I hope I am not imposing."

"Not at all." Ambrose smiled as Theo turned towards the stairs.

After changing and washing up, he stood before the mirror in his room and looked at his haggard face. He was clean, but his eyes were circled in black as though he had not slept in days. He sighed. There was little more he could do to improve his appearance. He turned from his reflection and hurried to the dining room.

Kate and Ambrose waited for him at the table. "Please sit down Theo. It will be such a pleasure to have a guest for dinner." She nodded to a footman to begin the service. The meal was eaten in silence. He felt the eyes of his hosts on him as he ate. Now that he was here with his friends, he had no idea how to begin to confide in them. The tension in the room was palpable.

"Out with it, Theo," Ambrose said. "You look terrible. I would be willing to wager something has occurred with that pirate wife of yours. You might as well tell us what has happened."

"She is not a pirate. Ambrose. She is a smuggling captain. There is a difference," Theo said in a weary voice and sighed.

"Whatever." Ambrose brushed the distinction aside. "What has happened, Theo? You would not be here if you were not planning to confide in us. Let's get it done with."

Theo recapped the events of last week. When he spoke of Arabella's pregnancy, he had to squeeze his eyes closed for several minutes before he could continue. Ambrose and Kate were silent. When he had completed his tale, Kate reached over and patted his hand.

"I am not surprised. Oh, my poor Arabella. What a trial this must have been for her." She shook her head sadly.

Theo and Ambrose looked at her with a curious expression.

"I, too, would have struggled to give up my designing for this marriage." She nodded at Ambrose. "Fortunately, we are able to go to town frequently which allows me to keep abreast of the fashions. And then, of course, I can arrange my days to allow me to work here."

She motioned to her footman to serve tea.

"The way I see it…" She took a sip of tea. "Your problem is her occupation is illegal and therefore dangerous. What you need is a solution which allows her to run her little business on the right side of the law."

She took another sip of tea and reached for a square from the dessert platter. Both men stared at her as she munched her brownie.

"One can hardly expect a woman of Arabella's nature to give up her whole life for her marriage, and she needn't have to." She took another bite, chewing thoughtfully. "It is simple, really. She needs apparatus and freedom to engage in legal trade. Then *voila*, problem solved."

She reached for a second treat. "I mean, have the two of you even discussed the idea of her pursuing a captain's role in legal trade? Surely if she was accepted by the ruffians on the coast, she will be able to make her way in the shipping world."

Holding her brownie like a pointer, she gestured toward him. "My aunt has run several businesses for years. Of course, she has a manager for propriety's sake, but the management of the operation is hers." She took a bite of her dainty. "It can be done, with a modicum of discretion of course."

Theo stared at her with his mouth ajar, rising slowly from his chair. "Kate!"

He rushed over to her and hugged her. She had to struggle with her brownie, to keep him from knocking it from her hands in his exuberance.

"You are a genius. That's it!" He hugged her again. This time he dislodged the brownie. Kate frowned as it fell to the floor.

"I will leave for London immediately. There is a solution!" He leaned down and kissed Kate hard on the lips. Ambrose half rose from his seat to protest. "I can design her a ship. There is much to be done!"

"Whoa. Theo, sit down," Ambrose said in his commander's voice.

Theo instinctively followed his order.

"It's Bristol you want, Theo. It is where you will find a shipbuilder. You are not thinking clearly. Finish your meal, then you will stay the night. Anyone who looks at your ragged face can see you need some rest." He frowned at him. "There is plenty of time."

"Yes," Kate added, "and after you have had a hot bath and are settled in your room, you can write Arabella a letter. I get the feeling she is beyond worry."

After supper, Theo did just that. Having sent the letter, he lay in bed making his plans. He was sure he would be unable to sleep in his enthusiasm to bring this idea to fruition.

A ship of her own, and the opportunity to command it. It was such an obvious solution. He thought of the woman of power and expertise he had seen on the Bella. She had rightfully earned a position of respect among her crew and peers. Her courage was evident in her escape from the revenue captain. She had done what few others could have accomplished. Even he would have been hard pressed not to give up when in that predicament.

He began to understand what he had expected her to give up. It had been too much. Captain Ara was a part of her. It was a huge chunk of the strong woman he had married.

He laughed aloud. "My god, I think I too would miss that part of her," he said. It was a strange epiphany. He let the knowing of it settle into his being. "I would truly mourn its loss."

His mind jumped back to the solution with renewed enthusiasm. Arabella would have to approve the ship's final design. She was sure to have requirements of her own. If it was to be her ship, she needed to be part of its creation. He would surprise Arabella with a plan she could alter, not a final product.

"I am coming home to you, love," he whispered, as he fell into a deep sleep.

Chapter Thirty-Five

Arabella diligently cleaned her teeth and washed her hair, looking all the while at the folded letter Theo had sent her. She picked it up and returned to her room to sit on the edge of her bed and stare at the paper. She was afraid. She had never been so afraid in her life. Her stomach twisted, and she knew that had she not vomited already she would do so again now.

Finally, she took a deep breath, flipped open the letter, and read.

My Dearest Wife,

I hope this letter finds you and our baby healthy and well. You have been forever in my thoughts. Though distance separates us, know you are with me each moment. I have been to London, then Kent to visit Ambrose and Kate. Kate sends her warmest regards.

It seems I have spent a lifetime thinking about you, and about us. Kate has helped me to see our situation from a new perspective. I will be eternally grateful to her. I know now I cannot be forever hopelessly competing with your persona Captain Ara, and your love of the sea. I know too that we have been able to compromise in the past. There was always a deal to be made. I have thought of an excellent bargaining chip. I have come to realize you will be forever unhappy without at least the sea in your future and the title of captain before your name. I plan to rectify that.

As you know, the journey home to you is a long one. There is still a matter of business I must accomplish. I will be at least another week, perhaps longer. For the love of god, try to stay out of any life-threatening situations until I return.

Your loving husband,
Theo

Arabella held the note to her breast and wept. She had her Theo. This time, she would hold him with more care. Somehow, she would find a way to make this marriage work. She wiped away her tears and, smiling, she massaged her belly.

"Well, my children," she thought aloud, "we still have your papa, and this time we will not disappoint him."

She vowed to get through the whole week without a single misstep.

She hired three men from the village and began to reconstruct the garden. Her plans to revive the beauty of its former splendor filled her days. It was there she was able to restore her energy, and concentrate on something other than Theo. The time ticked by too slowly for her to simply wait, counting the hours.

Once most of the underbrush had been cleared away, it began to look like a garden. Flower beds were dug and replenished with soft humus. The fountain was a project. It took several days just to clean it. Jem stood beside her and watched the men scrub the tarnished marble.

"The captains are making runs again. It seems the way is clear once more," he said, watching her face with interest.

When she only shrugged, he put his heavy arm around her and gave her a little shake.

"It's proud of you I am for that," he said. "I will have one of the captains check the lace stall at Gravelines for word of Aran."

She smiled up at his big, scarred face. "Did I tell you I will be having a child? Two, actually."

"I knew it would be soon," he said, well pleased. "You will make a fine mother and wife."

"I hope so."

They both turned back to watch the stone fountain emerge from years of dirt and grime, his heavy arm still wrapped around her shoulders.

Each day, more of the property was reclaimed from the wilderness, marking through its progress the time Theo was away.

Ten days after she had received his letter, she awoke late in the night to the sound of him washing up in his room. His door had been left open the whole time he was gone. She had wanted to feel his presence. Now she waited impatiently for him, hoping he would come into her room. And hoping too, that he had forgiven her.

When he finally leaned against her doorframe, she could only smile widely at him.

"Still alive, I see," he teased. "But I suppose I will hear the tales of your adventures soon enough."

"Oh, Theo, I have been perfect. You would be proud to see the exceptional wife I have been."

"Well, that is good, because I have not yet spanked you

for your escapades the last go around." He threw off his robe and grabbed her.

She was laughing and he tickled her before flipping her over and pulling her across his knees.

"No, Theo!" she squealed, but he tickled her again until she was laughing helplessly. He pulled up her nightgown until he had her bare butt exposed. "I have dreamed of doing this since I first heard you had climbed the draw that night and by god, I will have my wish."

He patted her butt playfully.

She twisted beneath him. "Theo, you cannot be serious."

He tickled her again, and she began to laugh.

He smacked her hard across the buttocks.

"Theo!" she cried out. "That stung!"

He only laughed. Twice more he spanked her hard. She tried to squirm away from him, but he held her firmly.

Then he flipped her back facing him and kissed her with all the passion she had missed and dreamed of while he had been away.

They spent the night loving each other soundly. Theo was insatiable and gloriously happy.

He was curious about the changes in her body and spent much time analyzing even the smallest difference. He declared her breasts to have grown even larger and was astonished with how they had swelled and darkened around her nipples. He massaged her tight belly and announced that he was able discern a slight rounding between her hips. And after his complete examination, he had made love to her again, slowly and lovingly. She told him she loved him more than anything in her life and she knew it to be true.

When morning came, she slid luxuriously across the sheets. She felt sexy and wonderfully alive.

"Come on, get up. There is something I want to show you." Theo stood at the foot of the bed. He was dressed and watched, smiling, as she pulled on her robe. "What? No vomiting this morning? I miss my belly holding."

She grinned. "Sometimes they give me a reprieve."

"They?"

"There are two of them. A boy and a girl." She grinned up at him.

For some reason, he found that announcement hilarious and throwing back his head in the manner she loved so well, laughed heartily.

"Eat. Then meet me in the library."

Arabella ate her breakfast wondering what it was he was so eager to show her. She had yet to have an opportunity to explain herself to him. She needed to tell him about her determination to be the wife he wanted.

Last night, she had tried to bring up the topic, but she was loath to remind him of her choice to go to the point as Captain Ara. It seemed impossible to discuss her new resolutions without bringing up her foray to Bergen's Point. This she could not do. Not yet. She was too afraid of losing Theo to renewed anger and disappointment.

She would have to speak to him about it eventually. She wanted to tell him she was ready to give up Captain Ara forever. Just not today.

Chapter Thirty-Six

Theo laid out the plans for the ship he had designed for her on the wide desk in the library. Spreading the blueprints out, he secured the corners with paper weights. He pulled the curtains back to allow for as much light as possible.

His face flushed with pride in his accomplishment. The basic blueprint had existed. He'd just had the designer make a few adjustments. This vessel was devised with the capacity to cross the ocean if that was what she wanted to do, god forbid. Unlike The Bella which belonged to Harwood, and her brother Aran, this ship would be hers. It would carry a large cargo, not the smaller secluded loads of smuggling luggers. There was much legal trade to engage in. Time would tell what she chose to do.

After the baby, or babies, he amended with a grin, she could sail her or hire a captain if she wished.

It solved several problems. When Aran, her brother, returned it would be time for her to leave Harwood. The estate she loved and had dedicated her life to, would no longer be her responsibility. He hoped this blow would be relieved at least in part by the knowledge she had a future of her own. The more he considered the ship, and the possibilities it would provide for his Arabella, the more pleased he was with the purchase.

And she could be the captain once more. He mentally sent Kate another heartfelt thank you.

Arabella entered the room. Pausing in the doorway, she looked at him curiously, her head tilted to the side. Then she strolled to the desk and looked down at his designs.

"It is yours, Arabella. It will be yours to do with as you wish." He leaned back on his feet, spreading his arms wide, and grinned at her. "My only stipulation is that whatever you do, it is legal."

"Theo, it's...it's too much. You do not have to give me this."

The smile slowly died on his face as he watched her face fall into an expression of pure misery. She burst into a flood of tears. Hurrying around the desk to hold her, he frowned in confusion. He had thought his gift would make her happy; instead, she seemed devastated. Arabella sobbed with great painful heaves.

"What is it? Do you not want this ship? Arabella, I only want your happiness." His words seemed to bring on another rush of tears. She cried aloud. He rubbed her back and murmured to her, but nothing could comfort her.

It took forever for her to calm. Theo gave her his handkerchief and she mopped her face and blew her nose. He led her to a chair and nudged her down to sit.

Kneeling in front of her, he asked, "What is it, love? Please let me know what is bothering you."

"Oh, Theo. I love you so much." She hiccupped and blew her nose before continuing. "When you were away, I realized how much I love you. That I should be such a... a poor wife that you must give me this."

She rested her forehead on his chest. "I do not need this to love you, Theo. I feel as though I have shown you that you must buy my love and it is not true."

She looked up at him and said more firmly, "You are enough for me, Theo. I can be your countess now. I am ready to be the wife and mother you want. I have been so wrong, Theo. You must forgive me."

"No. No," he said, "I didn't buy this, my dear, to earn your love. I have known you loved me for a long time, Arabella, maybe even before you recognized it yourself."

He pulled her back and looked at her. "It is true. I think you have loved me since that first day at the mill. And I have always known what we have together is special; that you will forever be the love of my life. I love you with my whole heart, Arabella."

He took her face in his hands and held her steady. He looked directly into the wide mahogany eyes he loved so well and brushed the dark, tearstained skin of her cheek with his fingers.

"This ship was not a gift purchased to buy your love, my wife. This is a gift for the Ara in you. I love her too. When I saw the proud and fierce part of you, it scared me. I feared for you. But I soon learned that like everything about you, it is precious. I have decided I selfishly want to keep my Arabella, with her Ara. I love every part of you, my love."

"Oh, Theo." She flung her arms around him. She cried again. This time it was for pure joy.

He looked at her fresh tears, threw back his head, and laughed.

Epilogue

The Resurrection sailed slowly up the Thames towards the docks in London's busy harbor.

Arabella yelled to her crew, "Drop the mainsail, boys. We'll glide her in."

Theo left the rail where he and his son Jacob had watched the city slowly emerge. He stood behind his wife where she commanded from the helm and slid his hands around her waist, feeling the massive bulge with pride. This new baby would be born at home. It had been a very productive trip indeed, he thought with a grin.

The ship carried coffee, tea, silks, and spices, some from distant East Asia. They had gone as far as South Africa's Port Elizabeth on her eastern coast. The winds were always high around the cape; it was the season for its famous brutal storms.

Arabella had refused to chance it with the children on board. They had instead purchased their goods in Port Elizabeth. Arabella seemed satisfied with their load. She was pleased with her profit margins. After this trip, she hoped to purchase a third ship and expand her business once again. Increasingly she had begun to rely on her captains to sail for her. This excursion had been the first in a long while. Now with her pregnancy, she was determined to retire from the actual operation of the ships completely and concentrate on managing her business from home.

Theo saw a blur swing down towards the deck. Realizing it was Faith, his wayward daughter, he was about to yell a reprimand, when Arabella beat him to it.

"Faith, leave the rigging be," she ordered. "Go join your twin at the rail and behave yourself."

He watched amused, as Faith stomped in indignation across the deck and stood beside Jacob. Jacob only glanced at her before turning his serious eyes to shore. He was eager to be back on land. Of the two of them, it was his black-haired daughter who most loved the sea. Jacob tired of the endless vistas of blue. He was bored with the tedium of life on the Resurrection, wanting desperately to get home.

Not so Faith. She gloried in life at sea. She was everywhere, learning everything she could. Despite her constant questions and sometimes dangerous presence underfoot, she was the favorite of the crew. Thankfully, they looked out for her. Keeping Faith out of mischief on board was a full-time job for all of them. Once after a suspiciously quiet interlude, they heard her voice singing from high up in the crow's nest. And there she sat on her dangerous little perch, with her chubby legs swinging to the beat of her tune.

Though Theo had enjoyed this trip, he too would be glad to have his feet firmly on the ground. There had been only one terrible day off the coast of Africa on their journey home. A pirate ship had emerged over the horizon. It was then he had been grateful for the changes Arabella had made to the ship's design.

When they had discussed the blueprints for The Resurrection, she had demanded, "I want her narrower, with a crafted carvel hull. She needs the extra sails, including one on an extended bowsprit."

Theo, who managed the accounts, had objected, "If she is narrower, you will cut down substantially on the hold space. Your cargoes will be limited."

"I think it is better to carry less and be fast enough to keep it should we meet up with renegades, don't you?" she had asked him.

"I think, my lovely wife, that you just like your speed," he had said with a laugh.

But when the pirate ship took a run at them, he admitted she had been right.

Arabella had aimed her telescope on the ship. "She is a nasty one and she's coming hard. We'll have to make a hell of a run."

Theo had turned to the cabin boy. "Take the children to the captain's quarters. Lock yourself in with them."

When he turned back to Arabella, she was already at the helm, issuing orders.

"Rig them up, boys. All sails. And make it quick!" She spun around.

There was a loud snap as the sails unfurled and caught the wind. The ship lurched forward.

"To the bow! Hook up the bowsprit."

Another sail unfurled at the bow of the ship. The Resurrection caught a strong tail wind. She broke through the waves at breakneck speeds. But the pirate ship still came.

Arabella held her steady, pushing the Resurrection and her crew to their very limit. For hours, the pirate ship tailed them. Always it gained ground, and always Arabella pushed her crew for more. And still the pirates stubbornly loomed on the horizon.

Theo stood beside her as she used her telescope to check their distance. "Oh god, Theo. They are lighter and faster than us. It is only a matter of time before they board us."

A black storm cloud loomed on the horizon due north. Arabella turned directly into its path.

Theo looked at the ominous black clouds ahead. "The storm looks dangerous, Arabella."

"We are going to have a hard night, love, but it's the only way." Her eyes flashed with a fierce glint. "We can't let them take us with the children on board. It's the only option."

"If anyone can take us through, Ara, it's you."

As they moved beneath the mammoth clouds, it began to rain. Then the winds rose, and a frightening storm surge beat down on them, and still Arabella pushed forward. It was only when a monster wave washed across the deck in a fury, scattering anything not secured, even the crew, that she let up.

The Resurrection was dangerously listing to portside, pushed by a raging storm surge when at last she hollered, "Drop the sails."

After five hours of battling monstrous waves, Theo tried to relieve her. "Let me take the wheel, Arabella. Go below and get some rest."

"No, Theo. I will see us safely through this bloody gale," she shouted through the howling winds. "We've battled the worst of it."

She was drenched. Strands of black hair had pulled loose from her braid and whipped around her face in the wind. He knew there would be no reasoning with her. She would be at the helm until all danger was past.

When dawn broke, so did the winds and rain. The sea was smooth glass once more. The pastel colors of dawn reflected on the waters, gentle and serene. It was hard to imagine these very waters had only hours ago threatened their lives with its rage. And nowhere on the vast horizon was the renegade ship. They had lost her.

But Arabella was not to be deterred.

"All sails. Full speed ahead, boys," she yelled. The sails went up and the Resurrection glided through the water once more.

Theo handed her a warm mug of tea, then wrapped his arms around her from behind.

"I know you think you can battle through another day, but this little one," he said, rubbing her swollen belly, "and me, want you to get some rest."

He turned her in his arms and kissed her forehead. "Trust me. I will wake you if even a fisherman's trolley should dare to appear on your horizon."

Only then did she surrender the wheel to him, going below to get some sleep.

And now they were home. The Resurrection was docking. But there would be one more fierce battle to be fought. Duties and taxes would have to be paid on the cargo. Arabella had never grown accustomed to the revenue boys boarding her ship to assess her load. They would slap her with a steep tax before she could have her goods unloaded. It infuriated her.

"Here they come, the dirty thieves," she growled at the sight of a half a dozen green uniformed revenue men preparing to board.

Theo laughed. "Go below. Be the countess and mama. Let me deal with them."

She sighed. "I am ready to be home, Theo. I want to

lounge and nap. I will be as lazy and indolent as my grandmother."

Theo thought about those two old grandmothers who had brought them together. Once more, he thanked them for bringing the betrothal contract to his attention. He would be forever grateful.

He looked at Arabella's disgruntled face as she scowled down at the revenue boys standing on the wharf. He laughed, nudging her forward. "Go. Let me do this for you."

He kissed her once more before she turned to go below. As he watched her make her way to the cabin, he realized her walk had become a bit of a waddle. There would be no time left for her to laze about. Indeed, they would be lucky to make it back to his estate. He chuckled to himself. They had arrived home with little time to spare. His Captain Ara had, as always, pushed it to its very limit.

He too was ready for his sweet Arabella.

Author's Note

Smuggling along England's coast was a way of life since the first taxes on imports were imposed in 1688. By the nineteenth century, it had become an accepted norm. Some communities along the coast had almost a hundred percent engagement in the trade. Robin Hood's Bay, or Baytown as the locals called it, on the Yorkshire coast, bragged that a bale of silk could travel from the wharf to the town limits without ever seeing the light of day. Items were passed from house to house in a series of tunnels below ground. Records show that smuggling crews even paid a tithe to the local church. Furthermore, by the late 1800s, smugglers caught by revenue officers had to be tried at the Old Bailey in London because an unbiased jury could not be found locally. Beyond the coast, the population was not hesitant to accept the reality of the trade in exchange for duty-free goods. At one point, seventy percent of all the tea drank in England was acquired illegally. Brandy, gin, silks, and luxury goods were all often imported illegally from the continent.

Disputes between revenue men and smugglers were

commonplace. In coastal communities, the excise men were often at the mercy of a village mob. In Kent, near Reculver, two revenue men were identified. The villagers chased them through the streets. They were forced to barricade themselves in a local store. When the magistrate arrived, they were saved from certain death at the hands of the mob, but promptly charged with disrupting a local business.

That women played a role in the trade is indisputable. Though most of the actions of women were restricted to the transportation of goods on land, there were exceptions. Two notable captains were Mary Read and Anne Bonney. Mary (Mark) Read, an English woman, disguised herself as a man and fought two years for her country, serving in the English navy. When she enlisted, she was only a teenager. Upon her release, she stole and captained her own ship, working as a pirate in the Caribbean. Anne Bonney was an Irish woman who lived a similar life. Both were captured at some point, which accounts for the historical record of these female captains. As an interesting side note, some reports of Anne Bonney have her being released because of her pregnancy and living out the remainder of her life as a domesticated housewife on the coast of South Carolina.

Given these scenarios, it was not a stretch to create Captain Ara, and her wild Yorkshire home by the sea.

Next in the Regency Romance series

vinci-books.com/the-spy

The perfect spy needs the perfect cover story. Love wasn't part of the plan.

When Lady Alexis Betcher's scheming relatives threaten her with a forced marriage, she flees to join her father in Lisbon. But a twist of fate lands her in the arms of Aran Garscon, a dashing English spy masquerading as a wealthy merchant in Napoleonic France.

Turn the page for a free preview…

The Spy: Chapter One

This late at night the wharf at London's harbor was not a safe part of the city, especially if you were a woman alone, and she was. She needed to find passage aboard a ship leaving for Lisbon, and she needed to find it tonight.

At the marine terminal, an elderly watchman peered out at her through the wicket window.

When she asked about a passage, the old man squinted at her suspiciously. "Oh, aye. We have a galleon leaving at dawn. The Refuge. Bringing fodder for our troops over there. She's docked down at the far end of the wharf—still loading, last I seen." He poked his head out the window and surveyed her from her boots to her bonnet. "You look like a lady. This is not a place or a time of day for you, ma'am. I got a boy working with me. If you wait here a few minutes, I can have him escort you."

Waiting here at the terminal was not an option. She would be easily spotted, dressed in her travelling cloak, and clutching her carpet bag and reticule. She could not risk it.

"Thank you. I will find my way," she said and with a glance behind her, started her walk down the dark passage.

After only a few steps down the wharf, she began to regret her choice. The docks were eerie this time of night. The fog had rolled in and swirled around her skirts as she quickened her pace. On her right, ships lurked in the shadows, their great hulls rising and falling in the dark as though breathing the reeking water of the Thames. On the left, the dark shapes of warehouses loomed. Occasionally, a rat scuttled past.

Thankfully, she met no one for the length of the long wharf. With her carpet bag tight against her body, she walked as briskly as her skirts would allow. All she could hear was her boots echoing on the planks of the dock.

At last, through the haze of fog, the yellow glow of lanterns bobbing up and down a gang plank became visible just ahead, as a crew busily loaded a ship near the end of the pier. She stood back from the action and peered up at its hull. She could just make out the faded letters 'FUG' near its railing on the bow. And as the watchman had said, they were loading her with cargo.

This must be her, The Refuge. It did not look like a very prestigious ship. Indeed, for a ship hauling goods to the Royal Navy in Lisbon, she seemed downright derelict. But beggars could not be choosers, she thought as she looked back towards the terminal to check if she had been followed. With the heavy blanket of fog, she could only see a few feet behind her. After waiting for a break in the line of workman, she took a deep breath and hustled up the gang plank.

The captain stood on the deck hollering orders to his crew. Beside him, a boy held a lantern, which did little to light the gloomy deck. As Alexis approached, she was struck by the shabbiness of the captain. It was too dark to make out much about his person except that he wore a plain sailor's flat cap and a tattered long coat. He was certainly not one of the crisp uniformed captains she had often met in her father's company. If she had not heard one of the sailors address him as cap'n, she would not have recognized him as the man in charge.

Alexis stood at the captain's side while he ignored her. Unsure of what she should say or do, she shifted awkwardly, waiting for him to acknowledge her. Fidgeting with her reticule and scanning the wharf below for any pursuers, she tried clearing her throat several times to get his attention. The captain steadfastly avoided her gaze.

"I am looking to book a passage," she said at last, raising her voice to get his attention.

The captain froze. Turning slowly, he leered down at her. As he leaned into the lantern's glow, his face illuminated an ominous amber. His lips broke into a nasty smile. Alexis noticed he was missing several teeth. She took a step back.

"Are you, missy?"

Alexis had to grip her toes into the soles of her boots to keep herself from heading down the gangplank and back to the relative safety of the wharf. She had never travelled on her own before. On her earlier visits to her father, she had always been treated with the utmost respect. Every detail of her journey had been arranged for her.

Her father was a general in the British forces, much admired and respected. Furthermore, he was a wealthy British peer. Henry Betcher, Lord Salsbury, was a man who demanded the best for himself and his family; he invariably got it.

But she needed to board this ship.

"I will give you thirty shillings for my passage." she blurted out.

The captain did not answer her immediately. Instead, he assessed her from top to bottom as though she was a piece of merchandise.

"I suppose I can put up with the likes of you for an hour or two," he said with a sneer, "but it will be forty, not thirty, and you'll stay below. I'll not have you pestering my crew. Wouldn't haul your arse at all, except that I'm keen to do the madam a favor."

"Of all the..."

"Or ye can get off my ship. I don't like carrying passengers to start with." He scowled at her. "I like women even less."

Her cheeks flared with shock and indignation. Never in her life had someone spoken to her so rudely. She fumbled with her reticule as she struggled to count her fare. Only the thought of the report she would make to her father, and imagining his retribution, gave her some relief from her chagrin.

She handed her coins over to the man and attempted her haughtiest voice. "My father is General Betcher of the Royal Guard. He certainly will hear of my treatment here, shoddy that it is."

The captain laughed.

"And my mother is the queen of Sheba." To her horror, he reached down and swatted her on the butt. Before she could recover from the indignity, he hollered to the lad at his side, "Take her below. Lock her in. I won't have her galloping about."

Once below, she paced the tiny cabin. Again and again, she rattled its locked door.

"I have made a mistake," she muttered to herself. "How

can I journey all the way to Lisbon locked in this disgusting hold? And the captain—"

She shuddered at the thought.

More than once, she reminded herself she was escaping a worse fate. Whatever indignities she suffered here were minor compared to what she would face at home. There was simply no choice. She wished she had lived a more adventurous life back in London, that she had been more than a society belle. All the skills she had so painstakingly learned to negotiate a soiree were of no use here.

Taking a deep breath, she decided to settle into her cabin and make the best of her situation. *I have done well so far. At least here in this cabin, I am hidden and safe.*

Only minutes passed before she felt the ship begin to move out into the harbor. She propped up the single pillow on the bunk and, lying on top of the covers, resigned herself to her fate.

The ship lurched as its sails filled. Already they were on the open sea. She closed her eyes.

When she awoke, the ship was still. Rising to her knees, she peeked out the porthole above the bunk. There was not much to see. They appeared to have docked but it was still too dark to make out much of anything.

We must have stopped at an English port along the coast. Good. I will jump ship here and board a proper vessel. Everything will work out for the best.

The rattling of her door caught her attention. It squeaked open a crack, just wide enough to allow the cabin boy from last night to poke his head into the room.

"Cap'n says you are to head out now before you get in the way of the loaders. You're to hurry, ma'am," he said, stepping into the room.

"I had hoped to wash up. Could you please fetch me a basin and some water, young man?"

"Nah. No time for that. Cap'n wants ye off and gone before we unload. The boys are already in the hold. We best hurry." He grabbed her arm.

She barely had time to snatch up her belongings before he shoved her out of the room and onto the deck. In moments, she was heading down the gangplank. She paused and adjusted her bonnet. Several locks of her red hair had loosened from her bun and straggled down past her shoulders. She tried to tuck them back under her hat but was only partially successful.

This is ridiculous, she thought, still only half awake and battling her confusion. Her father would hear of all the degradation she had suffered. She managed to balance her reticule and carpet bag as she negotiated the gangplank.

"There ye go," the boy hollered from the deck when her feet hit the dock. "Gravelines in record time."

She looked up at him where he held his lantern at the top of the gangplank. In faded letters on the hull to his right, she made out the letters of the word Fugitive.

She had boarded the wrong ship.

Gravelines was a smuggler's port on the coast of France, just across the channel. Napoleon had cordoned off the walled town to exclusively accommodate the illegal trade.

She had heard her father and his cronies speak often of the town. It was said to be inhabited by the worst element of British society: thieves and traitors to the crown. They had even debated pulling into the harbor and using their canon to level the place.

"Oh no," she moaned, her stomach rolling with panic. This was not Lisbon. She had been dropped at Gravelines, of all places.

The wharf was busy this time of night. Unlike legal ports, the cover of darkness was prime business hours for the sailors here. Men hefting tubs or crates scowled at her as they pushed past her to the docked ships.

Needing a moment to think and fighting the fear gnawing at her belly, she worked her way across the busy wharf to a well-lit area just off the docks. She had no idea where to go or what to do. Perhaps her aunt was right, and she was helpless and inept, incapable of managing even her own life. Her mind revolted at the thought. Now was not the time to wallow in self-pity. She resolved to find a solution to this fiasco.

Up ahead, a lane circled the loading area. It was cluttered with carts being loaded either directly from the boats or from a series of warehouses banking the wharf to her far right. She found a clear place beneath a streetlamp and, clutching her carpet bag, she began to contemplate her predicament.

Moving to the streetlamp was a mistake. Under the light, she was clearly visible to the sailors who were heading for the rowdy taverns up the street to enjoy a much-needed drink or even a tumble in the bawdy house at the end of the lane.

A group of sailors, five or six of them, left the wharf and walked towards her. She looked down, pretending to examine the clasp on her case, hoping she would go unnoticed.

The men circled her; she was surrounded by the scurvy crewmen.

"What have we here?" A sailor in his pea jacket grinned at her. "Looks like some fresh produce for Madame's hot house."

She whirled around, thinking to escape his attentions,

but found that several more men had come up from behind her. They stretched their arms out as though herding cattle, barring her way. Wherever she turned, she saw only their faces, laughing.

"Leave me be," she said, trying to use her haughtiest voice. She hung on tight to her carpet bag. It held her jewels and the money she would need for her journey. Convinced she was about to be robbed, she hollered, "Help! Help me, please!"

"Mayhap we should be the first to sample the goods, eh boys?" an older man with a scarred face said.

"Get away from me, you swine!" She tried to force her way through the human barricade but each time she lunged forward, she was caught and shoved back to the center.

The men laughed and jeered at her. One of them ripped her bonnet from her head. A round of cheers went up when her red-gold hair tumbled down her back. She was flung back once more. Someone grabbed at her cloak, and it was ripped from her body.

"That is enough. Keep your hands off me," she sputtered, beginning to panic. Filled with sickening dread, she realized it was not only her money they were after. "Leave me be. Let me go!"

Her cries only incited the men to further violence. One of them got a firm grip on the shoulder of her gown.

"Let's see what you got to offer, girl." He sneered into her face, ripping her sleeve from her shoulder to the top of her bodice. The skin on her pale shoulder shone in the lantern's glow. The men shouted out their raucous encouragement.

Grab your copy...
vinci-books.com/the-spy

About the Author

I wish I could say that I wanted to be a writer my whole life, that it was my dream. But it wasn't. I fell into it on a whim and discovered to my surprise that I enjoyed it. What I always have been is a reader. I will read anything. During the times I could not afford books, I read whatever sat on the shelves of the secondhand store. Sometimes it was History, sometimes Romance, and sometimes it was how to make macrame hangers.

But I am getting ahead of myself. I grew up in Brightsand Saskatchewan, in an immigrant family with six siblings. We were a hard-working troop, scraping a living out of a rocky mixed farm. I look back on those busy years fondly. I have plenty of stories about walking through miles of snow to school, uphill both ways!

I went to the University of Saskatchewan, studying History and English, which I converted into a career in teaching. I love my job. I teach a wild crew of junior high students. There is never a dull moment. It has been a passion of mine which has truly made life worth living. Much of my time is committed to coaching. I can be found most mornings in the gym by six thirty, spending time with my teams. We have had some memorable seasons, winning basketball districts against all odds.

I was lucky enough to marry the love of my life. My husband and I share another passion, gardening. He does the vegetables and I do the flowers. Together we spend many peaceful evenings, enjoying the beauty and bounty we have created.

I squeeze my writing into the bits and pieces of the day that remain. In many ways it is my personal time. I have been surprised by the writing process. Though I start with a plan, my characters always surprise me with their antics. I look forward to every new book, with its host of characters leading me into places unknown.